A Shocking Sign

Though he'd already started mending it, the fence showed definite signs of damage. None of the wires had been cut, but instead had been bent, as if some large weight leaned against it until it was low enough to crawl over.

I looked for any sign of cloth or fur stuck to the wires but came up empty. Finally, I reached out to grab the fence where it had been mangled the most. As I touched the wire, a jolt raced through my fingers and I yanked my hand away. A thin red line rose where my palm had touched the barbed wire. "Damn it, why didn't you tell me there's juice running through this?"

Jimbo gave me a quizzical look. "What are you talking about?"

With Murray peeking over my shoulder, I showed him my hand. "This is what I'm talking about. The minute I touched the fence, I got shocked."

"O'Brien, this fence ain't electrified. I don't have the bucks for that." His eyes flashed and I thought I detected a hint of worry behind that gruff exterior.

Murray turned to examine the fence. "He's right, no juice. Em, did you feel anything else?"

I closed my eyes, trying to remember what had been running through my mind, but the only thing that stood out was the blinding flash of pain as it registered on my nerves. "No. I have no idea what happened, but I don't like it. . . ."

Murder Under
A Mystic Moon

Yasmine Galenorn

BERKLEY PRIME CRIME, NEW YORK

THE BERKLEY PUBLISHING GROUP
Published by the Penguin Group
Penguin Group (USA) Inc.
375 Hudson Street, New York, New York 10014, USA
Penguin Group (Canada), 10 Alcorn Avenue, Toronto, Ontario M4V 3B2, Canada
(a division of Pearson Penguin Canada Inc.)
Penguin Books Ltd., 80 Strand, London WC2R 0RL, England
Penguin Group Ireland, 25 St. Stephen's Green, Dublin 2, Ireland (a division of Penguin Books Ltd.)
Penguin Group (Australia), 250 Camberwell Road, Camberwell, Victoria 3124, Australia
(a division of Pearson Australia Group Pty. Ltd.)
Penguin Books India Pvt. Ltd., 11 Community Centre, Panchsheel Park, New Delhi—110 017, India
Penguin Group (NZ), Cnr. Airborne and Rosedale Roads, Albany, Auckland 1310, New Zealand
(a division of Pearson New Zealand Ltd.)
Penguin Books (South Africa) (Pty.) Ltd., 24 Sturdee Avenue, Rosebank, Johannesburg 2196,
South Africa

Penguin Books Ltd., Registered Offices: 80 Strand, London WC2R 0RL, England

This is a work of fiction. Names, characters, places, and incidents either are the product of the author's imagination or are used fictitiously, and any resemblance to actual persons, living or dead, business establishments, events, or locales is entirely coincidental.

Murder Under a Mystic Moon

A Berkley Prime Crime Book / published by arrangement with the author

PRINTING HISTORY
Berkley Prime Crime mass-market edition / January 2005

Copyright © 2005 by Yasmine Galenorn.
Cover art by Lisa Falkenstern.
Cover design by Lesley Worrell.
Interior text design by Kristin del Rosario.

ISBN: 0-425-20002-7

Berkley Prime Crime Books are published by The Berkley Publishing Group,
a division of Penguin Group (USA) Inc.,
375 Hudson Street, New York, New York 10014.
The name BERKLEY PRIME CRIME and the
BERKLEY PRIME CRIME design
are trademarks belonging to Penguin Group (USA) Inc.

PRINTED IN THE UNITED STATES OF AMERICA

10 9 8 7 6 5 4 3 2 1

ACKNOWLEDGMENTS

My love, thanks, and gratitude to my husband, Samwise, who remains one of the greatest sources of inspiration and support I could ever hope for. No matter what anyone else claims, he's truly my #1 fan—and I'm his. And to my furbles, Luna, Pakhit, Tara, and Meerclar—for keeping me sane and for being my little fuzzy children.

Again, many thanks to Carolyn Agosta, my critique partner. Also to Meredith Bernstein—my agent, and Christine Zika—my editor, for helping me make this series a reality, and a fun one at that.

I have to offer my gratitude and love to the wonderful members of *Writers Will Be Warped*: Alexandra, Amy, Annie, Barb, Carol, Carolyn, Chris, Deanne, Deborah, Ellen (I miss you, Ellen), Glenski, Jenny, Judy, Linda, Margie, Mark, Paddy, Paula, Rebecca, Red, Robert, Shemah, Sue, Veryl. All of you understand the isolating life of a writer, and together, we keep each other sane. You are my family in so many ways. Cheers for community, be it cyber or "real life"!

And as always, thank you to all of my readers, both old and new. Welcome to the pages of a new adventure and I truly hope you enjoy the book. I love writing these stories, and am happy if they sweep you away, even if only for an afternoon. If you want to contact me, you may do so through my website: Galenorn En/Visions: www.galenorn.com

To forestall speculation: the Klakatat Monster is a figment of my imagination, born on the legends of Sasquatch—in whose existence I do believe. The Warriors of the Mountain are also fictional, though based on several legends from several lands. Strange beasties and energies inhabit these beautiful Cascade Mountains. I know, I've felt them.

Bright Blessings and thank you!
the Painted Panther
Yasmine Galenorn

This book is dedicated to:

All who promote and work toward the preservation of the wild and wondrous places that form the backbone of our world. Those working to keep alive the incredible beauty of the Cascade Range, the Olympic National Park, Hawai'i Volcanoes National Park, and so many other wonders borne from our Mother.

May we never face the day where nature is devoid of mystery, and where the wild woods no longer stand sentinel on the face of this Earth.

"All birds, even those of the same species, are not alike, and it is the same with animals and with human beings. The reason WakanTanka does not make two birds, or animals, or human beings exactly alike is because each is placed here by WakanTanka to be an independent individuality and to rely upon itself."

—SHOOTER
Teton Sioux

Chapter 1

❖

THE PHONE JARRED me out of my pre-caffeine stupor as I was eating breakfast. I'd woken to find the kids already up and halfway through their chores, hustling to make it down to the Chiqetaw Recreation Center before the swimming pool got too crowded. I grabbed the receiver on the third ring, trying to maneuver my tongue around a mouthful of jelly doughnut.

"'Lo?"

"O'Brien?" Jimbo Warren's voice came booming over the line. A biker and self-proclaimed mountain man, Jimbo and I had started out as adversaries and ended up as friends. Not only had he helped me save my son from kidnappers, but he'd insisted on paying me back every penny that he'd cost me and my insurance company for throwing a brick through my living-room window. Now that we'd put the past to rest, we actually got along pretty good.

"I need your help," he said. "My buddy Scar's gone missing. I want you to find out if he's dead."

Dead? Did he say *dead*? I glanced at the clock. Yep, it was eight in the morning, all right. Jimbo didn't sound like he was joking. Didn't sound drunk, either, so that eliminated any practical jokes he might come up with after a long night at Reubens. I squinted at the phone. Maybe I'd missed something along the way. I'd barely started on my espresso; the caffeine hadn't had time to hit my system yet and there was a good chance I was still running at half-speed.

I licked my fingers. "Say what? Who's Scar, and why do you think—?"

"I'm not kidding, O'Brien," Jimbo interrupted. "I need your help. Scar's my best buddy. He lives in the biker enclave out in Klickavail Valley, and he's been missing for a week. I think he's dead, and if he is, I was thinking that you might be able to contact his spirit. You owe me one."

He had me there, but did he have to pick this way to collect? Things had been going so well for a change. Nobody had died on me in months. I was thoroughly enjoying a break from the astral brigade that seemed to have set up camp on my doorstep over the past year and I had no intention of courting any more trouble. Events promised to be shaping up for a crisp, calm autumn. I wanted them to stay that way.

I grabbed a paper towel and tried to wipe the residue of raspberry jelly off my face, succeeding only in getting the paper stuck to my fingers. Exasperated, I told him to hold on for a minute and dampened the towel. Once my face and hands were reasonably clean, I said, "I'm back. So your friend's disappeared. Are you sure he's not just hiding out somewhere?"

Jimbo let out a sigh. "Do I have to beg? Okay then, *please* help me find out what happened to Scar. You know the cops aren't going to do anything about a missing biker, and his old lady's really upset. She's pregnant. Scar wouldn't up and leave her. I really have a bad feeling about this."

I straightened up. Jimbo never begged anybody for anything. For him to say "please" meant that he was dead serious. I glanced at the clock, gauging my list of errands for the morning before I headed down to my shop. "This morning's booked, but if you come down to the shop around noon, I'll buy you lunch and you can tell me what's going on."

"Thanks. And . . . O'Brien, you know I wouldn't bug you about this if I had any other choice." He hung up and I stared at the receiver, listening to the dial tone. Somewhere, out there in the universe, the cosmic scales teetered and I could feel all the balance and order I'd managed to regain over the past few months list to the side as it went crashing to the floor in a heap. I glanced out the window. The sky stretched out cloudless and sunny, but I had the feeling I'd better lash the mast and batten down the hatches. A storm was making its way to shore.

MY NAME IS Emerald O'Brien, and I own the Chintz 'n China Tea Room. My daughter recently suggested that I change the name to the Chintz 'n China Tea Room & Tarot Emporium, since I read the cards for so many of my customers, but I told her that sounded like a carnival sideshow. I preferred to maintain what little dignity I'd managed to scrape together over the years.

You see, I hold the dubious honor of being Chiqetaw's one and only "town witch." It wasn't my idea to dub myself that, but people say it with a smile, so I good-naturedly accept the teasing that goes along with the role. In some ways, the nickname fits, though I don't match any of the stereotypes people automatically think of when they hear the "W" word. I've never visited Stonehenge, I'm not an angst-ridden Goth girl, I don't wear a long black cape, and I'm only flaky when I haven't had my caffeine.

What I am is a thirty-six-year-old divorced mother of two wonderful children—Miranda, my star-struck daughter, and Kipling, who just happens to have been born with a strong dose of second sight. Granted, some folks think

I'm a little wacko, but I don't care as long as I've got my family and friends. Over the years I've met more than my fair share of ghosties and ghoulies, both good and bad, and I know how to handle them thanks to my grandmother. Nanna taught me to work folk magic the same way that *her* grandmother taught her. I miss Nanna, but her spirit still pops in from time to time to give me a little advice or a helping hand when I really need her.

And even though I seem to be a beacon for the entire spirit world—the blue-light-special of the "other side" so to speak—I really didn't sign up to be Buffy the Vampire Slayer or one of the Ghostbusters. I honestly have no idea where the universe got the notion that my idea of a good time consists of hunting down astral spooks and mortal murderers. But when destiny knocks, you don't slam the door in its face.

So when the bad guys come calling, I take it for granted that I'm going to end up with bruised knees, nasty welts, torn clothing, exploding cars, virtual visions, astral journeys, the occasional haunting, and all sorts of delightful jaunts into the netherworlds. Score one for the karma police, zero for me.

In the meantime, I just try to keep my children safe, make a success of my business, and enjoy life as much as I can.

As I gathered my keys and purse, my mind lingered over Jimbo's call. In the pit of my stomach, I knew that my temporary reprieve from adventure was over. I took a deep breath, opened the door, and plunged back into the maelstrom.

CHIQETAW'S ANNUAL EARLY Autumn Breeze Celebration ran from Friday through Sunday during the second weekend in August. Designed to attract shoppers eager for end-of-the-summer bargains, the street fair encompassed most of the downtown businesses. When I opened the Chintz 'n China Tea Room a couple of years back, I happily joined in the fun.

Since western Washington had the well-deserved reputation for being the rain capital of the Northwest, there was a definite benefit to luring customers downtown while we still had shirt-sleeve weather. In a little over a month, the rainy season would start and the sky would be overcast again for months on end.

I studied the layout of miniature gift baskets, glancing at the clock. Five minutes to ten. Almost time to open the doors. Friday mornings usually were a little slow, but with the advertised sales going on along Main Street, I expected business to pick up as the day wore on. I adjusted one of the baskets, admiring my handiwork. Brimming with honey and crackers and packets of orange spice tea, they looked so inviting that I thought I should make up a few to take to my parent's anniversary party next month. My sister Rose had roped me into helping her plan a huge affair that I knew my folks wouldn't like, but Rose was a force in her own right, and with Grandma McGrady on her side, even the devil himself wouldn't stand in her way.

Satisfied with the display, I surveyed the entire shop. The windows blossomed with color, sporting arrangements of Indian corn, giant sunflowers in tall urns, and baskets overflowing with poly-resin mushrooms, silk autumn leaves, and bottleneck gourds. The faint essence of cinnamon lingered in the air from the incense I'd burned earlier, a subtle but perfect invitation to stock up on harvest supplies. A lot of the town matrons canned their own fruit and put up preserves at this time of year; they'd be in the mood to pick up a box of spiced tea or a pumpkin-shaped teapot.

Like most small stores, half my yearly revenue came from holiday shoppers. I hadn't resorted to putting up a Christmas tree the day after Halloween, but I had caved in to some of the retail traditions, subliminal suggestion being the best of them. And, of course, I supplemented my business savvy with a few little charms for abundance that I'd tucked away in the nooks and crannies. They were the icing on the cake, adding to the general ambience of the Chintz 'n China, and to my family's prosperity.

"Are you ready?" I asked Cinnamon, grateful I'd been able to extend her hours to fulltime. She was a good worker, and she needed the job.

Cinnamon finished arranging the last of the china plates and cups on the sideboard, then fished out a box of Irish mints and fanned them onto a silver salver, setting it on the counter. "Almost. What should I call today's menu?" She picked up the chalk, poised to write up the menu on the new floral motif board that my friend Murray had made for me.

"Let's see, what do we have? Petit fours and pound cake and raspberry tea and lemonade? Hmm . . . why not 'August Garden Party'?" I gave the shop one more look-see, unlocked the front door, and propped it open to let the morning breeze drift in.

"Are the kids coming down today?" Cinnamon asked, as she finished writing up the menu. "Or is Kip waiting until Lana gets here?" My nine-year-old son had a crush on our part-time clerk that had been going on for months. Lana took it in stride, and I was grateful for her patience with him when he followed her around like a puppy dog.

I shook my head. "They went swimming this morning, and this afternoon, Kip has computer class and Miranda volunteered to clean the shed." My daughter's birthday was coming up and I knew she was trying to win me over for some new astronomical gadget. In July, she'd received the treat of her young lifetime—a long-coveted trip to Space Camp. The week-long experience had only intensified her focus on becoming an astronaut. Not quite fourteen, Randa was already studying up on colleges, intent on finding the best astronomy department in the nation.

The bells over the screen door tinkled and Margaret Files bustled in. My boyfriend's aunt, she was the only family he had around these parts. She had retired from her job as a file clerk several years ago, and had been coming for tea almost every day since I opened the shop. Like clockwork, she scheduled a tarot reading during the last weekend of each month.

"Emerald! You're looking so pretty today. That sundress matches the green of your eyes perfectly." She gave me a big hug and planted a petunia-pink kiss on my cheek. I discreetly wiped off the lipstick, grateful for her support. She never made any mention of the fact that Joe was ten years younger than I, and seemed genuinely happy that I was involved with her nephew. "The store looks absolutely lovely, like a painting."

I escorted her to the tearoom. "Have you heard from Joe?" It had been a long week. Joe was at a conference for EMT's in Portland, Oregon. Though he'd called before bed every night since he'd been gone, I missed the scent of his woodsy aftershave and the feel of his arms curling around me as we fell asleep.

Margaret sighed. "Of course I have. He's a good boy, Emerald, but sometimes I wish he'd cut the apron strings. He phoned last night right when I had the hand of a lifetime. I told him to call back later. It isn't every week that I get a chance to shoot the moon, and Leticia and Iris were hopping mad." She rested her hand on my arm. "You should join us, dear. Sometimes Iris isn't feeling up to snuff; she has angina, you know. The girls wouldn't mind if you sat in for her."

I knew all too well about Margaret Files and her pinochle club. On the surface, they seemed like a nice, genteel group of older women who got together every week for cards. In reality, they played cutthroat pinochle for higher stakes than I could afford, and they played to win. Since no men were invited, and tea was served instead of beer, they had decided that what they were doing wasn't gambling, but when push came to shove, their strategy made cockfighting look tame. I didn't have the stamina to keep up with them and I knew it.

"Margaret, you know I'd be outgunned in an instant. I'm about as good at gambling as I am at keeping out of trouble." I gave her a wink and she giggled.

"So tell me when my nephew is due home?" She zeroed in on the platters of cookies and cakes, then lifted a lid on one of the soup vats to give it a good sniff. Today we were serving gazpacho and chicken noodle, as well as a selection of turkey and cream cheese sandwiches.

"Sunday night. I miss him." I straightened the stack of napkins, then rearranged a platter of cookies, trying to squelch a sudden flood of longing. Joe had wormed his way into my heart, all right, and his being gone left me lonelier than I wanted to admit.

She kissed me on the cheek, then settled at a table with her food and a book. "I don't know if you realize just how sweet he is on you, my dear. He always talks about you. Now go on back to your other customers; you don't have to fuss over me. I've got my petit fours and my tea and my latest Danielle Steel novel to keep me busy. I love the juicy parts, don't you?"

I winked at her. "A woman after my own heart. Okay then, if you're comfortable, I'll talk to you in awhile."

Cinnamon could handle the few customers milling in the shop, so I slipped outside to catch a breath of fresh air. Golden sunlight flickered through the trees standing guard along the sidewalk; it glinted off parked cars and reflected in the row of shop windows that lined Main Street. The city had planted them years ago, interspersing benches and flower boxes between the tall, smooth trunks. The snake-bark maples provided shelter in summer for pedestrians strolling along the main boulevard, and in the winter their bare branches twinkled with hundreds of Christmas lights, shimmering along the snow-shrouded streets.

I perched on the bench directly in front of my shop and leaned back, closing my eyes to avoid looking at the white lines marking the crosswalk just a few yards away. Back in April, one of my tarot clients had met his untimely end between those two white lines, thanks to a hit-and-run driver who sped through the red light, clocking a good forty miles an hour. The image had stuck in my mind and offered up an instant replay every time I looked at the intersection.

"Yo, O'Brien, wake up!"

I knew that voice. "I'm asleep. Go away."

"Come on, wench. It's almost noon and you promised we'd talk."

I opened one eye to stare at the familiar face. Yep. There stood Jimbo Warren, decked out in full leather and studs, towering over me. I didn't see the monster he called his "Sugar" anywhere. "Where's your chopper?"

He jerked his head toward Chiqetaw's downtown parking lot and I could tell he wasn't up for small talk. I still found it difficult to believe that this giant of a man and I had started out as enemies. Over the past few months, his drunken bouts had tapered off and he'd actually taken to stopping by my shop for a bag of cookies or an honest-to-goodness cup of tea.

"As I said on the phone, I need your help."

His sober expression got me moving. I stretched, then motioned for him to follow me into the shop. As we navigated our way through the display tables, several of my customers tossed us questioning glances. I returned their looks with a gracious nod, but Jimbo added a little half-bow with a flourish, his eyes twinkling.

"Morning, ladies," he said in an easy voice. "I trust the day's being kind to you?"

Flustered, they tittered back a few daring responses and one of them—I think it was Elvira Birmingham—positively beamed. I forced myself to keep a straight face. Oh yeah, women loved bad boys all right; especially the prim and proper matrons of the town.

I led Jimbo to the table I kept reserved for shop personnel and offered him a seat. Jimbo eyed the chair. The delicate scrolled backs were aged with a green patina, and the smooth leather seats belied their strength. "You sure that bitty thing's gonna hold me up?"

"It might look dainty but the framework is solid iron; it won't bend under the weight of a sumo wrestler." I motioned for him to sit down. "I'll get us some lemonade and cake." After I brought the food and drink back to the table, I settled into my own chair "So what's going on?"

He hesitantly perched on the cushion and swigged down his lemonade. He set the glass back on the table, staring at it for a moment before speaking.

"I told you that one of my buddies has disappeared."

I nodded. "Scar, right?"

"Yeah. Scar's been hanging around Klickavail Valley for the past four years. Now he's up and vanished. Nobody's seen him for a week. He wouldn't just wander off like this, O'Brien. I know something's happened to him." His lip twitched.

A biker who'd vanished spelled "road trip" to me. Or "jailbird." "I assume you've talked to the police and to his other friends?"

Jimbo grunted. "Scar's old lady hasn't seen him since Friday—a week ago today—and that's the last time I saw him, too. Seems Traci came into town to buy groceries. Scar told her he was going to head over to my place. When she got home, the lock on their trailer was busted and the place was trashed. Every drawer had been tossed. A real mess. I went up there and looked around. Whoever did it was searching for something and I don't think they found it."

"Thieves?" I asked.

"That's just it. Nothing was missing, except Scar. As soon as Traci saw the state of their trailer, she drove over to my place, figuring Scar and I would be out fishing, but he never showed up. I followed her back to the enclave and we asked around. Clyde—he runs the joint—was the last person who talked to him. Clyde said he asked Scar if he wanted to hang out and have a beer, but Scar told him that he was heading out for my joint. Then he vanished. We went to the cops Saturday morning when he still hadn't shown up."

Jimbo must have been worried if he'd actually brought in the police. "What did they say?"

"You know how they feel about the bikers. They keep hoping the whole lot will just disappear, and since they can't raid the place without a good reason, they're not about to do anything to help find a biker gone AWOL. They were total assholes."

"I can't believe they'd just ignore the fact that he was missing." I knew several of the officers, including my best friend Murray who had made detective earlier in the year. The Chiqetaw police were usually responsive to the public.

"Oh, they took a report all right, but then that paunchy old dude—what's his name? He's the head of detectives?"

"Coughlan?"

"Yeah, thanks. Coughlan, that's it. He took one look at the report and passed it off. He said that Scar was probably off on some road trip. Traci told them about the trailer, but they ignored it. Just said that they'd ask around at the bars. Real big freakin' help, huh?"

Jimbo scratched his chin, his beard still braided in the long cornrows that I'd suggested. The first day he'd showed up with them, I realized that I had no business offering fashion tips to bikers, but he seemed to like them so I refrained from commenting other than to murmur an "Oh yes, how nice."

"Coughlan, huh? That figures." The officers I knew took complaints seriously, checking things out as much as their constrained budget and limited force allowed, but Coughlan was another matter. Murray's supervisor, he'd made her life miserable ever since she got a promotion to his unit. They'd managed to achieve a truce, but I didn't expect it to last.

He shook his head. "Remember, we're talking about the

Klickavail Valley bikers. The cops suspect all sorts of trouble out there, most of it the product of their overactive imaginations. Since the enclave is housed on private property and the boys have permission to live there, and since there's no proof that anything illegal is actually going down, the cops ignore the place, hoping the group will get bored and leave. They're not gonna help anymore than they're forced to. Anyway, so Scar's vanished and Traci's freakin'."

"They have a fight, maybe?"

"Nope, no way. She's pregnant and they're happy as a pair of lovebugs. Kid's due to pop in about a month. I told the cops Scar would never run out on his old lady. All he can talk about lately is having the kid and settling down. He wants two or three more, after this one." Jimbo shrugged, but I thought I glimpsed the ghost of a smile behind his worry.

Curious. I'd have thought that anybody living in the biker's enclave out there would want to remain free, unattached. "What about you? Have you ever considered getting married?" The question slipped out before I could stop myself.

Jimbo picked at the crumbs of his cake. "Me? Nah . . . I mean, it just ain't the life for a woman. Hell, you know me. I spend most of my time in the woods. What would I do with a wife and kids? I got my land and my house and that's enough. Heck, I was here before most of those guys even knew the valley existed. I'm about as settled as I'm ever gonna get."

Jimbo's home, from what I had seen, had been built one room at a time; he just kept adding on as he needed to and it resembled a sprawling shack more than a house, but I wasn't going to nitpick over subtleties.

He continued. "But after years on the road, some of the boys need to settle down, plant some roots. Don't mean they get kicked out of the gang, they just keep the home fires burning for the rest. Anyway, so you see, Scar wouldn't leave Traci, and he sure as hell wouldn't run off without his new Harley. He just bought that baby and she cost him over thirty grand."

"*Thirty grand? For a bike?*"

"Hey, it's a customized Screamin' Eagle Electra Glide. They don't come cheap."

I didn't ask how Scar had managed to get his hands on thirty thousand dollars; the less I knew about the financial dealings of Jimbo's friends, the better. But something about the situation intrigued me. I'd shed a lot of my stereotypes over the past few months. If Jimbo was right about his friend, then Scar wouldn't have up and taken off without letting somebody know. On the other hand, could the man still have a wild streak that Jimbo had overlooked?

"Has anything else happened that strikes you as suspicious?"

He glanced around to see if anybody was eavesdropping. God knows, somebody probably was. I loved my customers but a select handful were firmly ensconced in the busybody boot camp. My tearoom had become a hotspot for the tea-and-crumpet set to pick up a little gossip along with their daily "cuppa." Whenever I had a few moments, I joined them, doing my best to keep tabs on local rumors and squash anything I knew to be wrong.

"My chickens have been disappearing. Last week, something tore up my fence—that's pure barbed wire, babe, and ain't much fun to tangle with."

"Cougar? Bear maybe? This is the time of year when they pack on the weight for winter, so they'll be out and about." Chiqetaw was nestled out in the boonies off Highway 9, about fifteen miles southeast from Bellingham. Quite a few wild animals wandered in from the woods to the outskirts of town, especially out near Miner's Lake and up on Jumping Jack Ridge.

Jimbo shook his head. "I don't think so. Whatever did it trampled my carrot patch and got into the corn. I found footprints in the dirt, and O'Brien, they weren't made by any four-legged animal. They were big and barefoot. Bigger than my feet." Jimbo stretched out his leg. Yep, his boot was mighty big, at that.

He leaned in closer. "My guess is that something's tromping around Miner's Lake, something dangerous. A few of the guys in Klickavail Valley told me that they've come up short on stuff lately. Food . . . blankets . . . stuff like that. Terry-T said his sleeping bag disappeared off the clothesline a couple weeks ago. And they've been hearing strange things in the woods out there, too. Noises, and seeing shadows that shouldn't be there."

A tingle pulsed in the back of my neck and it felt as if I stood poised on the edge of a cliff. "You said you thought Scar is dead. Why?"

He sighed. "I can't prove that he's dead, but I got one of those awful feelings in my gut that I ain't ever gonna see him again. This week I've had a couple dreams about him calling my name, but in them, I could never find out where he was. And then last night, I had another dream, and he was there, and he was all bloody and holding out his hands. Scared me shitless."

"So you want me to go ghost-hunting."

"Yeah," he said with a bob of his head. "Come out to Miner's Lake and take a look around. You can see these things better than me."

I took a deep breath. The situation didn't sound good, that was for sure. "What exactly do you want me to do?"

"What I was thinking was, seeing as how you're a hoodoo woman like my Granny, maybe if he's dead, his ha'nt is hanging around and you might be able to see him or hear him."

I leaned back in my chair, contemplating the situation. Over the past few months, Jimbo and I'd had several talks about his grandma, who practiced some sort of folk magic down in the bayous of Louisiana. Jimbo firmly believed in the supernatural, he'd had several interesting experiences as a kid, then again when helping me rescue my son. And apparently, I was the only one he could talk to about the paranormal without being labeled a wacko.

I took a long swallow of my lemonade. Chances were good that Scar had just dropped out of sight for awhile, but Jimbo had tweaked my curiosity. If it would set his mind at ease, I'd do it. And as he'd said, I owed him one.

"All right. How about Sunday? I can't promise results, but I'll give it a try. Do you mind if I bring my friend Murray?"

He hesitated for a second, then shrugged. "What the hell, it ain't like this is top secret. Why don't you bring some chips and beer, and I'll fry us up a chicken, fresh from the henhouse."

It was my turn to pause. "Fry a chicken? You can cook?"

Jimbo smirked. "Hey babe, I ain't just good looking, you know. My Granny taught me how to pluck a hen and skin a possum, and fry up catfish fresh from the lake. Hell, you think I could do the work I do if I lived on baloney sandwiches?"

We had more in common than I'd thought. Since my mother had worked in my father's business, I'd learned most of my skills from my Nanna, too, though I'd never once had to face skinning a possum. I shuddered, grateful for small favors.

He pushed back his chair and winked at me as he stood up. "I'll hide anything your cop-friend shouldn't see."

Oh yeah, that made me feel better. I cleared my throat. "Sounds like a plan." He stood up, but paused when I rested my hand on his. "Jimbo, what do you really think happened to Scar? You said you think something's prowling in the woods out there. Are you hiding something from me?"

He paused, his expression guarded. "You'll think I'm nuts."

I stared at him. "You do realize who you're talking to, don't you?"

He rubbed his hands together. "You know, those woods have a lot of secrets. There's some crazy-assed shit going on out there; always has been, always will. Rumors and stories float around. I laughed most of them off until lately. About two . . . maybe three weeks back, I start getting the feeling that I'm being watched every time I'm out there. I tell you, those woods are alive, and they seem agitated."

My psychic alarm clock began to ring. "So what do you think happened?"

He sighed, then jammed on his helmet and pulled on a pair of leather gloves. "I think the Klakatat Monster killed him and dragged him off somewhere. That's what I think." And with that, he saluted me and strode toward the door.

Klakatat monster? What the heck was that?

With visions of beasts and bogies dancing in my head, I glanced over to where Margaret sat, ostensibly reading her book. I could see her peeking over the top, her face a question mark. I leaned down next to her and gave her a gentle hug. "Jimbo's just a friend in need of a little help."

"Friend, indeed," she said. She shook her head, but looked relieved. "He's wearing enough leather to build himself a cow." I poured her another glass of iced tea, then got back to work.

Chapter 2

❧

MURRAY WIPED THE dirt off her face and took a long drink from her water bottle before bending back over the tangle of bramble creepers and clover. I'd enlisted her help to thin out my overgrown, weed-infested flower beds in the backyard. Earlier that spring I'd planned on planting a kitchen garden, but during my last adventure I'd bonded with nature a little more than I had intended. The experience turned me off from anything having to do with mucking around in the dirt.

By the time I'd managed to shake off the memories of being encrusted from head to toe with forest mulch while welting up from a nasty patch of stinging nettles, it was too late to start any seedlings. Now though, I was determined to get the beds ready and then, in a month—or whenever my neighbor Horvald Ledbetter told me to—I'd plant a bevy of spring bulbs for next year. Tulip lovers of the world unite!

My knees pressed into the soft dirt as I stabbed a particularly tenacious dandelion with my trowel. "Sheesh, these things don't want to give up!" I finally edged the tip of the garden tool under the root and pried until I'd dislodged the tuberous plant enough to yank the whole thing out.

Frustrated, I tossed the trowel aside. "Time for a break." Leaning back onto the warm, soft grass, I stared at the clouds that wandered across the evening sky. There went a sinuous sea monster, and there, a griffin. Thoughts of sea creatures and legendary beasties brought me back to my conversation with Jimbo.

"Mur, have you heard of the Klakatat Monster?" I glanced over to where she lay, sprawled out on her stomach, face down in the grass. I leaned over and poked her gently in the side. "Hey, you awake?"

She grunted. Anna Murray was my best friend. One of two, actually. We'd known each other since high school and had been roommates during our college years. A detective with the Chiqetaw Police, she was carving a niche for herself in a department headed by a man who didn't particularly welcome Native Americans or women.

Actually, I had a feeling it wouldn't have mattered what ethnicity she was. Mur was a warrior by nature, who looked like a cross between a sturdy Amazon and an Indian princess. Stronger, faster, and smarter than most of the men on the force, her competence and stern beauty rattled a handful of the detectives with whom she now worked. Luckily, she still had stalwart friends among the patrol officers, including the chief of police; friends who would do anything for her.

She sat up and gracefully folded her legs into the lotus position. Just looking at her made my joints ache, though I had to admit, I envied her flexibility and good health. Lately it seemed like I was always catching the sniffles or something and I had the sneaking suspicion it had everything to do with my intake of gooey treats, my lack of self-discipline when it came to exercise, and the amount of caffeine I happily imbibed.

"How do you do that? I don't understand how the heck

you twist yourself into those positions." I tried to mimic her, failing miserably.

"They're called asanas." She grinned at me. "I keep asking you to come to yoga class with me. It's fun, and good for you."

I considered the idea. I hated the thought of going to the YMCA, which was the only gym left in town since my other best friend—Harlow—had closed the doors to her spa. I'd taken a self-defense course and felt confident that I could protect myself in an emergency, but the fact was that I'd turned into a sloth, spending most of my free time lounging around with Joe. I had no problem with my curves, but the only exercise I got lately was sex. I wasn't complaining, but the truth was that the mattress mambo couldn't replace a good set of weights or a treadmill.

"Will they start me slow?"

Murray nodded. "As slow as you need. The teacher's really good; she only advances students when they're ready. C'mon. I'm going tomorrow night. We can go together. It'll be like college."

I squinted, trying to figure out when we had ever worked out together. Then the memory flooded back. Every day, come rain or shine, we'd taken long walks together through the Washington Park Arboretum in Seattle. It kept us in shape, gave us time to gossip, and worked off the endless pizzas we'd ordered.

"Yoga is great stress release and it makes you look and feel younger." Murray frowned. "Em, I haven't wanted to say anything but lately, you're looking a little . . ." Her voice drifted off.

I shot a glance at her, warning her not to continue. After a moment, I snorted. "Yeah, yeah. Too cushy for my own good. You know, the thought of being able to relax on cue is pretty appealing."

I wasn't very good at getting rid of stress. In fact, I was the only person I knew who'd had trouble pulling a "C" out of my relaxation class in college. While everybody else was busy learning how to loosen their toes, I was still trying to find my pulse, a skill I never had mastered. I spent the entire quarter convinced I was one of the walking dead.

Maybe if I stopped drinking my daily ration of caffeine, it might help, but if I quit, I'd have to do something else for energy and *that* meant increasing my sugar intake, which wouldn't be good for my teeth or my waistline. I sucked on my lip for a moment. Nope, it had to be exercise.

"Okay, I'll go. I can always quit if I don't like it. Now, tell me about the monster? Do you know anything about it?"

"The Klakatat Monster? Yes, I've heard of it." She pulled a long blade of grass and began tying it into knots. "Why?"

I told her about Jimbo's request. "I can't figure out why the cops won't help him. Do you know anything about it?"

She shook her head. "Coughlan's not going to lift a finger to help the bikers. And Chief Bonner won't counter him. Bonner's a good man, but I can guarantee you he's not going to go out of his way to help anybody living out in Klickavail Valley. They've had a running feud with the cops since they first started gathering out there, what with the way they raise hell at the bars. And let me tell you, those boys collect speeding tickets like honey attracts flies."

"Do you really think they're running drugs and guns, like the rumors say?" I had first thought Jimbo might be into trafficking illegal wares, but once I saw his house and the setup out on his land, I knew that he was just a seasoned biker who liked his solitude and preferred a mountain man existence.

Murray considered my question. Finally she said, "Maybe. I don't have any doubt that a few of the guys out there are bad apples. To be honest, I doubt that any guns are making their way through the compound. But there are some pricey homes out that way owned by people who have clout. Those folks won't take kindly to any help the police give to the boys."

"I know you think Jimbo's a troublemaker, but he helped me save Kip, and I really feel like I owe him this. He's not so bad when you get to know him."

Murray gazed at me, her expression unreadable as usual. "You haven't taken a shine to our biker-boy, have you?"

"Oh sure." I snorted. "And I've also decided to beg Roy to take me back. We'd make a delightful threesome, don't you think?" Giving her one of my "you-know-better-than-that" looks, I pushed myself up to rest on my knees. "Now, why on earth would I drop someone like Joe for someone like Jimbo?"

Murray relaxed. "I just wanted to make sure. You and Joe make a great couple, Em. I'd hate to see anything or anybody come between you. Anyway, you wanted to know about the Klakatat Monster?"

"Uh huh." A dandelion waved in the breeze and I pulled it, pressing the butter-yellow pom-pom to my nose as I said, "What is it?"

"A large creature of some sort, supposedly cousin to the Sasquatch, though the Klakatat Monster isn't nearly as well known. You do know about Sasquatch, right?"

I shrugged. "Yeah, it's an manlike ape-creature that hangs around the forests here in the Pacific Northwest, though somebody on television said those footprints that guy found were a hoax. But I thought the local tribes have stories about Sasquatch that go back before white men arrived on the continent?"

She nodded. "We do. In some of the tribal dialects, his name translates as 'The Big Man.' He's also known by some as 'Brother.' Sasquatch is out there, all right, but I hope we never find him. Some local yokel or rabid scientist would shoot him or try to dissect him."

She was right. People always attacked the unknown, afraid of what it might bring into their lives. I'd experienced that particular prejudice first hand, but somehow, I'd managed to carve a niche for myself here in Chiqetaw—eccentricities, folk magic, ghosts, and all. But not everybody was as lucky as me.

"So, are the Klakatat Monster and Sasquatch the same?"

She stood and dusted her hands on the legs of her jeans. "There are similarities, but according to the stories I've heard, the Klakatat Monster is more unpredictable than Bigfoot. Sightings place him over seven feet tall, with long claws like a bear, and razor-sharp teeth. I think his fur is supposed to be gray, but I'm not sure about that. The reservation elders don't talk about him much; we believe that talking about something can bring it into our lives."

"Agreed," I said. Sometimes focusing on an energy or force did seem to beckon it in, so I was careful where I turned my thoughts.

"So, will you go out to Miner's Lake with me on Sunday?" I asked, arching my back until it popped. "Jimbo's going to show me where his garden got trampled and then I'm going to hunt around and see if I can find any sign that Scar might have been there." As an added enticement, I said, "Jimbo's frying up a chicken for us."

With a snicker, she said, "Frying a chicken? I hope he plucks it first. Hell, why not? Should be interesting."

Good, it was settled. "Come on. Let's get some apple juice and you can tell me more about yoga class."

As we strolled toward the kitchen door, the ground suddenly rolled under my feet and I reached out to steady myself. When it stopped, I realized that it hadn't been an earthquake—nothing had really moved. An astral jolt, maybe? I glanced at the yard but it was empty and still. Overhead, clouds were pushing in from the west, dark and heavy thunderheads, signaling the brewing of a storm. As a rush of excess energy raced down my spine, tingling pinpricks, I quickened my pace.

"What's the matter?" Murray asked, running to keep up with me.

I shook my head. "I don't know. A goose just walked over my grave, I guess." She gave me a questioning look but I couldn't answer. Something had shifted, and though I had no idea what it was, I had a queasy feeling we were going to find out.

WHEN WE TROMPED into the house, Miranda was sitting at the table, eating cookies and drinking milk, her nose stuck in a book as usual. Her gaze flickered our way. Without missing a beat, she said, "Mom, you're tracking again."

I glanced down at my sneakers. Encrusted with soft dirt from the flower beds, they were leaving a trail of grimy footprints across my clean kitchen tile. I sighed, stopping to untie them. Murray followed suit.

"Can't somebody come up with a floor that repels dirt?" I dropped them into the pantry next to the laundry basket, then snagged the sponge and a paper towel to wipe up the mess.

Randa smirked behind her book.

"Thanks a lot, kiddo." I tossed the paper towel in the garbage. After I washed my hands and poured the apple juice, I motioned for her to scoot over to the end of the table. "You just love it when your mother trips up, don't you?"

She grinned. "Hey, don't blame me for trying to even the score."

I peeked at the cover of her book. *Bad Astronomy: Misconceptions and Misuses Revealed, from Astrology to the Moon Landing "Hoax."* "Any good?"

"Yeah," she said with a satisfied smile. "It's a lot of fun." Ever since Miranda had returned from Space Camp, she'd been more determined than ever to become an astronaut. I still worried about her studying too much, but at least she'd traded in her standard Donna Karan–look for something more age-appropriate. In her cobalt polo shirt and khaki shorts, with her raven hair cut into a long shaggy mane, she looked her age, rather than thirteen-trying-for-twenty.

She closed her book and pushed it to the side. "Hey Mom, has the school called yet?"

"No, but I'll let you know as soon as I hear anything." Earlier in the summer, she'd taken placement tests to see if she could skip a grade or two. We were waiting for the results.

Murray wrinkled her nose and playfully snatched a cookie off Randa's plate. "These are good, who made them?" she said, biting into the crumbly golden round.

"Ida." I refilled the plate from the cookie jar on the counter. Yum. The scent of peanut butter drifted up to tickle my nose. "She's been trying to keep busy. That business with her nephew shook her to the core, so I've been encouraging the kids to spend a lot of time at her place this summer, helping out. She insists on paying them, but I think the company does her good."

Ida Trask was a local legend, a retired schoolteacher and baby-sitter extraordinaire. Practically everybody who'd been born in Chiqetaw during the past thirty years had ended up as her student. Now she ran a baby-sitting service and I'd relied on her to watch Kip and Miranda ever since we moved into the neighborhood a couple of years ago. With her living just down the street, she was handy as well as reliable.

"Poor Mrs. Trask," Miranda said. "I don't blame her for being upset. Say, what are we going to do for my birthday?" Her leap in subject matter was par for the course. Randa's self-centered nature had always managed to rear its head, though lately she'd been worse than usual. I knew she was going through the typical teen-angst phase, but the trait bothered me. Still, with her fourteenth birthday coming up in less than two weeks, I'd decided to write off the latest bout to excitement.

"What do you want to do? Do you want a party?" I wasn't about to plan some surprise gig that she might not like. I'd already made enough mistakes in the parenting department to last me a lifetime.

She shrugged. "Maybe just dinner and movies here. I guess Dad's going to forget again?"

For the millionth time I wanted to kill Roy. I bit my tongue, trying to figure out what to say when Murray broke in. "Say, what about a party out at my house?" she said. "I haven't played hostess for awhile. You can bring all the friends you want."

Randa flashed her a huge grin. Murray lived over on Sunrise Avenue, on three acres in a gorgeous, old Victorian, along with her two beautiful boa constrictors, Sid and Nancy. Her land was adjacent to Willowmoor Meadows, the biggest park in Chiqetaw.

"That'd be great," Randa said. "I'll invite Lori, and of course Kip and you guys and Harlow and Joe and the members of my astronomy club. Do you think Mrs. Trask and Mr. Ledbetter might want to come?"

Once again, it struck me that my daughter had very few friends her own age, but she seemed content and, in the end, that was what really mattered. "I think they'd probably like that."

We agreed on an evening barbecue on the twenty-second, which was still a couple weeks away, and then Randa grabbed her book and took off for the front porch, where she could read in peace.

After she left, I relaxed. "Thanks Mur, I've been at my wit's end trying to think up something she might enjoy. Randa never gives me any clue as to what she wants when it comes to stuff like this."

As we were headed into the living room, the screen door squeaked and Randa poked her head around the living room wall. "Mom, Harlow's here."

Harlow cautiously navigated the bench in the foyer, stopping to admire the bouquet blossoming out in the weathered marble urn that sat on the table next to the bench.

"Gorgeous roses," she said. "Love that dusky peach color. From Joe?"

"Nope, from Horvald," I said, grinning. Over the course of the summer, my neighbor had taken it upon himself to keep me in freshly cut flowers. I enjoyed the bouquets, and it was nice; it felt like Horvald had kind of adopted the kids and me.

Harlow waddled into the living room. Pregnant or not, she was still the most gorgeous woman I'd ever known. Her crimped golden hair was caught by a velvet ribbon, and streamed down her back. Standing five-foot eleven, she'd been a supermodel until her early twenties. Pregnancy had eliminated the angular, anorexic edge that she'd never before been able to shed and, while Harlow had always been beautiful, now she was breathtaking.

"What's shakin' hon? Besides that baby of yours?" I kissed her on the cheek and led her to the firmest chair we had. "Here, this should work. I thought you were sticking close to home now that you're near your due date."

"Yeah, but I was out this way for a meeting, so thought I'd drop by." She edged into the chair with a sigh of relief. "My ankles are swollen up as big as your boobs, Em."

Murray choked on her cookie and hurried to swallow the last of her apple juice, then curled up on the sofa. "You know, you make me really happy I decided not to have kids," she said, a twinkle in her eye. "I simply can't imagine myself as a mother, and certainly not pregnant."

Harlow waved languidly in her direction. "Glad to be of service. You're right. I can't see you having kids, either. You'd probably feed them to the snakes when they got out of line, or worse yet, let them take Sid and Nancy to show-and-tell and give the teacher a heart attack." She gave Mur a wicked grin.

Murray sputtered. "Hey! Hold on there just one minute. I happen to be great with kids—I just don't want any of my own!"

"Of course you're great with kids, you nit," I said, settling into the recliner. "Kip and Randa adore you, and so will Harl's little girl." I turned to Harlow. "So, what meeting were you at this time?" Every time I turned around, the woman had joined yet another committee. Most of them were volunteer charities, or out-and-out philanthropic organizations.

With a grimace, she shifted around until she found a comfortable position, then leaned back. "Shit, my back hurts. Whoever created the myth of the wonderful, carefree pregnancy had his head up his butt. I don't glow, I sweat!"

"Yeah," I said, "I have to admit, being pregnant with Kip and Randa made me all too aware of how unfair this universe is. If there was any justice, men would have an abdominal pouch and hatch the kids, just like in seahorse-land. But nope, we women got stuck with the job."

"Been watching *Animal Planet* again, have we?" Harlow snickered. "The meeting was for the Literacy Council—"

I reached for my purse. "Fundraising time already?"

She shook her head. "No, but all donations are welcome." As I wrote out a check she continued. "I actually came over to warn you about something."

"Warn me? Warn me about what?" I handed her my donation. "I don't think I like the sound of that."

She tucked the check into an envelope and dropped it into her purse. "Well, you won't like it even more when I tell you what I found out. Cathy Sutton was at the meeting tonight—KLIK-TV is running a special on local charities."

I groaned. Cathy Sutton was the local anchorwoman at KLIK-TV. She was always vying to win Reporter of the Year; but had about as much chance as a snowball in hell. Next to her, Hedda Hopper sounded discreet, and Cathy's to-die-for glamour didn't hide her lack of talent, or the crocodile smile behind those pouty lips. Over the past year, we'd had several run-ins that had left us less than the best of friends.

"So what's the ditz up to now?" I asked.

Harl cleared her throat. "She told me she's going to be covering the Early Autumn Breeze Festival. She'll be in town tomorrow to film some of the local shops, and I weaseled it out of her that she's planning on focusing on the Chintz 'n China, since you've become a local legend."

"Local legend" indeed. Just because I'd had the misfortune to get mixed up in solving several murders, I'd somehow acquired an aura of celebrity. Though it was good for business, it was bad for my peace of mind.

"Oh great. Well, at least it's only for the festival. Last time I threw her out of my shop, she flattened me like a bug on her damned show."

Murray guffawed. "If you'd exert a little diplomacy, she might get bored and move on to some of the other businesses."

"There's more," Harlow said.

"Spill it. All of it."

"She introduced me to some guy who's interning at KLIK-TV. When she said she was going to interview you, he begged her to let him come along. Apparently, you have a big fan. He was practically doe-eyed over you."

I groaned. Just what I needed—a fan base in town. "Uh, did he say why he was so star struck?"

Harlow gave me an evil grin. "He eventually wants to be a professional psychic, and he thinks you are just the person to give him advice."

"You've got to be kidding!" Great, another idiot wannabe poking around with forces he probably didn't understand or respect.

"Sorry, babe. His name is George. I can't remember his last name, but you're going to be meeting him tomorrow because I overheard Cathy agree to let him tag along."

Forewarned was forearmed. I tried to put the thought

out of my mind as we moved on to other, more interesting subjects, like Harlow's job. At the beginning of the year, Professor Abrams from Western Washington University had employed her as his research assistant. She'd been telecommuting, a real boon during the time she'd been wheelchair-bound. Now she was planning her own college education, to start after the baby was born.

"I'll keep working," she said, "but I think I'll take a couple night courses until I decide what I want to major in."

I didn't have the heart to tell her that between the baby, work, and school, she'd probably end up a frazzled mess. At least she had the money to hire help, and I knew that her husband, James, would support every decision she made.

The evening wound down and I walked them to their cars, waving them out of the driveway. As I returned to the house, the silence settled over my shoulders and I took a deep breath, breathing in the scents of the warm summer evening. Kip was staying overnight with his best friend Sly and, for a rare occasion, the house was at rest. No insistent hum of the computer, no *oofs* and *ughs* from his video games.

Soaking up the peace, I headed upstairs and peeked in Randa's room. Yep, just as I figured, she was out watching the skies. On one of our first nights in the house, I'd caught her attempting to climb out of her window. Rather than fence her in, I hired a contractor to reinforce the flat section of the roof right outside her room. He'd built a solid guard rail so that on warm nights she could crawl out of her window, telescope in hand, and stargaze the evening away. After a few months, the neighbors had gotten used to seeing my daughter perched on the roof. I glanced at my watch. Nine-thirty. Well under bedtime.

I stuck my head out the window. "Good viewing?"

She nodded. "It's really clear tonight. Want to join me?"

Surprised, but pleased, by her invitation, I climbed out

of the window and gingerly made my way over to the blanket on which she was sitting.

"What are we looking at?" I asked as I settled down next to her. The view from up here was wonderful. Our neighborhood sat up on a modest hill and on clear days, we could see the peaks of the Twin Sisters jutting up from behind the foothills from the second-story windows. At night the glittering street lights of Chiqetaw unfolded, laid out in long cross-strings racing across the flat, marking the boundaries of the town. It was a beautiful sight.

"I'm watching Mars tonight," she said, pointing out a fuzzy red light to the southeast. "Here, take the telescope. You can see Syrtis Major—it's a large, dark area." She scooted over so I could lean in and look through the scope, an expensive Christmas gift from last year.

I squinted through the eyepiece and sure enough, Mars came into view; the ruddy surface marred by shadows. "There she is . . . okay, I can see the planet. Now where am I supposed to look?"

"Find the equator, then follow the dark patch that extends to the north," she said. "See it? That's known as Syrtis Major."

And I saw. A blotch covered the rust-colored surface, stretching northward like a column of ash. Suitably impressed, I stared at the planet for a few minutes, then returned the scope to her. I folded my arms around my knees. "So what's on the celestial calendar for the rest of August?"

"The Perseids meteor showers are due in a little over a week. They peak late this year. We could see a meteor every minute from up here. More, with my telescope." The enthusiasm in her voice was infectious.

"Really? A meteor every minute? Maybe you and Kip and I should have a late-night picnic up here and watch together." I ruffled her hair, a habit she hated but one I hadn't been able to break.

The look on her face was repayment for all the snippy

comments she'd made in the past month. "Really? You'd like that?" Then her expression fell. "Shoot, my astronomy club is getting together that night to watch." She lowered the telescope and gave me a hopeful look. "Maybe you and Kip could come with me?"

I could tell she was torn between wanting to take me up on my offer to enter her world, and the desire to be among people who understood her passion. "Tell you what. We'll all go to your club meeting and then, if you like, we'll come home and have dessert out here on the roof and watch some more?"

Randa threw her arms around me and gave me an unexpected smooch on the cheek. "That'd be perfect!"

I stroked her back and nuzzled her on the head. "I know, babe. I know." I yawned, suddenly worn out. "Listen, I'm going to take a bath and read in bed for awhile. You be sure you're inside by midnight, okay?" She reluctantly let go of me and I cautiously made my way back to the window.

"Okay. Say . . . Mom?"

"Yes, hon?"

She paused, then shook her head. "Just . . . thanks. Sweet dreams, okay?"

"Sweet dreams." I blew her a kiss and climbed back inside. As I drew my bath, it occurred to me that a college course in astronomy might help me understand the passion that so captivated my daughter. We were still light-years apart, but if a little studying could bridge the gap, I'd happily make the effort.

Chapter 3

❧

I TOOK EXTRA pains with the cleaning on Saturday morning, making sure we were done ahead of time. Then I slipped into the bathroom and changed, donning a camera-suitable skirt and top. The bells tinkled and by the braying laughter that echoed through the store, I knew that Cathy had arrived. She was followed by Royal, her everpresent cameraman-slash-lapdog. Behind her stood another man; he was younger and dressed in pleated pants, a polo shirt, and loafers. He carried a large metal briefcase and shifted nervously as I fluttered over to greet them.

"Cathy, how are you? Don't you look nice, today? I'll bet you're here because of the Early Autumn Breeze Festival! Am I right?" I'd prove that I could schmooze with the best of them. I'd charm her right out of my shop.

Her jaw dropped. She'd probably been ready to dig in her heels for the fight, but now she did an about-face, attempting to recover her poise. "Emerald, I'm glad to see you're in such a good mood. The shop's looking lovely, by the way. You remember Royal—"

"Of course I do. How can I forget the best cameraman

west of the Cascades?" I flashed him a tight smile, show-ing just a hint of my teeth.

"And this is George Pleasant, KLIK-TV's newest in-tern." Cathy shoved the younger man forward.

Besides his metal briefcase, he had a camera and minia-ture tape recorder strung around his neck. As Cathy gave him the old heave-ho, he stumbled, managing to catch himself before he crashed into the nearest display table. I edged between him and a four-tiered stand of teapots, smiling all the while.

"Hello." I offered him my hand and he shook it a little too eagerly, squeezing a little too hard. His palm was clammy and I discreetly wiped off my hand on my skirt as Cathy interrupted, proceeding to ask me her usual series of inane questions. At least this time we were covering a sub-ject with which I was comfortable. I was proud of myself. I gave brief, concise answers and not once did I order her to get out of my face.

As we discussed the festival, I noticed out of the corner of my eye that George was nosing around the shop. Just what he expected to find, I had no idea.

Cathy was finally getting what she wanted—an inter-view in which I was cooperative—and it seemed to throw her off kilter. After about ten minutes, she lost interest and started to wrap things up. She eyed me suspiciously after Royal had turned off the camera. "You were certainly help-ful today."

"No problem. Now, I really have to get back to work—"

She interrupted. "Before you do, I have a favor to ask of you."

A favor? Oh joy. Give Cathy a lick and she'd steal the whole ice cream cone. "What is it now? I thought the in-terview was over."

She flashed me an ingratiating smile. "George is a big fan of yours. He asked if he could come along with me and meet you. He'd like to stay and ask you some questions about the tarot, and I thought that you wouldn't mind since that's your area of expertise."

Harlow had been right, damn her. I glanced over at George, who had edged up behind Cathy's right shoulder. He blinked. Behind the round lenses of his glasses, he looked for all the world like a belligerent owl.

Shit. My inner alarm clanging, I homed in on his energy for a moment, then quietly withdrew. No . . . George himself wasn't dangerous, but there were disturbing ripples in his aura and regardless of his last name, I didn't think he was as nice as he pretended to be. "Uh, I'd rather not—"

George suddenly came to life. "Please, let me stay, just for the afternoon? I've always been fascinated by the occult and when I found out that Cathy knew you, I wondered if I might entice you into a discussion about the tarot. ESP and the tarot have been pet studies of mine since I was fifteen and I think I've got what it takes to be a professional psychic. I've studied J.B. Rhine's experiments and read all of Hans Holzer's books and Edgar Cayce's work. I've even seen ectoplasm once at a séance that my best friend's sister conducted and I'm trying to learn remote viewing—"

Eager to shut him up, I held up my hand. "All right, all right. Just slow down, okay?" I flashed Cathy a look that said I'd like to send her someplace nice and hot. She blushed. Royal the cameraman leaned against the door, obviously enjoying the show.

"George, listen to me," I said gently. "I don't study ESP or psychic phenomena, so I really don't think I'm going to be much use to you. See, I've read the cards since I was a little girl and I learned all my traditions from my grandmother. These things are all just part of my everyday life."

His expression fell so hard that I thought he'd break his jaw. "You mean you won't talk to me?"

Cathy stiffened and I knew that if I said no, she'd find a way to make me regret it. For some reason, she'd taken this runt under her wing. I looked back at George, who could have passed for a basset hound on a sad day. What the hell. How bad could one afternoon be?

"Oh all right. If you want to discuss the tarot, I suppose you can stay, but please, don't bother me with questions while I'm waiting on customers, okay?"

The moment I acquiesced, Cathy made a beeline for the door. "Now that that's settled, Royal and I have to interview a few other business owners along Main Street. Thank you, Emerald. George, we'll meet you back at the station."

She and Royal took off out the door faster than a greased pig on speed, and as I watched them go, I couldn't shake the feeling that I'd just been scammed. I had to pat myself on the back, though. This was the first time she'd left the shop on her own volition.

I turned back to George. He held up the metal briefcase, the eager smile on his face a little too bright. "I want to film you while you're reading the cards for somebody. I've got my video camera right here."

Whoa! Since when had I agreed to that? "Slow down there, partner. No cameras. Any reader worth her salt maintains strict confidence for her clients. That means you can't listen in, either."

He scrunched up his face, his chin jutting forward. "But that way I could study your technique better."

"Well, I'm sorry, but that's not going to happen." I straightened my shoulders and put on my best face. "You'll have to be content with just asking your questions."

Pouting, he swung around, jostling the nearest display table as he did so. He jerked away, but only managed to destabilize it more. I dove, trying to steady it before disaster struck, but was seconds too late. The table tipped, sending two delicate and expensive rose-patterned teapots smashing to the ground. Four of the baskets I'd so lovingly prepared went flying, their contents skittering across the floor. Miniature jars of honey and jelly rolled everywhere, a few of them breaking and spilling their sticky contents all over the tile.

"Jeez! Please, be careful!" I stared at the remains, rubbing my brow. Oh yeah, headache looming on the horizon, prepare for attack. "Well, these teapots are history. You wait here while I sweep up these shards. The last thing I need is some customer cutting herself on them."

A cloud of gloom settled over his face. George waved at the mess on the floor. "I suppose you expect me to pay for those?"

Cinnamon, who had been watching this debacle from behind the counter, brought over the whisk, the dustpan, and a wet cloth. She shooed me away and proceeded to clean up the scattered bits of teapots and the honey that oozed along the floor.

After thanking her, I turned back to George. "You break it, you buy it." I pointed to a tasteful but firm warning tacked on the wall that informed customers of just that fact.

He rolled his eyes and pulled out his wallet. "How much?"

I added up the total amount of broken wares. "The damage comes to $152.80."

"Jeez," he said, flinging three fifties and a five on the counter. "They're just teapots. What'd you do? Pay the queen of England to hand paint them?"

I took a deep breath, counted to five, and then let it out slowly. "Listen to me. I agreed to answer some questions on the tarot. I didn't agree to any filming, or to having my shop disrupted, or to putting up with rude behavior." I rested my hands on my hips, staring him down.

He frowned, but shrugged and held up the video case. "Whatever. Can I put this somewhere safe?"

"Give it to me," I said, and took it into my office. When I returned, he was fiddling with his miniature tape recorder.

"Can I at least tape-record your answers?"

Already weary of the battle, I capitulated. "Fine, but only when we're alone. When I'm helping a customer, you back off. And I want a copy of those tapes after you're done. And for goodness sake, please, don't break anything else! Some of my inventory is far more expensive than you can probably afford and I'm not about to take a loss on it."

As he followed me to the counter, I began repairing a couple of the baskets that had received only minor dents. I could refill them and mark them on sale because of the scuffs and dings. As I worked, I tried to pin down George's energy. When I reached out, it was like poking the Pillsbury Doughboy. His ego was all puffed out of shape, as if he truly believed he had all the answers in life. I figured him for twenty-two . . . maybe twenty-four at the most. At any rate, George was like a number of young men who hadn't learned to see beyond their hormones. I sighed. I had better things to do than cater to a spoiled brat.

The day proceeded to go from bad to worse. After I finished helping Tansy Brewer find the right teacup to replace a broken one from her set, George cornered me near the alcove where I read tarot.

"I've got so many questions for you," he said. "Not many people I know are interested in—or capable of—discussing the occult on a professional basis. I know you haven't put in as much actual study time as I have but—"

"George, quit playing one-upmanship. I've been reading the cards all my life. Ask your questions." Might as well get this over with.

He took a deep breath. "Okay, first: Do you think the psychological benefits of tarot readings outweigh the psychic benefits of what the querent learns? Or do you think they are better served by the information from the reading itself?"

Great. Just what I needed, Frasier Crane of the psychic realm. "Dunno, it depends on the person, I suppose. Most of my clients come to me for issues that aren't life-altering."

"Oh." He looked almost crestfallen. "But surely you've thought about this before? I mean, you don't just come in here and give readings and then forget about it until next time?"

How could I make him understand? For me, reading the tarot wasn't a hobby. Neither was it a religion, nor a study. It was just something I did, like my charms and the folk magic my Nanna had taught me. All of my quirks were part of my life, just as much as breathing or the beating of my heart. I felt neither the need nor desire to defend myself.

"George, I told you. This is all part of my everyday life. Can you understand? It was something my grandmother did, and something her grandmother did. Nanna taught me how to read them when I was a little girl. The cards are part and parcel of who I am."

His smile took on a nasty, condescending edge. "I see. So you really don't know much about what you're doing. You just 'do it'?"

I squelched the desire to slap that patronizing look off his baby-face and narrowed my eyes. "I advise you to remember that you are a guest in this shop."

He cocked his head. "Have you ever lied during a reading?"

"No, George, I have never lied during a reading."

"What about when the person wasn't capable of handling the answer?"

The pompous twit. "I don't make judgments about the emotional stability of my clients. If I have reason to think they won't benefit from a reading, I won't agree to give them one. However, that doesn't rule out the use of diplomacy when interpreting—"

"Isn't 'diplomacy' just another word for 'lie'?"

I'd had enough. I reached out and grabbed his tape recorder, clicked it off, then handed it back to him. "You need to learn some manners, boy. Don't interrupt me again. And may I advise you to find a better dictionary?

'Lie' and 'diplomacy' are hardly synonyms. Tact and diplomacy do not require one to resort to lying."

George stared at me, his round eyes beginning to smolder. "I can't believe you call yourself a professional and yet you're disagreeing with me! You actually think everybody you read for can handle the truth? Emerald, the vast majority of people are pretty stupid. Don't give them any more credit than you have to."

I folded my arms and stared at him. "When someone comes to me for a reading, it's my responsibility to be honest with them. I'd be a fraud if I lied to them. Worse yet, I'd be abusing their trust."

He scuffed at the floor. After a moment, he looked up, sullen and broody. "Well, what about money? Don't you think that accepting money for parlor-game readings taints your work? It's not like you're giving them serious psychic counsel."

I took a deep breath, holding it to the count of five. When I spoke, I made sure my voice was so low that no one else could hear. "You have crossed the line. Listen to me, and listen good: The only thing that might taint my work is if I strongly *dislike* the person I'm reading for, and then I wouldn't offer to read the cards in the first place. Money doesn't interfere with psychic power unless you get greedy. And I have always discouraged people from getting readings when I think they can't afford them."

We were almost nose-to-nose and yet George crowded still closer. Uncomfortable, I took a step back.

"Take me in as a partner," he said, his eyes blazing. "I can help you. You can teach me to read for the public and I'll teach you all the stuff you've ignored, that you really should know. We could make a killing at the psychic fairs in Seattle. We'd make great partners."

Oh good God, so this was what it was all about? "I'm sorry to disappoint you," I said, "but if you're looking for a mentor, you'd better drop the idea right now, because it's not going to happen." The headache that had been looming since Cathy first came in the shop struck, and struck with a vengeance.

"Why not? Are you afraid of the competition? What would you do if another tarot reader set up shop in town?" he asked, a look of triumph in his eyes. "Isn't it better to have the competition working with you rather than against you?"

I snorted. "What would I do? Nothing. We live in a free country, or so the government claims. If someone wants to open a tarot shop in Chiqetaw, I'm not going to stop him. Get it through your head. The Chintz 'n China sells—gee, guess what?—china! I make most of my money off tea and teapots, which is the way I want it. So don't worry yourself about me. My clients come to me because they like how I read the tarot. If they want to go elsewhere, they're free to do so."

I put my hands on his shoulders and firmly pushed him back a few steps. "And George," I said, "don't ever get in my face again. I have a strong sense of boundaries, and babe, you crossed the line but good."

With a snort, he said, "Want some free advice?"

"I think you've said enough as it is."

"Fine, so you think I'm some punk and you don't need advice from me. Go on giving your penny-ante readings. But man, you've got real psychic power. The dead show up in your house and ask you to solve their murders. You could open up a ghost-busting type of outfit. Or a psychic institute. You could probably make some real money. I'd work with you! But will you help somebody who really wants to study the path to enlightenment? No, you just want to play tea party."

I'd had enough. I pointed toward the front door. "Leave. Now."

"Sure. Kick me out. You think you're such hot shit around here, but you're just a two-bit carnival queen. I'm telling you the truth right to your face; if you can't handle it, then it's not my problem." He wheeled and strode out of the shop. By now, everybody was listening. They watched him exit, then silently turned to me.

Astounded, I stared at the door as it swung shut. That little bastard. How dare he come into my shop, break my merchandise, and proceed to treat me like dirt! I leaned against the counter and tried to shake off my anger, studiously avoiding the questioning glances. Just then, Lana popped through the front door and I motioned to her.

"Take over here, please. I need a break, and I need it now."

I slipped into the bathroom, washed my hands and splashed some cold water on my face. As I stared at myself in the mirror, I felt a wave of doubt rise up. Could anything he'd said be true? But then, reality took hold and I shook it off. I just needed some lunch and a quiet moment in which to regroup. I headed to the tearoom for a cup of soup and a sandwich when Jimbo wandered in.

"Hey, O'Brien, gotta minute?"

I flashed Jimbo a tired smile. "For you? Maybe even five. I've had the most horrendous morning. Have lunch with me?"

Jimbo grunted and selected two sandwiches and an assortment of cookies. He swung one leg over the back of the chair and stuffed his mouth with turkey and pastrami. I ladled out a bowl of soup and slid into the chair next to him, launching into a diatribe as I vented my frustration over the morning.

After a moment, I realized that my voice was a little loud. "Ugh, I'll finish telling you later. What's up?"

The shop bells tinkled as he stuffed the last bite of his second sandwich into his mouth, followed it with a swig of raspberry tea, and licked his fingers. He tossed a ten-spot on the table. "Good grub. I just wanted to make sure you remembered how to get to my place. Scar's still missing." His eyes flickered with worry.

I'd been out to Jimbo's a couple times during the summer, mainly to ferry the kids for a swim in Miner's Lake.

"Yeah, I remember how to get there, but why don't you draw a map so I can give it to Murray. I'm not sure if she knows and I go by landmarks, rather than street names."

Jimbo looked like he was about to say something, then grabbed a napkin and sketched out rough directions on it. "She should be able to understand these." He bit into a gingersnap and then held it out, looking at it with a critical eye. "Not bad, not bad. You set a good spread at this joint, I'll give you that. So, you read up on the Klakatat Monster?"

"Murray told me a little about it. Like Sasquatch, but more unpredictable."

"And a damned sight more dangerous. Did you know that according to local legend, this thing has racked up over fifteen deaths since when the prospectors first settled near Goldbar Creek? The creek runs out of the valley and feeds directly into Miner's Lake." He drew a map with his finger along the table. "Way I figure it, is the creature's coming down from Klickavail Mountain. That's supposed to be its home."

A flicker crossed his eyes and I noticed that he was sweating. Just a few beads of perspiration dampened his forehead, but it was enough to make me nervous. If Jimbo was scared of this thing, then I really didn't want to get close enough to shake hands. That is, if it actually existed.

"I didn't know all that. What do the authorities say about it?"

"Authorities-schmorities. What do you think they say? Cougar death, or bear mauling. Well, that happens now and again, but the cougars and bears around here are more afraid of us than we are of them. They don't use people as chew toys and then leave them for dead. If they kill it's for food, or because some idiot gets between them and their cubs."

"Yeah, I guess you're right. Okay, see you tomorrow. Remember, you promised fried chicken. And make enough so I can take some home for the kids."

Jimbo pushed back his chair. "Sure thing, O'Brien."

"Can I come along, Emerald? This would be the perfect chance to see you in action!" George stepped out from a corner where he had been eavesdropping on our conversation.

I stared at him, astonished first by the fact that he'd returned, and second, that he had the gall to try to invite himself along after I'd kicked him out.

"I forgot my video camera," he added.

No longer caring if anybody overheard, I exploded. "I thought I told you to leave! Didn't your mother teach you to behave better than this? Jimbo and I were having a private conversation. You have no business asking to go along. In fact, you've got no business ever darkening the door of my shop again! I want you out of here."

Both Jimbo and George stared at me; Jimbo's eyes were twinkling.

George snorted. "Man, you really turned out to be a bitch. I thought we were going to be friends, but you're such a tight-ass that now I wouldn't work for you if you got down on your knees and begged me to."

"If anybody's getting down on their knees, it's gonna be you, dude." Jimbo stepped in between us, tapping George on the shoulder. "The lady wants you to leave. If I were you, I wouldn't make her mad. I've seen her in action. She's scary." He pulled himself up to his full height. "And I'm scarier."

George stared up at Jimbo, who towered over him by a good seven or eight inches and outweighed him by at least seventy pounds. "Uh . . . uh . . . I'm leaving, okay? I just have to get my gear."

"You stay here. I'll get it," I broke in. "I don't want you trashing anything else on your way out." I headed into the back room and Jimbo followed me, to give me a hand. He lugged the metal case to the front door and dumped it on the sidewalk. George flashed me an odd smirk as he picked up his camera case and headed toward a brand-new BMW convertible. The kid wasn't hurting for money. Probably had rich folks, because you sure didn't make that kind of dough on an intern's salary.

George screeched out of the parking space and down the street. Jimbo said, "He's a little weasel. Be careful, he's the type to hold a grudge."

"Yeah," I said. "I think you're spot on. I'll see you tomorrow."

As the biker ambled down the sidewalk, it struck me that on one hand, there was George, who passed for a nice, well-situated young man until he opened his mouth. On the other hand, there was Jimbo, a rough-and-ready biker who looked dangerous but had turned out to be as good-hearted as he was rough around the edges. Books and covers, I thought.

I returned to the tea room, searching for the instructions to Jimbo's house. The paper was resting on the floor, beneath the table, and as I reached down to get it, a prickle of energy rushed up my arm. Maybe we weren't off on a wild goose chase after all.

Chapter 4

✦

SUNDAY MORNING, I woke up more than a little sore. Yoga class had gone better than I expected. Tina Gaylord, the instructor, had taken me to one side to assess me for placement in class. After touching my toes produced a loud grunt, and trying to balance on one leg for longer than a count of ten sent me toppling to the floor, Tina assigned me to the beginners' side of the room.

As I watched Murray lithely twist herself into one asana after another, I decided that it was time to kick the couch-potato habit. I might never be able to stand on my head, but by God, I was determined to be able to touch my toes without groaning.

A warm breeze cascaded through the open window overlooking the backyard. I winced and climbed out from under the new comforter I'd recently purchased. The color of peacock feathers, the blanket had been the inspiration for me to redo my entire bedroom, and I'd lucked out, finding matching accessories so that now I felt like I was sleeping in an opulent harem. Even during summer, the nights in Chiqetaw were usually cool enough to warrant a cozy blanket.

I took a quick shower, then slipped on the one-piece swimsuit I'd bought at the beginning of summer. The bra shelf supported my boobs so they weren't doing the jiggle-dance that all large-breasted women dealt with, but the leg holes rode higher on my hips than I felt comfortable with. Harlow had helped me pick it out.

A cautious peek in the mirror caught me off guard. Whoa. My, oh my. Apparently, Harlow knew what she was talking about when it came to fashion. Outside the glare of the dressing room lights, the suit looked good . . . real good. The high-cut legs made me look taller and less cushy around the middle, and the color was a gorgeous tone-on-tone embossed burgundy, which set off my peaches-and-cream skin, as Nanna would have called it.

I slipped jeans and a tank top over the suit, slid into a pair of loafers, and wove my tangle of curls into a French braid that fell just above my waist. Silver sparkled among the brunette.

In the kitchen, the feline brigade came bouncing into the kitchen, clamoring for food. Kip fed them while I finished making English muffin-and-egg sandwiches for breakfast. I fixed myself a quad-shot espresso and poured it in the blender, adding a dollop of vanilla ice cream, milk, a couple of ice cubes, and chocolate syrup. Might as well make it nutritious, I thought, tossing in a scoop of chocolate Slim-Fast that I kept around for emergency meals. As the blissfully thick, caffeinated shake ran down my throat, I sat down at the table with the kids.

"Why can't we go?" Kip said for the umpteenth time, his mouth full of muffin. His strawberry-blond hair reflected in the sunlight that beamed through the window, as he gave me that woeful puppy-dog gaze of his. Short for his age, he looked younger than his nine years.

Randa chimed in. "Yeah, I hate chlorine. The lake would be so much nicer."

"I already told you," I said. "A man's missing. We don't know what might be out there and I refuse to put you in danger. I tell you what, if everything seems okay, I'll drive back, get you, and you can go swimming this afternoon." I gave them my "no-more-complaints-and-that's-final" look. They quieted down. "Stay around the neighborhood today, okay? I'm taking my cell phone, and Horvald's going to be home, so go over to his place if there's an emergency."

They pouted the rest of the way through breakfast, but by the time I was ready to leave, they'd managed to find something to occupy their time. Kip was playing superhero out in the front yard, and Randa was on the phone, calling to see if her friend Lori was back from vacation yet. A horn sounded from the front of the house. Murray had arrived. We were driving out separately, just in case her boss, Coughlan, called her back to the station. The jerk was so lazy that he had taken to interrupting her on her days off to take care of grunt-work that he didn't want to do.

I headed out the door, glancing at the still-unfamiliar Mercury Mountaineer parked in my drive. Yet another change this year. I had finally given up hope of ever finding my beloved Grand Cherokee, which had apparently gone the way of a chop shop when it had been stolen in April.

I sauntered over to Mur's pickup and leaned in her window. "Do you mind if we stop at the store before we head out? I didn't want to torture the kids anymore than necessary by packing a picnic basket here."

She nodded. "Not a problem. I'll follow you, right?"

I shaded my eyes from the sun. "Yeah, do you have the directions in case we get separated?" I handed her the map that Jimbo had drawn up.

"I've been there before, remember? When I was checking out Jimbo's alibi?" She tucked the napkin into her pocket.

"That's right. He's changed in the past months, don't you think?"

She shrugged. "At least he hasn't gotten himself tossed

in jail since you dropped the charges against him. Okay, let's get this show on the road."

As I pulled out of the driveway, I turned on the radio to 107.7—The End. Nirvana came wailing out of the speakers and I chimed in, happily belting out the lyrics to "Lithium," even more off-key than Kurt Cobain himself. Fifteen minutes later, the back seat full of bread, chips, soda, and beer for Jimbo, I turned left onto Myerson Road, with Murray keeping pace right behind me.

Myerson forked into a "Y." I flipped on my right blinker and turned onto Oakwood, which would lead us northeast. A spacious country road, Oakwood was free from potholes since the loggers took a different route that led them around Chiqetaw instead of directly through it.

The road wound through patches of fir, cedar, and alder that were interspersed with sprawling country homes and vintage farmhouses. The big farms had been subdivided into one-to-five acre individual lots years ago, and the profusion of houses were surrounded by miniature corn fields and blueberry farms. Weekend gardeners made a killing at the farmers' markets around the area. I veered left when we came to Lakeshore Drive.

Miner's Lake was actually more of an overgrown pond than an actual lake. While the other side was clearly visible, the lake was wide enough to fish on and swim in. I slowed, bumping along the uneven road, wondering if the city was ever going to get around to repaving it.

Jimbo's chopper, polished and shining, was parked in front of a ramshackle house that had long ago passed its prime. The house was surrounded by outbuildings and sheds scattered across the property. Half-finished projects, from engine motors to plumbing to woodworking, littered the yard, and a big old truck peeked out of the main garage. One of those rounded cab affairs, it had been jacked up for off-road use, probably for when Jimbo went hunting and trapping.

As I pulled to a stop, Murray eased in behind me and

Jimbo sauntered out into the yard. It still seemed odd to see him in his home environment. Instead of his leathers, he was wearing a mesh tank top and jeans. His perpetual bandana was nowhere to be seen, instead he'd caught his hair back into a ponytail that was hanging down his back. Roo, his brown and white three-legged dog, hopped along beside him, barking and wagging her tail. She was missing her left rear leg, but the pooch seemed happy enough.

Jimbo shushed her. "They're friends, you dimwit. Good girl, that's a good girl."

The dog came loping up to greet us. The first time I'd laid eyes on her, I'd been surprised to see how well she functioned with only three legs; but she ran and played just like any other dog.

"Hey Jimbo. You remember Murray?"

Jimbo's eyes flickered from my face to hers. He gave her a wry grin and spread out his arms. "Yeah, yeah . . . Hey, Detective, you want to frisk me?"

I choked back a snort as Murray cleared her throat. "Thanks for the offer, but I'll pass. I heard you were frying up a chicken and decided to find out if you can really cook, or if you're blowing smoke again."

As I watched them, a tiny bell went off in the back of my brain, but it flickered and vanished as quickly as it had come. I shrugged it off and looked around. "You know, before we eat lunch, why don't you show me where your fence got torn up?" If there was something nasty out here, I might be able to get some sort of energy trace on it and at least figure out whether it was a cow gone rogue, or something more sinister.

"Good idea. This way." Jimbo led us past the jumble of fix-it projects sitting around the yard, to a field that spread out for a couple of acres. I inhaled sharply; his garden was more than a small patch of vegetables—it was huge, taking up the space of two city lots. Thick patches of zucchini and squash dotted the ground, and vine after vine of peas trailed up makeshift trellises.

When we came to the carrot patch, however, it looked like Bugs Bunny's evil twin had come calling. The carrots were trampled, and a number of them had been uprooted and gnawed at, then dropped. A nearby corn patch had received similar treatment, the stalks bent and broken. I knelt down, looking at the footprints Jimbo had been talking about. Whatever had made them had been big, all right, and barefoot.

"Mur, what do you think?"

"Got a giant in the neighborhood? I've never seen prints that big, but they could be a hoax," she said. "Lot of kids out here get bored during the summer."

The raised beds had been torn apart. "Well, if it's kids, it's more than a prank." I gauged the damage that had been done. "They really ripped up this section of the garden. But why did the culprit stop here and not rampage through the whole field?"

"Because I heard it, that's why," Jimbo said. "Roo was barking her head off so I came out with my shotgun. Thought it might be a coyote or a fox after the chickens. I told you five of my chickens went missing over the past few weeks. I saw something loping back into the woods, and it was moving fast. Big, running on two legs. Look at what it did to my fence."

Though he'd already started mending it, the fence showed definite signs of damage. None of the wires had been cut, but instead had been bent, as if some large weight leaned against it until it was low enough to crawl over.

I looked for any sign of cloth or fur stuck to the wires but came up empty. Finally, I reached out to grab the fence where it had been mangled the most. As I touched the wire, a jolt raced through my fingers and I yanked my hand away. A thin red line rose where my palm had touched the barbed wire. "Damn it, why didn't you tell me there's juice running through this?"

Jimbo gave me a quizzical look. "What are you talking about?"

With Murray peeking over my shoulder, I showed him my hand. "This is what I'm talking about. The minute I touched the fence, I got shocked."

"O'Brien, this fence ain't electrified. I don't have the bucks for that." His eyes flashed and I thought I detected a hint of worry behind that gruff exterior.

Murray turned to examine the fence. "He's right, no juice. Em, did you feel anything else?"

I closed my eyes, trying remember what had been running through my mind, but the only thing that stood out was the blinding flash of pain as it registered on my nerves. "No. I have no idea what happened, but I don't like it. Okay, well, it's obvious something came through here. I dunno what."

"Bear maybe?" Murray said. "Bears are good for that sort of thing, when they aren't trying to get in your car." She gave me a snarky grin, as if I needed a reminder that a big ol' bear had been cozying up to my late and lamented SUV.

Jimbo shook his head. "Bear would have gone sniffin' around the garbage, not digging up carrots."

"True enough," Murray said. "What say we go get the groceries?"

We wandered back to the driveway and wrestled the food out of the Mountaineer. I looked over at Jimbo. "Where should I stow this stuff? Down in the clearing where the kids go swimming?"

"Yeah. Here, give me that." He snagged the heaviest bags out of my arms, carrying them as if they were made of Styrofoam. Murray and I gathered up the rest of the supplies and set off behind him, with Roo hopping right alongside.

"You're one heck of a doggie," I said, stopping to pet her.

Jimbo glanced back at me. "Roo's a keeper, all right. Found her out there on the road a couple years ago," he said. "Some dumb-ass hit her with a truck and kept on

going. I took her to the vet down the road and he ampu-
tated her leg. The bone was shattered, and he said it would
be harder on her for him to try and fix it than to amputate
it. She healed up just fine. I named her Roo 'cause she reminds me of a kangaroo."

Yet another side of Jimbo that had only recently showed
itself. He also had a couple of cats, Snidely and Whiplash;
a couple of nanny goats, Billy and The Kid; and a huge pen
of chickens. He only named the egg-layers though, never
the ones culled for roasting.

As we entered the clearing, I saw that Jimbo had been
doing some landscaping. The foliage had been cut away
since the last time the kids and I were here. The shore was
easily accessible now. The water was so shallow in this
area that you could easily wade out till it hit your knees before the lake bottom dropped off suddenly, plunging to fifteen feet deep within a single step's range. A couple of
inner-tubes floated nearby, tied to a rickety walkway that
led out to a rowboat. Canary grass, waist high, was sprinkled with thick stands of cattails and horsetail and skunk
cabbage, whose brilliant yellow flowers filled the air with
a fetid smell.

The day was shaping up to be hot—at least eighty de-
grees. I fished through the bags for sunscreen. "I'll start
looking around after lunch. I'd rather do it then, when I've
eaten enough to ground my energy."

Jimbo shrugged, looking a little disappointed. "Sure.
Whatever works for you. If Scar's dead, well . . . I guess
he won't be going anywhere. And if he's not, then I'm
back to square one." He headed up the trail. "I'll go check
on the bird. It should be ready in a few minutes."

As Jimbo disappeared toward the house, Murray and I
spread out the blanket and arranged the food.

"Do you honestly think you'll find anything?" she
asked.

I shook my head. "Ten to one, no. My guess is that Scar
took off, got freaked by the idea of fatherhood or something

like that. He'll probably turn up in a few days. I can tell that Jimbo's a lot more worried about Scar than he lets on. But I have to say, it's this mysterious intruder that confuses me. He's right, whatever did it was big. And if it was a person, they'd have to be incredibly strong to bend that fence."

The soft lapping of waves against the shore and the drone of buzzing insects lulled me into a drowsy state. I stretched out on the blanket, propping myself up on one elbow as I shaded my eyes. Across the lake, a scattered handful of homes dotted the shoreline.

"Those houses over there look expensive."

"They are. The developers scam people for every buck they can get." Murray arched her back, then pulled off her clothes to reveal a lovely two-piece tankini suit. The brilliant cobalt set off her dark skin and eyes. She shook her hair out of the ever-present braid. Loose, it hung down to her butt, a little longer than mine, but her hair was so straight that it gleamed in the sunlight.

I stared at her, unable to wrench my eyes away. "You look absolutely amazing, Mur." And breathtaking she was: tall, curvy, sturdy, with well-muscled legs and arms.

She swatted a bee away from the bread. "Thanks. I thought I might as well get some swimming in while we're here. Yoga class has given me a lot of extra energy."

"I was stiff as a board this morning. I sure hope I end up enjoying it as much as you do," I grumbled.

She settled on the blanket next to me. "Give it time. You just started. Your body has to adjust to the movements."

A rustling through the grass told us Jimbo had returned. He was carrying a platter of fried chicken. "We'll eat, then you can do your hoodoo thing and see if you can find out what happened to Scar."

The smell wafting up from the plate was incredible, and the saliva began to churn in my mouth. As I bit into the drumstick, a wave of flavor rolled down my throat that almost brought tears to my eyes. "I've never tasted chicken so good. You say your grandmother taught you to cook like this?"

"Yep," he said. "Last time I visited her, she gave me her recipe for fried chicken and catfish. I wrapped up some drumsticks and thighs for you to take home to the kids."

Murray gave him a smile, her chin covered with chicken grease and butter from the French bread. "Well, you were a good student, I'll say that much." We polished off the entire platter along with most everything else I'd brought. I passed around the wet-wipes.

"Oh man, another bite and I'll explode." I dried my hands on a paper towel. "Jimbo, tell us a little more about Scar. What's his real name? How long have you known him?"

He settled back against the ground, hands under his head. "I don't know what Scar's real name is. The boys in the valley have a code when it comes to information. If it's not offered, don't ask. Some of the guys out there are carrying baggage from the past that they don't want to talk about. Scar showed up four or five years back, said he was from the Midwest and had been on the road since 1986. We're good buddies, but he's never volunteered anything about his past. He's a good guy, though . . . good-hearted."

Murray nodded. "I guess tracing him by his social security number would be out of the question?"

Jimbo snorted. "And just who's going to have that information? Scar was what you call an entrepreneur."

I broke in. "But you told me he just bought a thirty-thousand-dollar bike. How did he get the money to pay for it?"

"The boys in the valley don't have regular jobs, Em," Murray said. "Most are legit, I think there are a several good mechanics out there who make a pretty penny and I know there are at least two jewelry makers and a fix-it guy. Others earn a few bucks through odd jobs and whatnot. And still others . . . You're right, though. Thirty thousand dollars is a lot of money to be dropping on a motorcycle when you don't have any visible means of income."

Jimbo sat up and expelled a loud sigh. "Will you two get off it? I don't know where his money came from, but I do know he wouldn't hurt a fly. Scar loves his girlfriend. He likes the idea of having a family and kids, and he just wants to hang out and have a beer with his buddies in the evening. See what you can find, okay?"

Obviously this was getting us nowhere. I stood up and dusted off my jeans. "Guess I'll get started. It'll do me good to walk off some of this food. Where does Scar usually hang out?"

Jimbo pointed to a path that cut around the lake. "His favorite fishing spot is back there, through the woods and over by that little spit that comes out of the trees there."

It looked to be close to half a mile. An easy hike. "Have you gone out there looking for him? Maybe he showed up, fell, hit his head on something."

The big biker hung his head. "O'Brien, I've scoured everywhere else on this property, but for the past couple of weeks, that path's given me the creeps every time I go near it. Never bothered me before but now, the minute I get near, I turn tail and hoof it back to the house. I wanted to check it out but I just . . . get scared out of my wits. I don't know what's going on, but I don't like it."

Jimbo was, for the most part, ESP-blind, so whatever was out there was either unusually strong, or his imagination was playing tricks on him. Neither possibility reassured me. "Okay, why don't you clean up this mess. If I'm not back in half an hour, come find me."

He checked his watch, then nodded as I turned to Murray. "Ready to go?"

She shook her head. "Give me a few. I ate like a pig and I'll explode if I move around too much. You want to wait for me?"

"Slacker! I'll just go all by my lonesome and you can

catch up." I tossed her a grin, then flounced off in the direction of the path.

"I'll be along in a bit—don't go too far until I get there," Murray called after me.

The area near Miner's Lake was one step away from deep wilderness. Cedars and fir grew thick in the hushed shade of the forest, their tall trunks buttressed by dense thickets of waist-high deer ferns and thick shrubs of drooping salal, its leathery, shining leaves and clusters of waxy indigo berries ready to gather for wine and jelly making.

I stopped by a fallen log covered with the ever-present moss and mushrooms that permeated the area, and settled myself on the end, where I drifted into a light trance, touching on the droning of bees, the bird song that echoed through the trees, the gentle burble of a nearby creek. Sunlight beat down through the forest canopy, dappling the ground with the sparkles of peridot light that filtered through the leaves.

As my thoughts came to rest, I began to notice an undercurrent of energy. The welcoming path ahead suddenly loomed daunting and shadowed. I tried to pick out the chord that disrupted the otherwise tranquil woods, but it was almost as if the land wore a thin veneer of energy, much like a blanket of weaving colors that hid its secrets from prying eyes.

Unsettled, I wondered if I should turn back. No, I'd promised Jimbo I'd find out what I could, and Murray would be joining me soon. Surely, if there was anything out here, I'd see it before it saw me. Inhaling deeply, I reached out, searching for any sense of human life nearby, focusing on the copse, breathing slowly. *Slow, go slow, deeper, a little deeper.* And then, before I could shield against it, a presence intruded.

Thick tendrils of energy rumbled up from the soil. I tried to pull away but the vines coiled around my conscious thoughts, dragging my focus deep into the mulch of the forest floor. I couldn't think, couldn't break away, couldn't do anything but succumb to the encroaching force. On the verge of passing out, I sought for a handhold, an anchor to ground me into the tangible world.

A sudden noise in the bushes broke my concentration, and I leaped to my feet, shaking myself out of the trance. A large brown hare scurried out of the bushes, loping across the path. The animal stopped long enough to turn and gaze at me through golden, glowing eyes, then vanished under a huckleberry bush as quickly as it had appeared.

Alice, I thought. Was I headed down the rabbit hole next? Jimbo had warned me there were strange energies hiding in these woods and he hadn't been exaggerating. This patch of land was rooted in the glaciers and volcanic flows of these mountains, remaining relatively untouched by human development. The forces here were powerful, older than civilization. Who knew what might be lurking in the shadows?

Should I go on, or give it up? I glanced back, looking for any sign that Mur was on her way. Torn between my sense of duty and the feeling that I wasn't altogether in a safe situation, I was about to go back for Murray when a beam of sunlight blinded me; reflecting off something in the clearing ahead, just beyond a low-growing patch of ferns. I hesitated. Since I'd come this far, I might as well take a look. If my eyes were playing tricks on me, then I'd head back to Jimbo's.

I veered off the path, pushing my way through the undergrowth into the glade. Now I could see that the object that had caught my attention—a pair of eyeglasses, sitting on the ground. The light was reflecting off their lenses. Focused on them, I stepped over a small, leaf-covered log half-buried in the dirt and my toe caught on a root or a twig. I wavered for a moment, but couldn't catch my balance and tumbled to the ground.

What the—? Reeling from the sudden fall, I pushed myself to my knees. No damage, as far as I could tell. I turned back to the log, my nose twitching. Something smelled horrible. Had an animal died out here? I leaned in closer, scattering a few leaves away from the branch that had caught my sneaker. Hell and high water! An arm! I'd tripped over somebody's arm! Panicking, I scrambled away, but nothing moved. Ever so cautiously, I crept back and began to brush away more of the leaves and soil.

The man had been haphazardly buried under several bushels of mulch. He was face down, but by what I could see of his leather vest and the green bandana wrapped around his head, I had a sinking feeling that I'd discovered our missing biker. The stench and the cloud of flies that swarmed up when I disturbed the leaves told me that he'd been out here for awhile. I made no move to turn him over. My imagination filled in blanks all too easily. I backed away, shaking.

Blood had spattered the tree trunk beneath which the man rested. Now dried, it resembled ruddy brown paint splattered on the bark. If this was Scar, he hadn't met his end in an easy manner. I leaned against a nearby tree until I could compose myself, unable to wrench my eyes away from the sight. This was no accident. I had to get back to Murray. We had a murder on our hands.

Chapter 5

❖

I JOGGED AS fast as I could, panting all the way. Oh yeah, I'd be sticking with yoga class, all right. As I broke into the clearing where we'd had our picnic, I received my second shock for the day.

Jimbo and Murray were entwined on the blanket. His hands were tangled in her hair, she was straddling his legs, still wearing that gorgeous swimsuit. Their lips were locked in a way that told me they'd done this before. Leaning against a tree, I stared in disbelief. As I opened my mouth, the only words that I managed to squeak out were, "Oh, my God!"

"Emerald!" Murray jumped up, tripping as she scrambled away from Jimbo. The two of them looked for all the world like a couple of school kids who'd been caught necking under the bleachers. "We were—I was about to come after you—"

I shook my head at her. "Later. Jimbo, I'm sorry, but I think I just found Scar's body and I'm pretty sure he didn't die of natural causes."

Jimbo's expression changed from crimson to crushed. He scrambled to his feet. "Goddamn it."

Murray grabbed her jeans and slid them on over her suit. She looked around for her tank top, then stopped to give Jimbo a gentle kiss on the cheek. "We don't know that it's Scar, Jimmy. But we'd better go out there and take a look. Let me get dressed and I'll call for the coroner and a couple of the boys." Stepping to one side, she pulled out her cell phone.

I knelt down next to the distraught biker. What could I say without sounding stupid? After all, I'd just found his best friend—dead, and I'd just found out that Jimbo and my best friend were probably doing the mattress mambo. After a moment, I reached out and put my hand on top of his. "I'm sorry, Jimbo. I really didn't expect to find anything."

He began to pace. "Scar was my best buddy. Did you sense anything out there? Anything at all?"

"Yeah, I did. Like you said, freaky. I wouldn't want to hang out there alone for long. I'm not sure what's causing it, but whatever the source of the energy, it almost knocked me unconscious. Whether it's tied into Scar's death, I dunno. But those woods aren't very friendly once you scrape below the surface."

Murray finished her call. "Go on ahead," she said. "I'll leave a note for Deacon and Sandy with directions and then catch up."

As Jimbo and I started down the trail, he eyed me nervously. "Listen, O'Brien. Anna and I didn't mean to keep you out of the loop. It's just . . . uh . . . well . . ." he stopped, then tried again. "You know, she's a cop . . . and I'm . . ."

Touched by his clumsy attempt to explain, I put my finger to my lips. "Shush. Don't worry about it. Right now, we need to find out if this is actually your friend. I think everything else can go on the back burner until then."

He gave me a wan smile. As we made our way into the

woods, I sensed yet another disruptive force, this time coming from behind a nearby cedar tree, and this time, distinctly human. Oh great. The signature was loud and clear and one I had hoped never to sense again. Spurred on by the adrenaline rush of finding Scar's body, I whipped aside the ferns that were covering the trunk. There, squatting in a crouch, was George.

Furious, I waded into the bushes and grabbed his arm, dragging him out to the path. "You weasel, you were spying on me!"

George squirmed away from me as Murray came jogging down the path.

"Who the hell is this?" she asked.

"Remember I told you about George Pleasant? Cathy's cohort? It seems that he's decided to follow me." I glared at him. "What now, are you stalking me because I told you to get out of my shop?"

Murray gave him the once-over. "All right, suppose you tell me what the hell you're doing out here?"

George, wearing a preppie polo shirt and a pair of Bermuda shorts, had a camera hanging around his neck. I reached over and grabbed for the strap, but Murray stopped me, stepping in between us. She flashed her identification at him.

"My name is Detective Anna Murray, and I asked you a question. I suggest you answer me. Now, what are you doing out here, and why are you following Emerald?"

He gulped, staring at her badge. "Okay, okay. I overheard Emerald and biker-boy here talking about the Klakatat Monster and wanted to tag along. I copied the directions off the paper she left on the table while she and the Hulk were in the back, getting my camera. I've got a right to investigate. Why are you getting on my case?"

"Your 'rights' don't extend to my property, Bub." Jimbo took a step forward, glowering, as I moved in between them. "Emerald told you to back off. I ought to—"

Mur held up her hand. "Mr. Pleasant, I'm afraid I have to ask you to step up against that tree over there. I need to make sure you aren't carrying a weapon."

"You can't frisk me! You haven't read me my rights," George protested.

"That's because I'm not arresting you, nitwit," Murray said. "However, a body has been found near here and, until proven otherwise, we are looking at a potential homicide. You, Mr. Pleasant, were found hiding in the bushes near the scene, so that makes you a potential suspect. Now are you going to cooperate or am I going to have to—"

George paled. "Homicide? Body?" Abruptly, he deflated, his bravado vanishing like wisps of smoke. He obediently leaned up against the cedar and Murray patted him down, then stood back, holding up a cell phone. She examined it briefly, then handed it back to him.

"Okay. Come with us, please. I'll need you to answer some questions." She maneuvered him in line, sandwiching him between Jimbo and herself. I was still boiling over his appearance. Not only did we have to deal with a dead body, but now we had to baby-sit a whiny, spoiled brat.

As we neared the clearing where I'd been sucked into the energy of the woods, George stumbled and Jimbo smacked against his back. With a low growl, the biker yanked George into the air, holding him by his collar. "You pinhead. Can't you watch where you're going?"

George, his feet dangling a good six inches off the ground, started to kick at Jimbo, but then apparently thought the better of it and stopped. Jimbo dropped him like a sack of potatoes and George hit the ground, scrambling out of Jimbo's reach.

As we entered the wild patch of woods, I stopped and raised my hand. Once again, the tendrils came searching for me.

Mur pushed her way forward to my side, where she

steadied me. "What is it?" she asked, interrupting the un-welcome trance.

"There's something hostile . . . this forest doesn't want us here." I noticed that George had slowed to a bare crawl. His face was pale and he turned toward me, the belliger-ence wiped clean from his face.

"I've never felt anything like this before," he said, his voice hushed. "This is a bad, bad place. Something awful happened out here."

"Brilliant, Einstein." Jimbo shook his head in disgust.

I shushed him. "George, I know what you're feeling. I can feel it, too."

George searched my face for answers. Obviously he'd never dealt with energies as powerful as these before. "What is it?"

I shook my head. "Dunno yet, but whatever you do, keep your mind clear. Don't tune in to it." With a little luck, his aura wouldn't be strong enough to attract its at-tention. I turned to Mur. "What do you think about all this?"

She took a long breath, focused, then let it out with a shudder. "These forests are far older than mankind. I know too many legends about this neck of the woods to ever let my guard down out here. I'm not as good of a medium as you are, which is why I suggested that Jimmy ask you to come out here and check things out." She gave me a sheep-ish smile. So, she'd been in on this.

We were nearing the point where I'd veered off the path and found Scar's body. I led them through the thrashed ferns, dreading what was ahead. As we approached the tree under which Scar now rested, Jimbo moved forward and knelt down, brushing away the flies that were circling the back of the man's head. A cloud of stench rose up and, shaking, Jimbo backed away and squatted near the tree. He let out a low sigh.

"Yeah, it's Scar. I don't need to see his face. That jacket . . . I bought it for him on his last birthday."

Murray winced and pulled out her notebook. "Jimmy, it's going to be okay. We'll find out who did this."

"No, you won't," he said. "Regardless of your prodding, the cops ain't gonna beat themselves up looking for whoever killed one of the Klickavail Valley bikers." He shook his head. "Besides, I think the Klakatat Monster got him. Remember the footprint in my garden? And the boys have been hearing some strange things go on up there the past few weeks . . . hoodoo strange. I think the monster's awake."

He impatiently stood up and strode across the clearing, staring into the deep woods that stretched for miles beyond this point. Murray let out a long sigh, then went back to examining the body and the area. At a loss, I looked around for George. Somebody ought to keep an eye on the pipsqueak.

He was standing near the edge of the clearing, talking on his cell phone. When he saw me looking at him, I heard him say, "Yeah, right, later," and he folded the phone and stuffed it in his pocket.

Wondering just who had he been talking to, I meandered over to his side. He gave me a questioning glance, then jabbed his finger toward Scar's body and said in a loud voice, "That's got to be the grossest thing I've ever seen. So, his ghost tell you who did it yet?"

I stared at him. "You really are a callous little bastard, aren't you? Scar was probably murdered, and all you come up with are one-liners?"

"Sorry," he said, shrugging. "Guess I'm just not used to this stuff like you are." A clouded expression crossed his face and he froze. After a moment, he wiped his sleeve across his eyes. "Shit!"

I rolled my eyes. "What's wrong now?"

He blinked. "Emerald, I know you don't like me but I gotta tell you, honest to God, I just had a vision."

He was right. I didn't like him. But I knew he was telling the truth. His aura was swirling so bright I didn't need to be in a trance to feel it; his energy had been caught up in some sort of vortex. Yeah, he'd seen something all right. Whether or not the vision was accurate was another matter.

"Tell me what you saw."

His voice went ringing through the clearing. "I saw a creature, a beast that's not a beast. And then I saw that dude . . . there was blood everywhere . . ."

Murray heard us and whirled around. "Don't encourage him, Emerald. And you—" she pointed to George. "If you start any rumors, I swear I'll find a reason to run you in. Keep your mouth shut unless you know something concrete about the murder."

Just then we heard noises coming from the main trail. The police and the coroner had arrived. Murray called to them while Jimbo found himself a log to sit on. George edged his way to the outer circle of the clearing.

Deacon Wilson and Sandy Whitmeyer were two of the best cops on the squad. They were followed by a stocky man, wearing a suit that was too small and too shiny. He was older and looked more out of shape than I felt. He eyed Murray with a look that told me immediately who he was. Jeez, Coughlan, her supervisor!

He scratched his head as he stared at the body, as the coroner tried to scoot around him, finally tapping him on the shoulder so he could get through to do his work. Murray sidled over to me, and I could tell just how thrilled she was that her nemesis had decided to oversee the case.

Deacon started to take photographs, while Sandy began skimming through the dirt, looking for evidence.

Murray asked me to tell Bob Stryker, the coroner and also the M.E. for Chiqetaw, how I'd found the biker. He had already turned the body over, and I didn't want to see what poor Scar looked like face-up, so I averted my eyes as best as I could. Since I was pretty sure that Stryker wouldn't go in for all my psychic "mumbo-jumbo," I just told him that I'd gone for a walk after lunch and veered off the path because I'd seen the eyeglasses reflecting in the sun. Which was the truth, essentially.

Stryker grunted.

Coughlan leaned over his shoulder. "Look at those slashes. Looks like an animal attack to me."

The M.E. cocked his head and stared at the detective. "Maybe. I can't be sure until I autopsy him, though."

As I watched the interplay, Coughlan casually reached over and squeezed Stryker's shoulder. Hmm . . . what was going on here?

"Cougar was spotted a few miles from here the other day, Bob," Coughlan said. "Almost got hold of a poodle. Woman was frantic when she called in. Trust me, it was a cougar. I'm sure you'll come to the same conclusion once you've had a chance to thoroughly autopsy the body. We'll discuss it over dinner. Laura's making pot roast tonight."

An undercurrent ran between the two men and I squinted, staring intently at Coughlan, who must have sensed my observation because he looked at me, narrowed his eyes, then motioned to Murray. "Get your ass in gear and take her statement, *Detective* Murray. Tell Whitmeyer and Wilson to talk to the others."

Murray nodded. After a quick word with Sandy and Deacon, she drew me away to one side where we wouldn't be overheard. Since she'd already jotted down everything I'd told her, she pretended to write while leaning close enough to whisper.

"That overgrown buffoon makes me so mad. Head of detectives, my ass. Jimmy's right. He's a lazy SOB. He's also right about the fact that Coughlan won't look very hard to find Scar's killer."

"So you don't think a cougar did this?" I asked.

She shook her head. "I've seen cougar attacks. I suppose to the untrained eye it could look the same, but no, I'll wager ten to one that Scar was murdered."

"Why would Coughlan try to cover it up, though?"

"Eh, he's not really trying to 'cover it up.' More like he just doesn't want to deal with an in-depth investigation that could take months to solve. He probably figures that nobody will give a damn since the victim is from the Klickavail enclave. Coughlan's a lazy SOB, and he's just putting in time until he retires a few years from now. If he passes this off as a cougar attack, you can be sure nobody's going to question him. Now, if one of the town financiers showed up, mangled like that, then you'd see Coughlan scramble. Double standard, Em. And no, it's not right, but it exists."

I gazed at the head of detectives, who was whispering in the coroner's ear. "Coughlan and Stryker seem to be pretty cozy."

She nodded. "Coughlan married Laura Stryker, Bob's sister. Rumor has it that Bob borrowed ten thousand dollars from them last year and hasn't paid them back yet. So you know he's going to do whatever he can to keep the peace."

"Nepotism in action, huh?" I shook my head. Political corruption, all the way to the ground level.

Mur shrugged. "Not much we can do right now, except watch." After a pause, she added, "Em, will you do me a favor, as my best friend?"

I knew what she was going to ask. "You want me to keep quiet about your relationship with Jimbo?"

She blushed. "We were going to tell you pretty soon, but with me being a cop and Jim having such a long rap sheet, it's bound to stir up trouble. My friends won't understand because he's got such a reputation for being a roughneck. And his friends won't talk to him if they think he's dating a cop. But I was wrong about him, Em. He's a sweetheart. Yes, he's bullheaded, and I'll admit he doesn't have the best record in the history of Chiqetaw, but he's a good guy."

I looked into those deep, obsidian eyes of hers and knew that she really was happy with Jimbo. When I'd found them in the clearing, there'd been a spark between them that told me this was more than a mild flirtation. And I wasn't going to play party to taking that away from her. "Of course, I'll keep my mouth shut. But I want to hear all about it when this is over. You owe me that!"

"You're on. And . . . thanks, babe."

Coughlan barked an order for her to get her ass over there, so she headed back to the body. Sandy and Deacon were still questioning Jimbo and George.

I decided to nose around the outskirts of the clearing. I had just set foot through the tangle of ferns past the crime tape when, to my dismay, I found myself staring into the face of Cathy Sutton. Oh God, why her? Why now?

"So Emerald, we meet again!" She trampled her way through the bushes to where I was standing and thrust her microphone in my face. "I suppose you're on the case, helping solve yet another murder? Have the police called you in as a psychic?"

How the hell had she gotten wind of what was happening? Maybe they'd been listening to a police scanner? I glanced back into the clearing. Wait a minute. *George and his cell phone.* George worked for the station as an intern. Yep, he'd called in the big guns. I turned back to her.

"I found the body, that's all. I don't know anything more about it."

"Oh come on, Emerald. Surely you know what's going on!" She motioned and Royal appeared, edging in for a close up.

Once again, unable to muster my diplomacy, I ground my teeth together. "Take a hike, Sutton. If you want answers, wait and talk to the cops."

I left her there and returned to the clearing, where I mutely watched the police finish their tasks. There was a fluttering in the wind, and the faint whiff of bonfires and autumn decay swept past me. Scar hadn't been the source of the tumultuous energy I'd felt in the woods. And he hadn't been killed by a cougar, either. That much, I knew for sure. When a person had been murdered, there was a certain feel to the case, a certain edge that I had learned to pick up, much to my dismay. Scar had died at someone's hands, not some big cat's paws. And I had the feeling that whoever—or whatever—had killed him wasn't finished yet.

Chapter 6

❖

HOME AT LAST. I trudged into the house, somber.
Randa glanced up at me from her book. "What's wrong,
Mom? You look worn out."

Just dandy. Most moms complained about having to
herd their kids to baseball games or ice skating lessons. I
whined about body counts. I dropped into the recliner.
"We found Jimbo's friend."

Randa marked her place and closed the book. "He
wasn't okay, was he?"

I shook my head. "No, honey. He was dead. That's why
I didn't want you guys to come with me." I looked around.
"Where's Kip? And why aren't you over at Horvald's?"

She shrugged. "I didn't feel so good; I got queasy after
lunch so I asked him if I could come home and rest. Mr. Ledbetter has been phoning every half-hour to check on me."

I rested my hand on her forehead. She was a little hot,
but I suspected that her nausea was due to the fact that
she'd just started her period this summer and puberty was
hitting her hard. "Do you want me to draw you a bath or
make you some tea?"

With a little sniff, she leaned against me. "Yeah, mint tea would be nice."

"Okay, I need to take a quick shower but afterward, we'll sit in the kitchen and I'll make you tea and toast. Would you like some soup, too?"

A glint sparkled into her eye and I thought that maybe it wasn't cramps at all, maybe she just needed a Mom-fix. "Yeah, soup's good!"

"All right. Do me a favor and go tell Kip to come home. I'll be back downstairs in a flash."

Though I longed for a lengthy bubble bath, I made do with a quick rinse and scrub down. By the time I returned to the kitchen, Kip and Randa were both sitting at the table. Even though I knew they'd had a good lunch, I pulled out a box of Lipton Noodle Soup mix and made up a big pot, double-strength, just the way we liked it.

"Randa says you found Jimbo's friend?" Kip sounded too eager, as always.

"Yeah, and it wasn't very pleasant so I'd rather not talk about it."

Randa squirmed. "Mom, why do you get mixed up in this stuff? I mean, it's not like when we lived in Seattle."

I ladled the soup into bowls and set them on the table, then trickled hot water over the Moroccan Mint teabags that I'd draped in my Dancing Violets teapot. The gentle scent of mint wafted up to envelop my senses and ran through me like a good massage. I set out teacups and brought the pot over to finish steeping on the table.

As I took my seat and pulled my bowl of soup closer, I thought about what she'd said. True, nothing like this had ever happened in Seattle. Then again, Chiqetaw was proving to be quite the strange little town. There were energies here that I'd never felt in my life before we moved here.

"Maybe there's some reason I'm supposed to get involved. Maybe the victims need me to help them find some sort of peace. Chiqetaw seems to be a quirky town, so maybe it's just the energy here that draws me into these

cases. Or maybe this is all coincidence. Whatever the reason, please remember that I'll always protect you from
anything that tries to hurt you."

With a ghost of a smile, Randa scooped up a spoonful
of soup and swallowed it. "Sometimes I think you should
have been the cop and not Murray. My mom the cop!" She
sobered. "I'm glad you aren't, though. I'd always be afraid
you'd get hurt."

Kip bobbed his head in agreement. "Can I have some
toast?" he asked.

I fetched the bread out from the fridge and popped three
slices into the toaster, then set the butter on the table, along
with a knife. "What are you planning to do for the rest of
this afternoon?"

"The Chiqetaw Museum has a lecture on space flight
that starts at five o'clock. I thought I'd go," Randa said.
"That is, if you'll give me five dollars for the entry fee."

"I'm going to Sly's house," Kip chimed in.

I fished the money out of my purse for Randa, eyeing
Kip with trepidation. No doubt my morbid son was aching
to spill my latest news to his buddy. This kind of thing
racked up big-time points in the world of nine-year-old
boys.

"All right. Take your bikes, and both of you be home by
eight-thirty. And don't you eat anything over at Sly's. I
don't trust his mother to make sure the food's cooked
right." Sly's mother had about as much common sense as
a lemming. The last time Kip had dinner there, he'd gotten
a mild case of food poisoning and that had put an end to
dinner exchanges, at least on Kip's end. As for Sly, I always gave in and fed the pint-sized runt whenever he
showed up on our doorstep.

Kip planted a quick peck on my cheek and took off.
Randa followed suit, with me close behind. I crossed the
street to Horvald's place, as she grabbed her bike and
headed down the road.

Horvald was in his garden, hoeing. Ida Trask was there,

too, kneeling beside the main tulip bed. Horvald Ledbetter was a retired security guard and one of the best neighbors I could hope for. He had the most colorful flower gardens in town and kept busy with them night and day, in memory of his late wife.

"How goes it?" I gave him a quick hug.

He leaned on his hoe and wiped his forehead while Ida went on with her thinning. "Could be a tad cooler for my taste," he said. "But we'll miss the sun come next month, once the rains hit. Is everything okay? You look beat."

Ida leaned back, dusting her hands off on a towel. How she managed to keep her linen pantsuit clean while she mucked about in the dirt was a secret known only to her and her laundry basket, but somehow Ida managed to never appear in public with a single hair out of place. Her clothes were always wrinkle-free, clean, and neatly tucked in all the right places.

She beamed at me. "Emerald, sit down! We haven't seen much of you the past few weeks."

I flopped on the grass, thinking that if I took better care of my yard, it would still be a vibrant green field instead of a tangled maze of jungle. "What with getting ready for the Early Autumn Breeze Celebration, the past few weeks haven't left me much time for anything else."

"When's the street dance? Tonight?" Horvald glanced hesitantly at Ida, then said, "I'll be escorting Ida, but we lost track of the flier."

Each year, at the end of the Early Autumn Breeze Celebration, the downtown Business Owners' Association closed off two blocks, including one right in front of my shop, for a street dance. This year I was taking an active part; I'd keep the tearoom open, and Margie Wilcox, who owned the Corner Street Café, would stay open. Together we'd feed the masses descending onto Main Street. Several local bands provided music, and everybody in town was invited to "Come on down and dance the night away!"

to the music of The Barry Boys and the Don Wan Kodo Drumming Group.

The Barry Boys were pretty good—playing covers of 70's and 80's hits. They were scheduled to play until 10:00 P.M., then Don Wan and his drummers would take over and the entire dance would turn into one huge, disorganized, Stomp-like rave for an hour or two. Everybody brought drums and bells, or pots and pans and had one heck of a good time jumping around and making noise. With a strictly enforced policy forbidding alcohol, there were rarely any problems.

"The dance is tomorrow night, from seven until midnight."

Horvald frowned. "On a Monday?"

I shrugged. "Don Wan's playing at a wedding tonight, so we extended the festival by one day."

"Ah, I see." Horvald nodded. Don Wan's group was an institution at almost all of Chiqetaw's festivals; complaints would run like melted butter if we excluded the drummers from the program. Not only were they great musicians, but Don's wife made the best egg rolls in town, and she always fried up a huge platter of them for all the shop owners during the hours preceding the dance.

I yawned.

"Tired, dear?" Ida asked.

"Yeah, it wasn't the best of mornings." I filled them in on what had happened. Ida paled; ever since that business with her nephew, she wasn't handling talk of murder—especially messy murder—very well. I glanced at Horvald, who gave me a subtle nod and asked Ida to bring him some lemonade and his medicine.

As she disappeared through his front door, he turned back to me. "I don't like it, Emerald. Strange things have been going on in these parts for years. I *can* tell you that we haven't had a cougar or bear attack in awhile, not since a young bear cub got cornered by a nosy tourist and mama decided to intervene."

Pausing, he shaded his eyes and squinted at me. "I remember hearing about the Klakatat Monster some years back . . . story went that it killed some farmer who'd gone up to the mountain to hunt for mushrooms one autumn. Hunters found him. Coroner said it was a bear attack, but there was just something odd about it."

"I don't believe that Scar was killed by an animal, and I really don't think any monster did it. There's a certain feel to the energy of a body when the person's been murdered. Scar . . . he had that feel."

"Hmm." He gave me a keen look. "You know, Miner's Lake is an odd place. Some wicked things went on there a ways back. A couple of brothers—prospectors, I think they were—named Luke and Jake Wiley, decided that the best way to get hitched was to kidnap their brides. They picked up a couple of young Indian girls, thinking the law would look the other way. Well, the law did look the other way, and the girls were found out near Turtle Rock, beaten to death. Their families showed up to avenge them, and . . . well . . . let's just say that there wasn't much left of Luke and Jake when they were done."

He squatted and began weeding where Ida had left off. "A lot of abandoned mines up there in those mountains. A lot of bad blood and old bones. Sometimes skeletons from the past just don't want to rest." Horvald smiled then, and stood up, reaching out to push back a lock of hair that had fallen in my eyes. "Go home and take a nap, Emerald. You look like you need it."

I yawned again. "Yeah, I think I will. Give Ida a hug for me, would you? Though she looks like she's getting plenty of that already." I snickered and, blushing, he shooed me toward the sidewalk.

"You just mind your p's and q's, young woman!" He chuckled and turned back to his lawn. "I'll have a passel of bulbs for you in a couple days, so get those flower beds ready."

"Aye, aye sir!" I saluted him, then wearily trudged back

to my house and headed up to my room. Though I'd already showered, the memory of Scar's decomposing body made me itch. I shuddered and stripped off my clothes, then padded into my bathroom, where I drew a tub-full of rose-scented bubbles. As I soaked in the soothing water, I replayed the afternoon in my mind.

Fact: Ghost-hunting is not necessarily the most pleasant way to spend the afternoon. Case in point: One dead biker found in the woods near Jimbo's place. Even more nerve-racking fact: Said biker looked downright nasty. Add to that the knowledge that Jimbo was getting it on with my best friend, and I was ready for a steaming cup of raspberry tea. Damn it, why had my favorite magazine gone out of publication? I needed pretty mind-candy right now, and *Victoria Magazine* had always provided that for me.

My thoughts drifted back to the woods around Miner's Lake. Though I wanted nothing more than to just stay out of the whole mess, a rumble in the pit of my stomach told me I didn't stand a chance. In for a penny, in for a pound. Fretting, I stepped out of the tub and reached for my towel. The master bath was a luxury I'd grown to cherish. I yawned and meandered naked into my room.

"Hi gorgeous!"

Holy hell! I jumped about two feet before I realized that it was Joe sitting on my bed, not some renegade spirit come calling. "Nitwit! You scared the heck out of me!" Laughing, I held out my arms. "I'm so glad you're home."

He grinned, leaping up to encircle me in a bear hug. I melted into his embrace as I pressed against his chest, basking in the warmth that filtered through my body, through my heart. Oh, I was a lucky woman. His shirt rubbed against my breasts, setting off a tingling I couldn't ignore. I reached up, locking lips with him and held on for dear life as he enveloped me in a kiss that ran from the tip of my nose to the tip of my toes.

"Oh God, I missed you," I said, diving back in for another kiss before I reluctantly broke away. Heaven forbid the kids might accidentally wander in and find me naked in his arms. They knew Joe and I were involved, and it was obvious that we were sleeping together, but they didn't need the details spelled out in living color. I reached for my robe. Joe handed it to me, his fingers lingering on my own.

I slipped into the bathrobe and sat down beside him, taking his hand in mine. "How was the conference? When did you get back?"

"Good, and about two hours ago. I called but you were out, so I stopped at Aunt Margaret's and had lunch. I decided to drive by on my way home and saw your car in the driveway. You know, you should lock your doors, Ms. O'Brien, before some pervert sneaks in and takes advantage of you." He winked and ran his fingers up my thigh. "What do you think?" he whispered. "Should I take advantage of you?"

I gazed at him, feasting my eyes. Joe was an easy man to get hooked on. Everything between us felt so comfortable. He liked the kids and treated them with respect. He didn't interfere with my parenting. In fact, he went out of his way to include them in some of our activities so they wouldn't feel like he was trying to take me away from them. My only disappointment was that he seldom got the chance to stay more than a couple times a week; his schedule was so hectic.

I held my breath as he traced a route up my leg. "Well, how about if you take advantage of me tonight? Kip's over at Sly's, and Miranda is at the museum, they're supposed to be home by eight-thirty."

He sighed, but dropped his hand. "Oh, all right. I've had to wait an entire week, I can wait a few more hours." He looked closely at me. "Are you okay? You look a little pale. Been spending too many nights awake, pining for me?"

"I might have been pining for you, but that's not why I

look ragged." I sighed, planting myself on the bed. "I found a dead body today."

"Crap!" He leaped to his feet. "You what?"

So I told him the whole story, excluding the part where I found Jimbo and Murray in a lip-lock. When I finished, Joe snorted.

"Good grief. What next? I swear, Emerald, if they dropped you on a deserted island, you'd turn over a seashell and come up with a murder. So Murray's boss isn't taking it seriously?"

I shook my head. "Go figure. Remember, we're talking about the king of jerks here. He's a paper pusher, and about as energetic as a sloth."

"And this Scar was one of Jimbo's friends?" Joe had grudgingly entered into a truce with Jimbo once the mess back in April had been sorted out.

"Yeah . . . and Jimbo's convinced the Klakatat Monster's the culprit."

Joe narrowed his eyes. "Doesn't matter if the monster is real. There's somebody loose out in those woods who's dangerous." He sighed, his breath whistling through his teeth. "I suppose this means you're going to be out there, trying to figure out who did it." Before I could protest, he held up one hand. "No—don't even pretend with me. Just promise me that if you need help, you'll call me *before* you get yourself into trouble."

With a laugh, I agreed and went back to giving him welcome-home kisses. As I stared into his brilliant green eyes that mirrored my own, he wrapped his arms around me and laid me back on the bed, breathing softly into my mouth. Tongue flickering against mine, he fumbled with the belt on my robe.

"Wait a minute," I said, and he paused. I locked the bedroom door. At least we'd have some warning if the kids came home early. As I returned to the bed, Joe opened his arms, greedily drinking me up with his eyes. I leaned over and began to unbutton his shirt, sliding it away from his muscled chest, licking his neck as I did so. He slipped out of his jeans and I eyed his naked body hungrily. Wahoo—he really was happy to see me.

"Oh, Joe." I whispered, not wanting to disturb the stillness between us.

He reached out and pulled me down, lightly running his fingers over my body, playing me as if I were a violin. "Do we have any condoms?" he asked.

I handed him one from the nightstand, watching as he opened the foil-wrapped package. Leering at me, he was comical and sexy, all rolled into one. With a sudden hunger, I pushed him back on the bed and slid atop him. He grinned, cocky and joyful and lusty, as his lips and hands sought to stroke my aching body. And so, I rode my strawberry-blond Viking, and we celebrated his homecoming in the most delicious way two people can.

Chapter 7

❖

THE KIDS CAME trooping in within the hour. Knowing how tired I was, Joe offered to fix dinner. Kip wanted to help, so they decided to stage a "Man's Night" in the kitchen and chased Randa and me out while they set to clanging pots and pans, and whispered over the various beneficial effects cheddar and Monterey Jack had on pasta.

While I balanced my checkbook, Randa channel surfed. She stopped. "Uh-oh!" She turned up the volume.

I glanced at the television. "Uh-oh" was right. Cathy Sutton and a picture of me from their files. What the hell was she up to now?

"Ms. O'Brien found the body near Miner's Lake." The picture changed to a photograph of Scar, standing next to his bike, a blissful look on his face. "Fingerprints have positively identified the biker as Scott Anderson, fifty-two. Mr. Anderson disappeared from Grand Rapids, Michigan, during the summer of 1986, where he was wanted by police for taking part in a series of convenience store robberies. Also a suspect—though never charged—in the Tempah City Credit Union robbery, he managed to elude police while his accomplice, Ian Hannigan, a janitor at the Freeman Academy for Boys in Grand Rapids, was arrested. Police believed that Anderson may have fled the country. The stolen money was never recovered."

Scar had been a thief? A bank robber? Jimbo better find himself a better class of buddies.

After a brief commercial, the camera zoomed out to show George sitting in a chair, next to the anchor desk. Oh joy, what now?

"Tonight we welcome George Pleasant, an intern with KLIK-TV, and an amateur parapsychologist, to the studio. Mr. Pleasant was at the crime scene when Anderson's body was discovered." The camera cut to George, sitting there looking like the cat that ate the canary. "Mr. Pleasant. What can you tell us about this case?"

He straightened his tie, fidgeting in his seat. "Well, the body was off the path, buried under leaves and debris. The moment I laid eyes on it, I could tell that the man was murdered."

I snorted. Like George had even had the guts to look at Scar's body. He'd been shaking in his boots.

"Police aren't calling it a homicide. What makes you think this is the case?" Cathy made sure to cover her bases, all right.

George gave the camera a pompous smile. "Because I saw the murder!"

"You saw it?" Cathy's eyes widened.

I straightened up, staring at the television. What the hell was this pipsqueak up to now? George was claiming to be a witness to the crime? No doubt this would go over real big with the cops. Murray would have his head for dinner. Parboiled, no less.

He nodded, his face serious with a capital "S." "I had a psychic vision while watching the police sort out the evidence. Scott Anderson was murdered by the Klakatat Monster."

"Oh my God! Did he say what I thought he said?" I dropped my checkbook and rushed over to the sofa, where Randa handed me the remote. I gawked at the images flickering on the screen, both fascinated and repulsed. Yes, George showed evidence of possessing some form of psychic ability, but surely he had to know that he was on shaky ground making this kind of claim? But then again, he had already proved himself to be both arrogant and stupid, a dangerous combination.

Cathy asked him what he saw and he went on to describe a gigantic, manlike creature that had ripped poor Scar to shreds. Feeling ill, I leaned back and watched as George distorted the facts and basically exaggerated his way through the rest of the interview. Finally, I threw the remote at the television, missing it by a mile. "Doesn't he realize that he's making the psychic community look like a bunch of raving idiots?"

Joe peeked in to see what the commotion was about. I motioned for him to hush as both he and Kip edged into the room to see what was going on.

Cathy asked, "Emerald O'Brien, Chiqetaw's resident tarot reader and china shop owner, was the one who discovered the body. Do you know if she had the same vision as you had?"

I leaped up, ready to charge the television, but Randa grabbed my wrist and I slowly lowered myself to the sofa again, holding my breath as I waited for what he might say next. And then George dropped his bomb.

"I really don't consider Ms. O'Brien to be a legitimate psychic. She refuses to let anyone observe her in action, which obviously means she's hiding something—"

An appalled look on her face, Cathy frantically motioned to the camera man. "I think we have a breaking news report—" she started to say, but George went right on talking.

"Emerald obviously hasn't read much about how real psychics act. Most psychics wear black to draw in the spirit world when they're reading the cards or performing a séance, and they don't run around listening to rock music and playing tea party all the time. I think she's bilking the town and playing off of the gullibility of her clients—"

The screen suddenly cut to Jack Sullivan, who cleared his throat and said, "We seem to be having technical difficulties. Cathy will return in a moment. Meanwhile, let me remind our viewers that the opinions of our guests do not necessarily reflect those of the station, its owners, or its newscasters. KLIK-TV offers absolutely no opinion about the abilities of Ms. O'Brien, and makes no accusations or confirmations as to the validity of her claims." He hastily cut to another human interest story.

Everybody broke into shouts at once.

"Mom, how could he say that—?"

"He deserves a kick in the nuts—" This from my daughter. I gave her a long look, then sat back in shock.

"He'd better watch his back or he'll be in the next big news story." Joe crossed the room in two strides and grabbed the phone. I sat there, speechless, while he turned back to Kip. "Hey kiddo, lower the heat on the noodles so they won't burn, would you?"

Before I could stop Joe, he'd punched in the number of KLIK-TV. "Let me talk to your guest, George Pleasant. . . . Where can I find him? I know he works for you." He paused, then in a low, firm voice, said, "Oh really? Well you tell your boss not to be surprised when we slap a lawsuit against your damned station." He slammed the phone down.

Still in shock, I couldn't muster a single word. The phone rang and Joe grabbed it. "Yeah?" His voice softened and he held out the receiver. "Murray."

I took the phone as he disappeared back in the kitchen. Murray was about to blow a gasket.

"Of course I saw it," I said. "I always manage to tune in when Cathy's making a fool out of me. I'm not sure what the hell to do. Joe just called the station, on the hunt for George."

"I think he's out to get you, Em. You made him mad and he's acting like a jerk. He's young and cocky; you took him down a notch."

"I'll take him down more than a notch, if I catch him." Feeling at a total loss, I asked, "What do you think I should do? Will people listen to him?"

She laughed. "Oh Em, your regular customers adore you. Don't let this get you down . . . it's just more of Cathy's screwed up tactics to buy a ticket into a major station. Unfortunately, she picked the wrong guy to interview this time. She's never going to make it out of Bellingham, regardless of how smart she thinks she is. Please, don't worry about this."

Not worry. Right. I'd not-worry myself over to George's apartment and kick his ass right down the street. My son had labeled me a Lara Croft clone earlier this year and right now, I really wished I was.

"Anyway," Murray continued. "That's not the only reason I called. I just got off the phone with Stryker."

"And?" I held my breath. Murder? What else could it be?

"Stryker's caved. He's labeling it cougar attack. No investigation warranted." Her voice told me that she felt the same way as I did. "Scar was ripped up pretty bad . . . I guess it could be taken for an animal mauling."

"Stryker's a professional. He should know!" I stopped myself. Might as well beat my head against a wall for the good it would do. "What about the evidence? Did you guys find anything to suggest that it was murder?"

She lowered her voice. "Coughlan took the bags from Deacon and Sandy as soon as they got back to the station. I have no idea what's in them. I'm going to ask the boys what they found out there, but I have to wait for the right time. Can't do it around Coughlan, he'd have my head, but I'll find the time."

"Mur, that was no cougar attack. There are some heavy-duty bad vibes out in those woods and they have something to do with Scar's death." Now I was sounding like Jimbo. I paused, wondering if I really did believe in the Klakatat Monster. "Maybe Scar *was* a thief, but Mur, he was murdered."

"Well, cougar attack is the official verdict, but you're right. I've tended to cougar wounds before. My cousin Edgar managed to get between a mother and her cubs and he almost died. He was lucky I was there. But his wounds were different than the ones on Scar."

"How's Jimbo taking Scar's death?" I tried to keep my voice level; not wanting to spark off unwelcome curiosity. Randa was still in the room, watching *Nova*. She could hear me and I didn't want to spill Mur's secret.

Murray sighed. "Hard. They were best buddies. He can't believe the guy was really wanted for—get this—seventeen robberies. Of course, they all took place a long time ago, and nobody was hurt, but still . . . he trusted Scar."

It suddenly occurred to me that Murray knew a whole lot more about Jimbo than I did, or probably ever would. I wondered how long they'd been hiding their relationship. It couldn't be more than a few months. But she was right. If the Chiqetaw police force discovered her secret, they'd find a way to fire her. Chief Bonner liked her but Coughlan was a bastard of first measure, and in the last tarot reading I did for her, the cards showed he was just lying low, waiting for her to make a mistake so he could begin his harassment campaign again. Come to think of it, the Lovers card had also shown up and I'd mentioned to her that maybe somebody was in the wings, waiting to enter her life.

"Em, Em? Are you there?"

Startled out of my reverie, I coughed. "Sorry, just wool-gathering. They say the mind goes first."

She laughed. "Okay. I promise I'll drop by the shop to-morrow and fill you in on Jimmy and me. Okay?"

"Okay. Mur, you know we're going to have to find Scar's killer on our own."

With a sigh, she said, "I know, but I can't do anything in an official capacity since Coughlan closed the case. Whatever I do has to be off the record."

"Gotcha. And tell Jimbo . . . tell him, I'm sorry that he was right about Scar."

I hung up, and Randa and I joined the boys in the kitchen. Joe and Kip had prepared a marvelous smoked salmon fettuccine and Caesar salad and we settled in for a late dinner. I took a deep breath, held it, then exhaled slowly. I refused to think about Scar or George Pleasant or monsters during dinner. As I looked around the table at my children and my boyfriend, I realized that, regardless of all the mayhem and violence in the world, the universe had given me with an abundance of joy, and I'd do my best to live up to the blessing.

AFTER DINNER, WE puttered around until I glanced at the clock.

"Nine-thirty, kiddo. Half an hour until bed, Kip."

I flipped on a CD—Talking Heads, *Speaking in Tongues*—and took over the computer while Joe helped Kip finish building a model plane. Randa went racing up-stairs for an early evening of stargazing. I plugged in the words "Klakatat Monster" into the search engine and watched as the results came up. Not many, but enough to start my search. Too tired to read at the screen, I printed off page after page of information.

As I settled on the sofa with my reading material, Joe

and Kip high-fived each other. "We did it!" Kip grinned at me. "Joe helped me get the last few parts on; I was having trouble but he showed me what to do. See?" He held up the plane and I cheered.

"Yippee! That looks really good, honey. What are you going to do with it?" I admired the model. My son really did have a good eye for detail.

"Put it in my room, on the shelf over my desk. Sly made the same model but it kinda looks dumpy. He's not too good at getting things straight." Kip gave me a goodnight peck on the cheek and took off for the staircase.

Joe watched him go, then curled up next to me on the sofa. "He's got a lot of talent for his age."

I set aside my reading and stretched out, leaning into his arms. "It's been one hell of a long day. So, when's your next shift?"

He folded his arms around my shoulders and nuzzled my neck. "Tuesday night. May I stay here tonight?" He always asked, even though by now he was a regular fixture in my bed, and I appreciated the gesture.

I nodded, too exhausted to do more than smile when I thought of our afternoon tryst. At least we'd gotten in one private celebration today. I poked at the papers. "I should read these, but I'm so tired."

"Then read them tomorrow." He hauled me to my feet. "Time for bed. The dishes are done, the house is clean. Get your butt upstairs, woman."

I stuffed the papers in the shoulder-bag briefcase I'd finally broken down and bought when the strap on my aging but beloved Perlina handbag finally bit the dust. I'd take the information to work with me and read it there.

After arming the alarm system that monitored the front and back doors and the windows on the lower level, we headed upstairs, with the cats following. I made sure that Kip was getting himself to bed. Nigel—our male orange tabby—had joined him and was curled up on his pillow. When I peeked in on Randa to make sure she hadn't fallen off the roof, Noël and Nebula crawled up on her bed.

"Inside by midnight and don't let the cats out on the roof," I called. She waved at me and held up her wrist, her watch clearly visible.

Samantha padded into my room, curling up in her usual place on the bottom of the bed. I opened the window a crack for a breath of fresh air. Joe gave me a gentle kiss and brushed the hair back from my face.

"Time for my girl to get some sleep." He climbed into bed and patted the space beside him. I rested my head on his chest as he enfolded me in his embrace. Within seconds, my eyes were closing and I was off in dreamland.

THE MORNING SUN broke through the window, splashing us with a brilliant wash of color. I struggled out of the fog that always enveloped me during sleep, and turned over to find Joe staring at me. I blinked, trying to focus.

"Hey you." I cleared my throat and fell back against the comforting, cool sheets.

He leaned over and planted a kiss on my nose. "It's still early, the kids aren't up yet, and I've got a surprise for you." With a grin he lifted the sheets.

Oh my. Surprise, indeed. "You know me." I let my eyes travel up his body, and followed the look with my lips. "I love surprises."

BY THE TIME we headed downstairs to breakfast, Randa was trudging out of her room wearing a pair of grey shorts and a navy top that looked like the same ones she'd worn yesterday. I suspected they were. My lovely daughter often slept in her clothes. Kip was in his Spiderman pjs.

The second they spotted one another, they both dove for the bathroom. Kip made it first and Randa immediately began pounding on the door.

"Kip! You got to shower first yesterday!"

I tapped her on the shoulder. "No whining, please. Go use the downstairs shower."

"Can I use yours?" She flashed her big dark eyes at me, trying to look winsome.

"You know the answer to that. Now go downstairs and shower and I'll make breakfast before I head to the shop. And when you dress, make sure you put on some clean clothes." She grumbled her way back to her room.

When we were all gathered in the kitchen, I scrambled up the eggs while Joe buttered the toast, Kip set the table, and Randa made my espresso for me. Joe watched as she poured the four-shot serving into a mug and added three tablespoons of Nestlés Quik and two teaspoons of Coffeemate.

"Emerald," he said. "How the hell do you drink so much caffeine without turning into a basket case? I'd be climbing the walls if I drank what you do."

I grunted. "The only way caffeine is going to hurt me is if I try to stop." I offered Randa a plate of eggs and toast in exchange for my mug. "I couldn't get through the day without this little jolt of black gold."

Joe coughed. "Have you by any chance, checked your blood pressure lately?" I stuck my tongue out at him and he responded by giving me a quick kiss. Kip groaned, while a faint smile flickered over Randa's face.

Over breakfast, Kip toyed with his food. "Mom, what's the Klakatat Monster? Is it real?"

Oh boy. I should have known this was going to come up.

"Hold on." I retrieved the pages from my bag. "Okay, let's see here. According to legends—and keep in mind, we don't know if the stories are real, Kip, they may just be old folk tales. Anyway, the Klakatat Monster is a little like Sasquatch."

"Bigfoot, right?" he asked.

I nodded. "Yeah, only this creature is supposed to be more unpredictable. Legends place it around these parts since before the white settlers came into the area. Murray's heard tribal stories about the creature."

Randa took a long drink of her orange juice. "Is it dangerous?"

I shrugged. "If it really exists, it might be. There have been several unexplained deaths attributed to it, but nobody came up with any conclusive proof. The wounds might have come from animals."

"What else do those reports say?" Joe spread jelly on his toast.

I thumbed through the pages. "Let's see . . . the prospectors used to hear growling and screaming in the woods at night, they thought it was the monster. Over the years, there were several sightings, especially near Goldbar Creek at the point where it flows out of Klickavail Valley, down toward Miner's Lake. That's where I was yesterday."

"What's this thing supposed to look like?" Randa asked.

I skimmed until I came to one eyewitness description. "Over eight feet tall. Stocky, covered with a gray fur. Jet black eyes. Strong, hunched over, a little like an ape walking upright." Setting the papers to one side, I finished my breakfast and eyed the espresso machine wistfully. Two more shots sure would be nice.

Kip polished off his breakfast. "I'm still hungry, can I have a doughnut?"

I sighed. "One, and something without a lot of frosting, please."

He dug through the basket until he came up with a cinnamon roll. "Do you believe the monster's real?"

With a sigh, I pushed back my chair. "I can't say I do, and I can't say I don't. There are strange things in this world that a lot of people don't believe in, things I know exist because I've seen them. Maybe there *is* a creature like this out there in the woods. But I'll tell you this—if there is a Klakatat Monster, I'll bet you anything that it's more afraid of us than we are of it."

I gathered up everything I needed for the shop. "Okay, guys. Chore time." During the summer, they took over most of the housework while I was at the shop. It taught them responsibility, and I paid them for the time they put in as long as they did a good job and didn't slack off. "Randa, clean the bathrooms, vacuum, sweep and mop the kitchen, please. Kip—dishes, cat box, empty the garbage, and dust. And no—"

"Internet while you're gone." He had it down pat.

"You've got that right." I fought back a smile. "And no turning on the computer until your chores are finished. When you're done, if either of you decides to take off, call me before you leave to let me know where you'll be. And remember to set the alarm, please."

Joe gave me a kiss and waved at the kids as we headed down the porch steps. I loved my house. Set back well away from the street behind a jungle of rhododendrons, forsythia, maple, cedar, and oak trees, it was truly a haven from the storms of life.

"What are you doing today?" I asked as he headed for his truck.

"Going to put in some time at the gym and then drop by the station, make sure everything's in order." Even though he didn't need to be there until tomorrow night, I knew that Joe would stick around, make sure his men were okay, inspect the rescue units to ensure that everything was in order, and in general, keep an eye on things. He was devoted to his job, a trait that both endeared me to him and made me uneasy. He worked under hazardous conditions, and thought nothing of putting himself in jeopardy to rescue someone in danger. His men respected him, even for the short time he'd been captain.

I watched him drive off and took a deep breath. Joe had wormed his way into my heart over the past few months. He brought me flowers when I'd had a hard day, he made me soup when I was sick, he even went to the store and bought me tampons when I ran out. But could I really be falling in love again, after all these years? Without a single hesitation, I knew that the answer was yes.

Chapter 8

❖

THE MINUTE CINNAMON opened the door, a handful of my regulars crowded in, but I didn't kid myself that they were all here to shop. Nope, my money was on Cathy's newscast; these folks wanted the inside scoop. I never knew how to deal with these sorts of things. Diplomacy just wasn't one of my strong points and too often, the words tumbled out before I realized I was about to say something stupid.

Frustrated and uncertain what to do, I puttered around my office, picking up the porcelain panorama egg that I'd found at an estate sale a month ago. The ones made out of sugar were more delicate, but porcelain lasted far longer. The autumn vista inside of the ornament made me glad that summer was nearing an end. Four more weeks and we should be entering the rainy season. I placed the egg on my desk, deciding to take it home. I'd been intending to sell it, but didn't have the heart to let it go.

Unable to procrastinate any longer, I took a deep breath and headed out to the counter. As I entered the room, I felt the inquisitive eyes of my customers, peeking at me surreptitiously. Their questions churned just beneath the surface, a whirlpool of curious energy.

It was old Mrs. Purdy Anderson who broke the ice. She planted herself in front of me, flowered straw hat flapping as she walked, muumuu encasing her voluminous figure in a brilliant field of fuchsia hibiscus, handbasket filled to the brim with tea and crackers. In voice loud enough for everybody in the shop to hear, she said, "Emerald, I want you to schedule an hour tarot reading for my daughter, and another for me. You've never led us astray."

I blushed. "That's very sweet of you, but you don't have to do this—"

"Nonsense!" She cut me off. "Trisha and I love coming to you for readings, and we wouldn't go anywhere else."

Grateful—for as eclectic as she looked, Purdy's whims and declarations led the charge for many of the other ladies who frequented my shop—I escorted her to the front desk, where I penciled her into my appointment book. That opened the floodgates; eight of the women rushed the counter, all clamoring for tarot readings. As I scheduled appointment after appointment, the rustle of gossip began.

"Can you believe the nerve of that young man—"

"He didn't have a lick of sense in him—"

"Heavens, you'd think that he'd be more careful, bad-mouthing a woman like *our* Emerald—"

"You ought to sue him for slander, Emerald! That's what *I'd* do, in an instant—"

Within five minutes, my bad mood had turned around. My friends and clients trusted me, they didn't believe some idiot's ranting. I looked around at the ring of women, all waiting for me to speak. My eyes moist, I gulped down a maudlin urge to sniffle.

"Thank you, thank you all. I can't possibly express how much your support means to me . . . but at least I can show my appreciation by offering you free tea and lemonade today!"

Cinnamon, who had been watching the proceedings,

ran over to the reader-board, where she chalked "Free Tea & Raspberry Lemonade Today." That was enough to turn the tide of conversation and the wave of women moved over to the tearoom, where they began oohing and aahing over the pastries as they made their selections.

Feeling a glow of warmth, and gratitude for a potential disaster forestalled, I busied myself, humming under my breath. Tonight was the Street Dance and I wanted the shop to sparkle. I polished and rearranged and tidied until the shelves gleamed, then stood back to survey my work. The Chintz 'n China was in its best condition ever. Ready for my lunch break, I headed toward the tearoom when I heard a familiar voice.

"Hey chick!" Murray, dressed in a grey pantsuit, gave me a hug as I turned. "Thought I'd have my lunch here today since I was in the neighborhood." She leaned closer so no one could overhear us. "I've got some interesting things to tell you about Scar's autopsy."

I nodded toward the tearoom. "I'll be over in a sec. Cinnamon?"

"Yes, Emerald?" Cinnamon had just finished ringing up a sturdy old-fashioned brown teapot for Maeve Elliston. Maeve seemed like an interesting woman, and I wanted to get to know her better. Around fifty, she kept herself in shape, never wore any makeup other than pale pink lipstick, and always dressed in jeans and cardigans or rayon blouses.

Aside from having a name straight out of Celtic mythology, Maeve didn't quite fit into Chiqetaw. A newcomer to the town, she'd shown up at my shop during late springtime and was a regular customer now. Within the space of four months, I heard that she'd planted an herb garden the size of my entire house, that she was raising llamas for her hand-spun yarn, and that she worked a loom and sold blankets, caps, and sweaters from her home.

I glanced at the clock, wishing I had time to do more

than say hello. I waved at Maeve as I told Cinnamon, "I'm taking lunch. I'll be in the tearoom if you need me."

Maeve abruptly spun around, blocking my way. "Emerald, may I give you a piece of advice? Ignore the idiots of the world. He'll find his little tantrum coming back to slap him in the face. You know what you can do, and so do your friends. That's all that matters." Before I could say a word, she marched out the door, bag of goodies in hand.

Cinnamon raised one eyebrow. "She's . . . a little abrupt."

"Yeah." I glanced at the door. "Very."

Lana had brought Murray a chicken salad sandwich, a bowl of gazpacho, and a slice of chocolate cake. I selected a cheese-and-watercress sandwich and a bowl of chicken soup. I added a slice of strawberry-rhubarb pie to my tray. Please, don't ever let me lose Larry, I whispered to the universe. He was my source for all the delicious food we served, delivering it fresh every morning.

Murray was two bites into her sandwich when I sat down. She swallowed and wiped her mouth on her napkin. "Busy?"

I gave her the rundown on what had happened after we opened. "I guess my regulars won't be paying much attention to George, thank goodness. I'd hate for them to think I've been cheating them."

"They know you're not like that, Em. Don't sweat it." She took a sip of her lemonade. "Okay, here's the deal with Scar's autopsy." She leaned in. "I talked to Bob Stryker's assistant. She says that he told Coughlan the fact that Scar had bat guano stuck to his shirt might place Scar somewhere else than Miner's Lake when he was killed. Now, if that's true, then somebody had to move the body. For one thing, no animal could have buried him in leaves. And for another, there aren't any bat colonies right near the lake. But Coughlan told Stryker that a bat must have pooped on Scar when it flew overhead, so they're still calling it an animal attack."

I frowned. "And if somebody moved the body, that somebody is probably the person who killed him. What about the rest of the evidence?"

Mur thoughtfully chewed her sandwich. "Deacon and Sandy are a little put out about that. They insist there were several potential clues, but when I called the crime lab, the report said that all the evidence was pretty much dead-end material. Just forest debris, stuff like that."

"Hmm," I said, picking up my sandwich. "Interesting. Cover up?"

"I don't think Coughlan would deliberately tamper with evidence, but he might conveniently look the other way if it's vague. I have no idea what to do about all this, Em." She was quiet for a moment, then pushed away her plate. "Coughlan has closed the case and he'll have my head if I investigate any further. Officially, that is." She gave me a long look, and I knew she was taking as keen of an interest in this case as I was. Maybe more, because of Jimbo.

If Coughlan had his way, Scar's death would be swept under the rug. It wasn't fair, not to Scar, not to his girlfriend, not to his unborn child, and not to Jimbo, his best friend. "So what are we going to do? What's our plan of action?"

Murray warily raised one eyebrow. "Hmm . . . talk to the bikers, I guess. If they'll speak to me. Maybe I can find out more about Scar's past; that might tell us something useful. I can't help but wonder now if he got his money for the Harley the old-fashioned way . . . by stealing it."

I sighed. "You know the guys out there would clam up in a second if you brought up that possibility. I guess we should start with Jimbo. He's convinced the Klakatat Monster's to blame, but maybe he'll remember something. Somebody who had a grudge against Scar, or maybe some woman he jilted. We could go from there." Before she could change the subject, I grinned at her and added, "Speaking of Jimbo, you promised to tell me everything."

Murray seldom blushed but when she did, her cheeks

grew fire-engine red. She lowered her eyes to her plate, playing with the remains of the chocolate cake.

"C'mon on, spill it."

She coughed. "Well, shortly after you two rescued Kip last April, I hand-delivered the notice that we had dropped all charges. Considering how much he helped the two of you, it seemed only polite to give him the news in person rather than just drop some bureaucratic note in the mail."

I nodded. Jimbo had come through all right. "Go on."

"I drove out there on one of my days off. Jimmy was out seeding his kitchen garden. I noticed that he was starting to plant the carrots next to the tomatoes and told him to stop—that they'd do better next to the onions, and that he should plant basil next to the tomatoes and then ring the whole bed with marigolds. We got into a discussion on companion planting, and I ended up helping him finish up the beds. We had fun, Em. The kind of fun you have when you're not worrying about what the other person is thinking about you. Before I knew it, the afternoon disappeared. He asked me to stay to dinner, and we ended up talking for the rest of the evening."

There was a softness in her eyes that gave her a glowing radiance. "Tell me the rest," I said gently.

"I went home. Three days later, he called me and hemmed and hawed, then finally asked if I wanted to go hiking. I knew that I shouldn't get involved, but there was something about him when we were alone, a vulnerable side that shone through. I went. We got trapped in the middle of a ravine during a sudden rainstorm." She shrugged helplessly. "By the time we got back to his place we were cold and wet. I took a bath, he knocked on the door and handed me a cup of tea. One thing led to another and . . . well, it was wonderful. I can't deny it. We click together."

I knew she was waiting for me to bitch at her, to tell her I thought she was making a mistake, but how could I? The softness in her eyes told me that she was happy. Jimbo seemed good for Murray; whether he was good for her career was another matter altogether.

"So you've been seeing each other all summer?"

She nodded, again looking helpless. "It's getting harder to keep it secret. Can you imagine the uproar it would cause if our relationship became known in town? Coughlan would see to it that I'd lose my job. Jimmy would lose a lot of his friends. We've gone over and over the situation and can't figure out a way to resolve it. All we know is that we don't want to stop seeing each other."

I thought of my own relationship with Joe and how easy it was. Even though he was ten years younger, nobody put up an argument or made any nasty comments. Murray was walking an uphill road when it came to people at her work. I knew Jimbo had a good side, and Joe, Harlow, and James would all accept him because they loved Murray. But not everybody would see it the way we would. And Chiqetaw was a small town, where word traveled fast.

I reached out to take her hand. "I'm happy for you, Mur. And things will resolve themselves in time. I won't say a word until you give me the go ahead."

She gave me a grateful smile. "Thanks, Em, for understanding. I need the support. I'm so glad you know, I hated keeping it a secret from you. Even Jimmy felt bad about it." She pushed back her plates. "I'd better get back to work. Coughlan will be on my ass if I'm late."

As she left, I couldn't help but think about her situation. I hoped that it worked out; she seemed so happy, but there were a lot of sticky issues involved and, no matter how optimistic I wanted to be, I couldn't foresee an easy resolution.

I wandered outside. The street detours gave us two full blocks in which to prepare for the dance. City workers were hanging banners from the lampposts. In Chiqetaw, all the towering street lamps downtown had given way to shorter, old-fashioned black steel posts shaped like the old-time gas lanterns, giving a quaint, old-world flavor to the shopping area. In a couple of hours, the vendors would start setting up their stalls; mostly artisans with home-crafted wares and artists willing to wing a pastel sketch or a caricature, but a few hotdog stands and cotton candy vendors would also find their way into the evening's event.

I perched on the bench in front of my shop, breathing in the warm air. Even though I was an autumn person, I had to admit that the summers here were beautiful; seldom too warm, seldom too cold. I leaned back and closed my eyes.

"O'Brien! You ever do anything but sleep outside your shop?"

Startled, I sat up. Jimbo again. I patted the bench. "Sid-down and quit pickin' on me."

He slid into the seat beside me and snickered. "I pick on you because you ask for it, babe, and don't forget it!"

"You just missed Murray," I said, lowering my voice.

He set his helmet on the sidewalk next to his feet. "Oh yeah? Too bad, but then, we couldn't have said much to each other. Too many people around."

"Yeah." I didn't know what else to say so left the subject alone. "She told me about the autopsy report on Scar. Has she had a chance to talk to you yet?"

He nodded. "Yep. She did. Man, I just can't believe he was involved in those heists. You think you know somebody and . . ."

"Sometimes people aren't what they seem, Jimbo. You know that. I know that. Once in awhile, the past catches up to us."

He sighed. "Yeah, I guess. Anyway, I still think Scar was killed by that creature. Dead bodies don't just get up and move by themselves, and something big has been prowling those woods lately. Which brings me to the reason why I'm here. I got another favor to ask you."

"What is it? You do realize I'm not particularly keen on staging a repeat of the last favor?" I had no intention of playing ghost-hunter again.

He scuffed his boot on the sidewalk, leaving a black mark. "I think I know where Scar was killed."

"What? How—where?" My hope that we might be able to solve Scar's murder suddenly brightened.

Jimbo used his finger to sketch out a map on the bench as he spoke. "Remember I told you that Goldbar Creek heads through a short patch of woods, then opens into the southern tip of Klickavail Valley?"

I nodded.

"Well, there's an access road back there—a fire road. Once you ease out into the valley proper, to the left you'll see the biker's enclave. To the right is a narrow stretch of woods and behind that windbreak, a thin meadow girds the base of Klickavail Mountain. There are caves in that mountain. And there are several bat colonies that hibernate in those caves."

"Which might account for the bat guano they found on his clothes." I eyed Jimbo speculatively. "You know, I have to ask this. Could one of the other bikers have done him in? Considering his background, maybe Scar had a beef with somebody? Maybe one of the guys knew about his past and threatened to expose him and they got in a fight?"

Jimbo looked shocked. "You think one of his buddies killed him? Get outta here! Regardless of what they did in the past, the guys out in the valley live by a code. They cover each other's asses. Some of them dudes have been there for years. They rode together while they were on the road and now they're building a place where they feel accepted instead of outcast."

He let out a long sigh. "Listen, O'Brien . . . the way it works out there is like this. If a couple of the boys start mixing it up, Clyde—who pretty much runs the enclave—makes sure that the fight is fair, with no weapons allowed. Afterward, all grievances are left in the ring."

"Reminds me of *Mad Max Beyond Thunderdome*."

"A little," he conceded. "But these aren't death matches

and both men come out alive. Besides, everybody liked Scar. He was always laughing, cracking jokes. Always had a joint for you if you needed one, or a bottle ready, or a buck or two for beer or food. And not many people know this, but he sent a lot of money to the Bread & Butter House."

That didn't surprise me. The Bread & Butter House offered the homeless a place to stay, and a food bank for those in need. Anybody who'd ever made use of the place usually gave back at some point, when they could. No doubt a number of the bikers had relied on the charity from time to time.

"Scar seems to have been pretty flush," I observed.

"Sure, he had the bucks, but I don't think for a minute that he was still out knocking off convenience stores. I think he earned them fair and square."

I pressed the issue. "And how did he do that? What did he do?"

Jimbo let out a loud sigh. "I dunno," he said, his voice gravelly. "I just don't think he was still hanging in that lifestyle. He had a girlfriend and a kid on the way. He wouldn't endanger them."

I sighed. Jimbo sure could turn a blind eye when it came to his friends, but then, if anybody came to me suggesting that Murray or Harlow had committed a murder, I wouldn't want to listen, either. Since Jimbo wasn't willing to entertain the idea that somebody in the Klickavail enclave might have betrayed Scar, I backed away from the subject. "Okay, so we'll go on the theory that nobody had a grudge against him."

Jimbo stared at the sidewalk, scuffing it with his boot. "Well, I guess I don't know that for sure," he said slowly. He tugged on his beard and once again, I cringed at the cornrows. Finally, he shrugged. "Maybe somebody might have had some beef against him, but I never heard a bad word turned his way. Considering all the other creepy stuff going on, as far as I'm concerned, the Klakatat Monster killed him."

"What was the favor you wanted to ask?" I gently brought the conversation back on track.

Jimbo shifted into shy-mode, scuffing the pavement with his boot. Finally, he blurted out, "I want you and Anna to go up to the area near the caves and do your hoodoo thing. Keep the monster from hurting anybody else. You know, slap a hex on it or something."

Slap a hex on it or something? Had I heard him right? "Let me get this straight. You want us to go up there and cast a spell on a creature that's supposedly older than mankind? Just what do you expect us to say? 'Back off and don't eat anybody?' "

He gave me a sheepish grin. "Sounds good to me."

"And what did Murray say when you asked her about this?"

He pretended to stare at the snakebark maple overhanging the bench. The leaves were swaying in the gentle breeze. Rather hypnotic, actually.

"Jimbo, what did Murray say?"

He sighed. "Well, she didn't exactly say she would, but she didn't say she wouldn't, either."

Jeez, getting a straight answer out of him was like pulling teeth. "Then what did she say? *Exactly.*"

"She says she's game if you are. She really doesn't want to mess with it, but agreed that if you would take charge of the . . . whaddaya call it? Oh yeah, the ritual, she'd go along and help out."

Great. The entire decision was resting on my shoulders. If Murray didn't want to do it, then she had good reason. On the other hand, I knew Jimbo was feeling mighty helpless. He desperately wanted to be of use somehow, and he didn't know how, so he was turning to me.

I held his gaze. Yes, he was a ruffian, and yes, he was frequently on the wrong side of the law, but he had saved my son and, against all odds, was making my best friend happy. "All right, I'll do it, but I do it my way, on my terms, and if something creepy happens, that's it. Okay?"

He flashed me a bright smile. "O'Brien, you're all right. You know that?"

I punched him playfully on the arm. "Uh huh . . . you too, you big baboon. I know I'm going to regret saying yes. I always do." Sobering, I cleared my throat. "However . . ."

"However, what?"

"However . . . I want you to listen to me and listen good. Murray is my best friend, and I won't see her used or abused." I poked him in the chest, no longer joking. "If you ever hurt Anna, in any way, I will dig out Nanna's nastiest spell and make your life a living nightmare, do you understand me?"

Even though he forced a laugh, he knew I could—and would—do it. He nodded and said gruffly, "I hear you, I hear you."

"Okay then. I've got to get back to work. I'll talk to Murray and we'll let you know when we're going up there." Actually, I thought, this wasn't a bad idea. While I didn't believe that the Klakatat Monster was responsible for Scar's death, going up to Klickavail Valley would give us an excuse to poke around for information leading to the real killer. I headed back inside as Jimbo took off down the street.

Chapter 9

❖

THE STREET DANCE was a rousing success. Men, women and children flooded the two-block area, and my tearoom was packed. Most people ordered their tea and pastries to go, then wandered back outside to the dance, so we were able to handle a lot more customers than usual. I wiped my hands on a towel as Cinnamon offered to stay and wait tables while Lana enjoyed herself at the dance.

"It's not like I've got a boyfriend," Cinnamon said glumly. "Darren is back in jail and won't be getting out for another year."

I shook my head. "Hon, let him go. He may be the father of your children, but he's always in trouble and he never helps you with child support."

She shrugged. "I know, I know . . . but the kids . . . and I still love him . . ."

There was nothing more I could say. She was caught in a cycle and had to find her own way out. At least she'd passed all her night classes for spring quarter and had one year left before she earned her associate's degree in accounting. Maybe I could convince her to go on for her B.A., I thought. Once she had her degree, I'd probably be saying goodbye. Even though the thought pained me— she'd been with me since I first opened and was a huge help in the shop—I knew she needed to be able to earn a good living to support her kids.

The Barry Boys were in full swing when Joe and the kids wandered in, followed by Horvald and Ida. Joe sidled up to me, took me in his arms and gave me a long, leisurely kiss. Not so long that the kids would be embarrassed, but long enough to let me know that he was thinking about me.

Horvald and Ida beamed at us. "We thought we'd grab a bite here, then go out and try our hand on the dance floor," Horvald said. "Emerald, you and Joe get out there, too! No hiding in the shop. I want to see some fancy footwork from the two of you."

It occurred to me that the older couple had been keeping close company lately. Hmm . . . wedding bells in the future, perhaps? It would be so nice for them to both have somebody special again. Ida had lost her husband long ago, when she was young. Horvald had been alone for over a decade.

I ushered them into the tearoom where Cinnamon fixed them up with iced tea and cookies. When I returned to the counter, the kids were waiting, hands open wide.

"Can we have some money?" Kip looked so hopeful that I decided to ignore the fact that his allowance had already disappeared.

I dug in my purse and pulled out two ten-dollar bills. "Here, but that's it, and no more till next week's allowance. You understand?"

Kip grabbed his money and ran out the door. Randa grinned and stuffed hers in her pocket. "Thanks. Need any help around the shop?"

"Why don't you go have some fun?" I frowned.

She shrugged. "Lori's on vacation, and there's not much

out there that interests me. I'd rather stay in here. I'll help Cinnamon."

Lori Thomas was Randa's one-and-only friend from school. I could hardly wait until she got back in town. While I was happy Randa could entertain herself, I really wanted to see her branch out and meet more kids her own age. If something should happen to her friendship with Lori, it could easily devastate her.

I gave Joe a helpless look. "Okay, if that's what you want. Just watch the counter though, since you aren't licensed to handle food or wait on people." As Joe escorted me toward the door, I said, "I love that she's so helpful, but sometimes I get a little worried about her."

"She's fine, Em. She's just different than you are and it bugs you."

"Yeah, yeah, I know. That's what everybody keeps telling me and you're probably right. But I'm her mother; I've got a right to fret."

He laughed, then pulled me out into the street in front of the shop and we strutted our stuff. I loved to dance, and Joe humored me. Whenever we went out to a romantic dinner together, he made sure there would be dancing.

Horvald and Ida waltzed by, spry and graceful. Several of my customers wandered past, all of whom who waved at me. We whirled to the music, stopping between songs to grab our breath. Then the band struck up one a B-52's classic—"Love Shack"—one of my technopop favorites. The crowd started to clap in rhythm, and then Joe and I were off, head-banging away, singing along as we shimmied until he dipped me back in a sudden fit of boogie madness. My hand slipped off his shoulder and I tripped, promptly bumping into the person behind me. I scrambled up.

Before I could turn to apologize, a voice I knew all too well caught my attention. "Watch it, will you—"

I groaned. Cathy Sutton. Why did she always have to be

in my way? Cathy steadied herself, her newly platinum hair shimmering like bleached straw.

"Couldn't resist trying to knock me over, could you?" A greedy glimmer flickered in her eyes. She gave me one of her crocodile smiles. "I'm sorry my interview with George got out of hand, but you know that I'd be happy to give you rebuttal time. Maybe we could set up a debate between you two. After all, you *are* our local psychic!"

I shot her a withering look. "What the hell have you been smoking? What are you trying to do? Audition for Jerry Springer's job?" Oh yeah, I could see the headlines now—"Psychics Duke It Out On The Astral Plane." Nope. Wasn't gonna go there.

With a sputter, Cathy narrowed her eyes. "Emerald, you aren't the only game in town. By now, I'd think you'd learn how to cooperate with the press . . . maybe even learn to use us to your advantage, rather than demonize us." She turned on her heel and sashayed off. Good riddance. I needed her around like I needed another ghost in the attic.

Joe grinned. I turned my oh-so-nasty look on him and he burst out laughing. "Slow down there, partner. Deep breath! Breathe, Emerald, breathe! The dragon lady is gone. You can calm down."

Too angry at Cathy to cope with his jokes, I headed for the shop door but he caught my arm and whirled me around.

"You're laughing at me," I said, hearing a whine in my voice. I sighed and tried to calm down. "Joe, I'm just so mad I could spit. Maybe you'd better leave me alone for a few minutes."

He refused to let go. "Yes, I am laughing at you," he said with a twinkle in his eye. "But honey, I can't help it. You and Cathy are oil and water, yet somehow you always manage to bump into each other. Maybe you have some sort of . . . what do you call it . . . karmic connection?"

"If karma sent that woman here to punish me, I must

have been a horrible person in another lifetime!" Abruptly, I shut up. He'd called me "honey." Joe had called me "honey." Everything I'd been fuming about went out the window. He'd called me "Em" and "babe," but he'd never used any of those endearments that men use when they're falling in love. "You've never called me 'honey' before."

With a slow smile, he asked, "Does it bother you?"

Hurriedly, I reassured him. "No, no! In fact, I like it." He took me into his arms, gently rocking me back and forth, I closed my eyes, content to bathe in his glow. He rubbed my back and I began to feel a little better.

With a gentle brush of the hand, he smoothed my hair away from my face. "Have I told you lately just how special you are? How much you mean to me?"

I basked, letting the waves of his energy wash over me like flickers of sunlight trickling through my heart. "Joe— you know how I feel."

"Yeah, I know," he whispered. "Now, let's go show that shrew how to shake a leg."

Laughing, I took his hand and let him lead me back out into the street. We'd managed to break a sweat to Don Wan's Kodo Drumming Group when Lana came running up.

"Emerald!" She stopped, pausing to catch her breath.

"What's wrong? What happened? Is it Kip?" I immediately began to look for my son but she shook her head.

"No, he's over at the cotton-candy vendor, but there is something you should know. I was almost at the corner of Main and Woodruff when I decided to stop at one of the vendors and grab a burger, and I couldn't believe it. You'll never guess what I saw—oh, I just hate telling you this! I know it's going to upset you."

Perplexed, I asked, "What? What did you see?"

She took a deep breath and let it out slowly. "I saw a card table there, near the far corner of the street fair. That really obnoxious guy who was in the shop the other day asking you questions . . . he's giving tarot readings, and his sign claims that he's the only accurate reader in town!"

Stunned, I looked up at Joe. "This can't be right. He's not a professional reader, he hasn't got the experience or the wisdom to be dispensing advice."

"Come on. Lana, tell Miranda we'll be right back." Joe grabbed my hand and we jogged down the sidewalk through the thinning crowds. There, near the end of the fair, right where Lana said he would be: George was sitting at a card table with a sandwich board propped on the sidewalk that read, "Ready for a change? Ready to find out what the tarot is really about? Get a reading from the only accurate reader in town. $15 per question." The word "only" was in bold letters, underlined twice.

"Boy, he didn't waste any time, did he?" I said in a low voice. "First he insults me, then tries to ruin my business, and now he's even undercutting my prices!" I couldn't believe he had the nerve to do this to me, but more important, I worried that his lack of experience might hurt somebody.

I strode up to the table and slammed my hands flat on the surface, knocking his cards onto the street. Nobody around us seemed to notice—this end of the street fair was almost empty. I leaned across the top until we were nose-to-nose. "Georgy-boy, just what do you think you're doing? You know you're digging yourself a mighty deep hole."

His lip curled until he was almost smiling. "I figured you'd show up eventually."

I pointed to the sign. "What the hell is that? You know I could sue you for slander after what you said on television?"

He shrugged. "I suppose you could, but I doubt if you will. You don't like bad publicity. It could have been different, Emerald. If you had treated me better, not like some punk kid, maybe I wouldn't feel this burning desire to prove what a bitch you are. We could have been partners. But no, you had to go and blow it big-time. Well, I've got a newsflash for you! You aren't the only tarot reader around, and you don't have a monopoly on the psychic world. Since you won't let me work with you, I'm just taking advantage of the free enterprise system we live with in this country."

"You little prig! If you had any idea of what you were doing, I wouldn't care if you set up a shop right next door. But you know perfectly well that you don't have the experience required to read for the public. All you're going to do is end up hurting somebody, and then you'll come whining to me to help you fix it. Well get it through your head—some things can't be mended, and if you mess up somebody's life, you can't always make it right. Get it?"

He snorted, but I was just getting warmed up. "By the way, you do realize that by slandering me, you're interfering with my livelihood? I hope you've taken that fact under consideration, because I can and will put a stop to it if you see fit to continue this little vendetta."

George laughed. "My mother can afford any lawyer in this state. You wouldn't stand a chance in court." He narrowed his eyes and let out a loud huff. "Maybe next time you won't be so quick to throw me out of your shop. Think about that for awhile." He looked around at the thinning crowd. "I'm packing it in—the dance is almost over and I've made several hundred dollars tonight."

Damned pompous little pup! Without another word, I turned to stomp away, but stopped when I heard Joe's voice. I whirled, only to see that Joe had backed George up against the wall of Elegant Evenings, a designer clothing shop.

"If you ever upset my girlfriend again, I'll wipe that smug little smirk off your face. Got it?" Joe's voice was low, but his intentions were clear.

"No!" This was getting out of hand. I couldn't let my

boyfriend mop the street with George, regardless of how much the idiot deserved a good thrashing.

Right about then, Greg and Deacon—who were on foot patrol during the fair—came sauntering up. "What seems to be the trouble?" Deacon asked, eying Joe. "Maybe you should let the dude go," he suggested.

Joe reluctantly backed away, crossing his arms. "All right, all right . . ." He nodded to George. "You just got lucky. Now, beat it, and don't come around Emerald's shop again."

With a snort, George shot back, "Don't sweat it, Mr. Fireman. I'm not sniffing up her skirt. She's too old for me, but I guess she's all you can get?"

Oh shit. That did it. Joe lunged forward, catching hold of George's collar. "Let me tell you, boy, you picked the wrong night to come downtown."

George let out a shriek as he struggled against Joe's grip. "Help!"

Deacon and Greg waded in, separating them. I gave Deacon a pleading look. "Please, don't do anything rash."

After a moment, Deacon shook his head. "Joe, my man, you can't just go around punching people you don't like, especially if they didn't hit you first."

Joe grumbled. "I tell you, this guy is a troublemaker."

"Aren't you going to arrest him?" George whimpered. "He threatened to hit me! He grabbed my shirt! You saw him!"

If I'd been close enough, I would have smacked him one myself, just for being a whiny brat. As it was, Greg dragged George over to one side of the table, while Deacon pulled Joe to the other side. I stood there alone, watching while they worked things out.

Finally Deacon motioned to me, giving me a long, deliberate look. "Emerald, you need to take your man home and cool him off."

I read him loud and clear, and grabbed Joe by the arm. "It's time to go lock up the shop." Looking dark as a thundercloud, he gave in. I knew he didn't want to back down, but we both knew that if he took one more step toward George, Deacon and Greg would be forced to cart him away to jail.

As we wordlessly trudged back to my shop, I thought about George's behavior. He'd obviously expected me to fall at his feet when he offered to work with me, and my rejection had stung, and stung bad. Yeah, it was his problem, but how far would he go to try to ruin my business in revenge?

Chapter 10

❖

STILL TIRED FROM the night before, I headed out for my daily trek through the jungle that was our front lawn. Our paperboy hadn't managed to get the paper on the porch or in the mailbox once in all the time we'd lived here.

As I waded through the weeds and wildflowers, it occurred to me that Kip had been neglecting to mow the lawn, one of his regular chores. I hunted through the usual places where our paperboy usually tossed the paper, then saw the rolled-up end sticking out from under the gigantic deer fern that occupied the center of the lawn. As I bent over to retrieve it, an argiope—those huge, orb-weaver, striped, garden spiders that like to hang around in webs and eat bugs—shimmied across the frond and brushed against my hand. I shrieked, the paper went flying, and the spider probably had a heart attack.

Okay, that did it. I gathered up the paper and marched back inside. As I neared the kitchen, Kip raced out of the room, heading for the stairs. "Whoa, kiddo! Slow down. Where are you going?"

"To Sly's. I'm not hungry this morning."

"Back to the table, buster." I gently herded him into the kitchen. "You are going to eat breakfast, and after breakfast, you will spend the day weeding and mowing the front yard. You skipped last week, didn't you?"

He grumbled. "Aw, Mom, can I do it tomorrow?"

"Today." I sliced up a cantaloupe and set it on the table as Randa dished up instant oatmeal. "If you finish early, and do a good job, you can go over to Sly's later this afternoon."

Obviously irked, Kip shoved a spoonful of oatmeal into this mouth, glaring at me as I poured evaporated milk over my cereal and liberally sprinkled on the brown sugar. Randa suppressed a grin as she said, "Mom, after my chores, I'm going to the library."

"Baby, isn't there anything else you want to do on your vacation except hang round the library?"

"I went to Space Camp. After that, everything else seems pretty boring. Lori will be back next week, though, so I'll be spending some time with her." She leaned over and gave me a pat on the arm. "Don't worry, Mom, I'm not turning into a hermit."

"Coulda fooled me." Kip licked the back of his spoon. "Okay, I ate my breakfast. Can I be excused?"

"*May* I be excused, and yes, you may go. Get busy on the lawn now, and you might have some time left over this afternoon. And I want the job done right!" I called as he took off running for the door.

Randa cleared the table as I opened the *Chiqetaw Town Crier.* "Klakatat Monster Strikes Again" jumped out at me in glaring black letters. Oh great. Ingrid Lindstrom had jumped on the bandwagon with her "Buzz About Town" gossip-fest. Chiqetaw's official rumor monger, Ingrid was also in charge of "Ask Ingrid," a woefully pathetic advice column. I pitied anyone gullible enough to actually follow her suggestions.

*Has the Klakatat Monster, a local legend that's been
slumbering in our town's history, woken up from the
sands of time? As you all know, the body of Scott Anderson was discovered on Sunday afternoon by our
own delightful town psychic, Emerald O'Brien. Emerald seems to have made a hobby this past year of dis-
covering and solving murders.*

*But rumor has it that the deceased may have been
the victim of a monster attack. The Klakatat Monster, to
be precise.*

*Sources tell this reporter that the body was slashed
to ribbons, not unlike reports from past deaths attributed to the Klakatat Monster. James Warren was overheard enlisting Ms. O'Brien's supernatural talents in
order to find Anderson. This same source reports that,
upon finding Scott's body, Mr. Warren reportedly
blamed the Klakatat Monster for the death.*

*Authorities cite Mr. Anderson's death as the result of
an "animal attack," but local legend reveals a more sinister possibility. This reporter wonders . . . can Emerald finger another murderer? And if so, is Chiqetaw in
for a spectacular reenactment of Beauty and the Beast?*

I snorted. What the hell was Ingrid thinking? It sounded
like she was trying to marry me off to the Klakatat Monster. She must be reading some pretty wacked-out romance
novels lately. And I didn't have to look far to figure out
who Ingrid's "source" was. George had been the only one
eavesdropping on us.

Dropping the paper, I pulled out the coffee grinder and
the black cat canister in which I kept my coffee. Randa examined the story while I scooped out a handful of the dark
espresso roast beans. "Mom, I thought newspapers were
supposed to print facts, not speculation? This is just silly.
Ingrid Lindstrom always starts all sorts of gossip and
rumors."

"Honey, newspapers like the *Chiqetaw Town Crier* print

just about anything they can think up to fill space. Trust me, though, I'd rather see them print this sort of tripe any day, than see Chiqetaw full of really newsworthy events— like murders and rapes and riots." I trickled the beans into the grinder and pressed the Start button.

Maybe Ingrid *was* a silly old busybody, but I was grateful that she didn't have to cover stories about the home invasions and drive-by shootings that commonly went down in Seattle. Even with our local disasters and barroom brawls and the occasional tragic murder that took place, Chiqetaw was the epitome of community.

And maybe our town did seem a little odd to strangers, with its Early Autumn Breeze Celebration, and the Midnight Reindeer Pageant held the week before Christmas, and the annual Sleepy Hollow Horse Race Faire on the weekend nearest the Hunter's Moon, but most of the townsfolk turned out for the events and everybody went away with smiles on their faces.

If our community included a few local monsters and mysterious legends and haunted houses, well then, they were just part and parcel of living here.

The smell of fresh coffee grounds sent me reeling as I tapped out a quad-shot measure into the little mesh cup that fit under the machine's spigot. Flipping on the switch to heat the water, I searched through the dishwasher until I found my favorite coffee mug. Delicately painted fans and old-fashioned parasols encircled the cup, turning a utilitarian object into an objet d' art.

As the espresso poured out in a thin stream, Randa rustled the paper. "Mom, look! Skies & Scopes is having a sale next week! Can you get my birthday present there?"

I knew better than to argue. "How about if I give you a budget and you can have a shopping spree?" Yeah, it would be the perfect present, even though it wouldn't be what I'd pick out myself.

She wrinkled her nose. "Thanks! You're the best, Mom."

As I finished lacing my caffeine with chocolate and Coffee-mate, the phone rang. Randa grabbed it. "Murray," she said, handing me the receiver.

"Hey Mur, I was about to call you before I went in to the shop."

She laughed. "Uh huh . . . you see the front page of the *Crier*?"

"Yeah. Looks like Ingrid managed to corner George."

"I doubt if she had much trouble. Hey, Greg told me about what went down last night. Tell Joe to keep his cool." She paused, then said, "So, I suppose Jimmy talked to you yesterday?"

Here goes nothing, I thought. "Yeah, he did. I said yes, Mur. I know you don't want to go out there, but I couldn't help it. Jimbo looked so upset and unhappy that I couldn't say no."

"Oh jeez. Well, all right, but you take charge. I've got your back, you know that, but your psychic gifts are a lot stronger than mine when it comes to this sort of thing." She sounded half-disappointed, half-relieved. "When do you want to do this?"

"The sooner the better. I was thinking that we can use the trip up there as an excuse to talk to the bikers; maybe get an idea of who might have had it in for Scar. What do you have going tomorrow night?"

"Tomorrow's Wednesday, isn't it?"

"Uh huh." I could hear the rustle of papers and knew she was leafing through her schedule.

"I was going to fix my porch railing, but that can wait. Let's get this over with. Can you come up with a ritual on such short notice?"

"That's a good question." I honestly had no idea what I could plan with one day's notice. "We'll do a general binding on anything nasty in the area, and then start asking questions. Jimbo will be happy, we might find out something useful, and if there are any astral nasties in the area, then we've done our good deed for the day."

After a moment of silence, she said, "Okay, I guess that will work. But Em, you can be sure that there is a creature out there—my people know this. If it *is* causing trouble, we don't want to go up against the thing, because we can't handle something that old or that big."

A wave of goose bumps puckered my arms. Leave it to Murray to remind me that we were only mortal. "Yeah, I believe there's something in those woods, too. Murray, I think Scar was killed by somebody human, but the fact that this creature—whatever it is—seems to have surfaced for the first time in years, tells me trouble's brewing. Now, maybe it's only coincidence, but I have a feeling the pieces do fit together. If we hunt for Scar's killer, maybe we'll figure out why the Klakatat Monster is on the move again. I feel an obligation to at least try."

Murray laughed. "Em, you feel an obligation to save the whole world. Okay, I've got to get back to work. I'll see you tomorrow night. Pick you up around six at the shop?"

"Sounds good." I jotted down a note to check whether Horvald or Ida could watch out for Kip and Randa. They were in that in-between age where they no longer required a sitter, but still needed someone close in case of emergency.

I hung up, grabbed my keys and purse, and gave Randa a kiss. "I'm heading out to work. I want you to ask Mrs. Trask if she'll be home tomorrow night—"

"And if she's not available, ask Mr. Ledbetter?" Randa gave me a grin and I ruffled her hair. She twisted away, but at least she was still smiling.

"Yes, now scoot." With a last look at the kitchen, I headed out for the shop. Another day. And, hopefully, more than just another dollar.

I SHOULD HAVE walked to work; the drive was so pleasant. Sunlight glimmered on the street, but not the heat we'd had a week or so ago. No, the first tangs of autumn were definitely filtering through the air, lingering on the breeze like a memory long forgotten, just now floating to the surface. The summer had been nice, but I was ready for the autumn, ready for the rain and the mist and the chill morning fog.

I parked in front of the Chintz 'n China and unlocked the door, beating Cinnamon by all of five minutes. The flurry from the street dance had left things in disarray.

"What a mess." I tossed my purse in my office, pulled off the navy blue jacket that looked so good with my tan khaki skirt and button-down ecru blouse, and rolled up my sleeves. "You take care of the dishes, I'll straighten out the front." We scurried around for twenty minutes, and by the time I opened the door to customers, the Chintz 'n China was once again respectably tidy.

The shop bells rang and I turned, surprised to see Maeve Elliston. She was carrying a large tote with her. Odd, she usually came in no more than once every week or so. I asked her if there was anything I could get her.

She hesitated, glancing around. "Perhaps some peppermint tea."

I knew that she grew her own peppermint. "Are you sure?"

With a shake of her head, she said, "Actually, may I speak to you in private for a moment?" I started to lead her over to the tearoom but she paused. "No, I mean somewhere where we can shut the door, where we can't be heard."

What on earth could she want? "Of course," I said. "Follow me." I led her to my office and offered her a chair while I slid behind my desk. I'd wanted to get to know Maeve better. Looked like I was going to get my wish.

"Emerald, we haven't had much chance to talk, but I've kept an eye on you since I moved to town. My family goes back many years in this area, though I only recently moved to Chiqetaw from Bellingham. My mother and father originally came over from Ireland, you know, as did my late husband's family." She sat quite still, hands never fidgeting, eyes never leaving mine.

I wasn't exactly sure what she expected me to say in response. Maybe *why are you watching me, please tell me you're not a latent stalker?* I finally settled for, "I'm sorry, I didn't know you'd lost your husband."

Maeve cleared her throat. "I didn't lose him. He died."

I bit my lip. She was blunt and to the point, that was for sure. "Yes, well, I'm sorry your husband died." I stared at my desk. How long was this odd exchange going to continue?

Maeve apparently wasn't one for idle chatter, she plunged right into her reason for visiting. "I suppose I might as well just come out with it. As I said, my family came over from Ireland. My mother had the gift of Sight, much like you. I never inherited it, though I did inherit her ability to work with herbs and to garden. Which brings me to why I'm here."

Finally, a point to the conversation. At least, I hoped there was a point.

She fished through her tote bag and came up with a cardboard box about seven inches square, which she planted directly in front of me. "This is for you. I have the feeling you need it. My mother owned it, originally, but I've no earthly use for such a thing, and I have no children so there's no one to pass it down to."

Hesitant, but curious, I cautiously opened the box, peeking up to glance at Maeve. An object was nestled inside, wrapped in several layers of black velvet. Oh man, I knew what this was. Even as I reached in to withdraw it, I knew precisely what Maeve Elliston was offering to give me.

"Are you sure you want *me* to have this?" I asked her.

"If I wasn't, I wouldn't be here. As I said, it belonged to my mother, but I can't make use of it. I don't have the gift. And my niece is a clumsy, churlish young woman. I wouldn't trust her with any family heirloom, she'd break it and then where would we be? My brother—her father—is Catholic and hasn't any use for scrying balls. No, I thought it best to see it go to someone with a good heart. I know you'll use it wisely."

As I carefully lifted the crystal ball out of its velvet wrappings, a tremendous rush of energy raced into my fingers. The wave was so strong that I started to slide right into trance. I forced myself to set the ball back on the desk.

"I'm not sure what to say, Maeve. This is an incredible gift. I don't know if I can accept it." And truth was, I wondered if perhaps there wasn't an ulterior motive behind her gesture. I'd learned long ago that some gifts came with strings attached.

She laughed. "Draw a card if you like or ask your spirit guide if you have one, or whatever it is you do." As I hesitated, she added, "Go on, I won't be offended. It takes much more to offend me than something as simple as that. You don't know me from Adam; why should you trust me?"

I pulled open my bottom drawer and took out my deck of cards. After shuffling, I rapped on the back of the deck three times and silently asked what I should know about the crystal ball and Maeve, then cut the deck and withdrew a card. The High Priestess. Clarity, intuition, magic, wisdom. The woman in the painting was holding a crystal globe. I couldn't have asked for a better answer.

"Thank you," I said graciously. "I'll do my best to keep it from harm." I replaced the deck in my desk and examined the quartz crystal orb again. Stunning. Simply exquisite, the sphere was clear except for a few internal fractures that shattered the light, reflecting through it into rainbows, like a prism.

"Use it as you need. Well then, I must be off. I've errands to run and llama-feed to buy." Maeve gathered her things, then paused by the door. "Emerald, this nonsense about the Klakatat Monster . . . what do you really think?"

I wrapped the crystal ball back in its velvet wrappings

and tucked it into the box, then set the box in my lower desk drawer where it would be safe until I could take it home. As I showed Maeve out of the shop, I gave her a faint smile. "I don't know for sure, but I think there's more going on than an animal attack."

She nodded, then strode away, forgetting all about the peppermint tea she supposedly wanted.

Chapter 11

❦

THE REST OF the day was a blur of customers who had decided that since I'd been mentioned by Ingrid in the article about the Klakatat Monster, I must be an expert on the subject. My afternoon was taken up by one question after another.

"Where does the monster come from—"

"Does it eat cats? Should I keep Tiger in at night—"

"What kind of evolutionary path do you think this creature has taken—"

"It's all poppycock. You tell them, Emerald—balderdash, pure and simple—"

"Is it going to kill anybody else—"

"Do you think its movements correlate to the full moon—"

"Are you going to try to contact it? I'd love to attend a séance—"

Finally, at three P.M., I decided I needed to hide out for awhile. I was jonesing for a large mocha, and herbal tea wasn't going to cut it. Purse in hand, I motioned to Cinnamon. "I'm heading over to Starbucks. I'll be back in fifteen minutes or so. Hold down the fort and don't let them give you any guff!"

As I made a beeline for the door, I glanced into the tearoom alcove. All tables were full, the blur of conversation embracing one subject: The Klakatat Monster. I managed to slip out unnoticed and took off up the street, breathing deeply on my walk to the nearest Starbucks where I lucked out. No line at the counter.

"A triple shot grandé iced raspberry mocha, no whip, please." I'd developed a taste for flavored mochas, and was going to have to shop around for a good brand of syrups to add to my home-brewed concoctions. While I was waiting, my cell phone buzzed. I flipped it open. Randa was on the other end.

"Mom, the school called, they want to talk to you. They asked me to give you their number and have you call them back. I bet they've made their decision about whether I can skip ahead or not!" She was so excited that I could barely understand her.

"Okay, just a minute." I grabbed a napkin and pulled out a pen. "What's the number?" She told me and I jotted it down.

"Ask for Mrs. García de Lopez. She's the one making the final decision. Will you call now? Please? I really want to know what they say!"

It meant so much to her, I couldn't leave her dangling. "All right, all right. I'll call as soon as I get my mocha. And you remember your promise, young lady. No complaining, regardless of their final decision."

She was very quiet for a moment. Then, in a voice tinged with the faintest whisper of dread, she agreed. "I promise. Will you call me back as soon as you talk to them?"

"Yes, I'll call you." I hung up, retrieved my mocha, and found a quiet table from where I could watch the street. After I took a long sip of the raspberry-and-chocolate-laced espresso, I punched in the number, gave my name, and asked for Mrs. García de Lopez. Within moments, a woman with a rich Spanish accent came on the line.

"Ms. O'Brien, thank you for returning my call so promptly. We've made a decision on what to do with Miranda and hope it will be satisfactory for all concerned." She laid out their plan and, relieved, I thanked her, after making an appointment to meet in order to finalize arrangements. Then I called Randa back.

"Yes? Yes?" She'd probably worn a hole in the carpet; I had the feeling she'd been fidgeting in front of the phone the entire time.

"I talked to the school. They've made a decision, and I think it will work out just fine—"

"I get to skip a couple grades? I knew they wouldn't let me down, I just knew it!" She was shrieking so loud that I had to yell to calm her down.

"Randa! Shut up and listen to me. You are not skipping any grades—"

"What? You mean I'm stuck in the ninth grade?" All promises went out the window with the whine in her voice, just as I thought they would.

"Remember what you promised or I'll just leave it at that." After she'd quieted down, I continued. "You are not still 'stuck.' The school has decided to implement a program for gifted students that it's been planning for several years now. You are not the only genius at your school, whether or not you want to believe it. You'll spend most of your day in accelerated classes, although you'll still be required to attend gym class."

"Oh," she said quietly. I had the feeling she wasn't too happy about the decision but she knew better than to complain.

"The school would like you to contribute thirty minutes a day as a tutor for students who need remedial work in mathematics. Your studies will still cover the required subjects, but you'll be accelerated in those areas in which you have the highest scores. You aren't a whiz at English, young lady, and you know it."

Actually, I thought the idea was brilliant. The school would assign rotating shifts for their current teachers to monitor the children, and so they would only have to hire one new staff member to direct and organize the program.

Even with the budget cuts going on in education, Chiqetaw schools did their best to cover all their students' basic needs. Every year the local PTA held a fundraiser before school opened; all monies earned went to purchase supplies that teachers would otherwise have to do without, or pay for on their own. That was one committee that Harlow would probably be welcomed on. I jotted down a note to mention it to her. With her little girl due any day now, she'd be taking more interest in child-oriented activities.

Randa took a deep breath, then let it out slowly. "Okay . . . okay. I guess that's better than nothing. Thanks, Mom." She hung up as I smiled. Her ego had been bruised, but she'd snap back, and the accelerated classes would be good for her. Maybe being around other gifted students would take the edge off the superiority complex that she seemed to have been developing over the past year.

Picking up my mocha, I headed back to the shop. Man, I could use a few weeks on a quiet beach somewhere, with only the waves and Joe to disturb me.

JOE DROPPED BY the shop right before I closed; he was headed to the fire station to take over the night shift. I pulled him into my office, filling him in on my day. He plunged his fingers into my hair, mussing me nicely, then checked his watch.

"Damn, I have to get going. I work the rest of this week, but do you want to take the kids and go camping next weekend?"

"I've been thinking about taking a vacation." I leaned against my desk. "Next month is Murray's annual family

fish fry and I'd like to wait until then. We go every year.
You'll come with us, won't you? It's a lot of fun."

With a laugh, he grabbed up his backpack. "Just try and
stop me! Get the dates to me so I can make arrangements."
He laughed, then turned to go.

"Just a minute, buster!" Before he could dive out the
door, I pulled him back into my arms for another long kiss,
reaching up on tiptoe to meet his lips. Oh, I could get used
to this so easily.

He brushed my bangs off my face. "Hey, Emerald,
don't do anything stupid, okay?"

Stupid? Where did that come from? "Like what?"

"You know, this whole business with Scar and Jimbo.
Be careful, please? Stay out of trouble? For me?"

Blushing, I put my hands on my hips and huffed.
"Name me one time when I've gotten myself in trouble!"

He groaned, shaking his head. "Uh huh, tell me another
one, lady. I know you, and I know you're a danger magnet.
So, if you do end up gallivanting out to that valley, take
Murray and her gun with you."

I waved him out the door. Silly man. As if I deliberately
sought out danger. I had to admit, though, it felt good having somebody worry about me.

A glance at the clock told me it was time to head home.
I retrieved the crystal ball from my desk drawer and
packed it in my shoulder tote. Then, after arming the security system and making sure all the doors were locked, I
climbed in the Mountaineer.

"You really are a nice car," I said. "I should give you a
name." I patted the steering wheel as I started up the engine. "Let's see . . . you're a Mountaineer, and you carry
everything for me. How about Tenzing?" After all, Tenzing
Norgay had climbed to the top of Everest right alongside
Sir Edmund Hillary, as his Sherpa and porter.

Tenzing gave a satisfied purr of the engine, and we took
off for home.

•   •   •   •

WHEN I WALKED through the door, I could smell something cooking. Kip and Randa were in the kitchen. Randa was grating cheese and her lips were set; she looked like she was trying not to cry. A pot of noodles bubbled away on the stove. I could see a plate of chocolate chip cookies and a salad sitting on the table, where Kip was struggling to arrange a bouquet of zinnias in a vase.

"Mom! You're home early!" Kip jammed the last few flowers in the vase and rushed over to give me a big hug. Something was off-kilter; I could feel it.

Not sure what was going on but not wanting to immediately start demanding explanations, I watched as Kip opened the kitchen door to let in some fresh air, and Samantha came bounding in, followed by her kittens, Nebula, Nigel, and Noël. The youngsters were all a good ten months old now and were almost out of that awkward-gangly stage.

Kip filled their food dishes without being told. "Nigel's gonna be a big cat, isn't he?"

"Yeah, but I bet Nebula gives him a run for his money. She's starting to gain weight," Randa said. "Noël's probably going to be pretty small. She was the runt." Runt, indeed. But the little cat definitely had an appetite, as did they all. The furble brigade rushed the pantry at the sound of Kip pouring kibble.

I meandered over to the counter and nibbled on the cheese as Randa scooped it into the drained noodles and added milk and butter, just like I'd taught her. She started to stir and a fragrant aroma drifted up, whetting my appetite.

"So, how about telling me why you guys fixed dinner? To what do I owe this special treatment?"

"Can't we do something nice for you just because?" Kip tugged on my hand, trying to pull me over to the table.

I looked him straight in the eyes, then turned to Randa. "Okay, let's hear it. What's up? Don't think I don't appreciate this, because I really do. Dinner looks delicious, but something's going on and you might as well tell me now."

She fidgeted. Biting her lip, she said, "We didn't want you to be upset."

Uh oh. That didn't sound good. Just what had they done for me to get upset about? They were still on summer vacation so it couldn't be a "F" on a test. "Did somebody break something?"

They shook their heads. Kip took a deep breath and let it out. "Dad called today."

Oh shit. Roy, nightmare Father of the Year. "Oh yeah?" I modulated my voice carefully, trying to conceal my distaste. Roy seldom bothered with the kids, disappointing them over and over again, never coming to see them, never bothering to send them gifts, never talking to them on the phone. "Did he say what he wanted?"

Randa's lip trembled. "Yeah. He did. He had something to tell us."

My intuition reared, telling me that I should step carefully. The kids' energy fields were flaring with mixed emotions. "What did he say to you?"

Kip lost it then. He burst into tears. "Dad's . . . Dad's . . ."

"He and Tyra are having a baby." Randa broke in, her voice flat. She plunked herself down into the chair opposite me, her gaze focused on the table. "He never comes to see us, he doesn't give a damn about us, and now he's making himself a whole new family."

"H-h-h . . . he'll forget all about us, won't he?" What composure Kip had left crumpled as he started to stutter. I pulled him to me and motioned for Randa to join us. She crept over, and I slid my other arm around her waist, holding them both tightly; never wanting to let go. How could I erase this pain? How could I convince them Roy wasn't going to forget them when he already had?

I'd been wondering if this was going to happen, though I admit, the speed with which Roy had managed to knock up Tyra took me by surprise. He hadn't enjoyed playing father when I'd been with him, and he preferred his women slim, not pregnant. But then again, I hadn't been the perfect trophy wife. Tyra was young and blonde, without a thought in her ditzy head unless it was how to dig more money out of Roy-the-goldmine. She might have convinced him that she'd be able to regain her figure and not embarrass him with sagging breasts or that tummy that most women never get rid of after they have their children. I had no doubt that, after the novelty wore off, Roy would probably neglect his new child as much as he neglected Kip and Miranda.

I kissed my children softly on the head, first one, then the other. After a few minutes, Kip's sobs began to lessen. Randa looked up at me, her expression fluttering between hurt and anger. Roy had traumatized her too much for her to ever trust him again; and now he'd proved her mistrust right on target.

"Okay, here's the deal." I stroked Kip's hair out of his eyes. "Your father, well, we all know he's never been very good at being a father. He will probably go on exactly the way he has. You'll have a half-brother or sister, and I'd like for you to be able to get to know him or her, but that may not happen if your dad doesn't allow it."

"Does he even love us?" Randa bit her lip.

I never lied to my children except when it came to Roy. "I'm sure he does, honey. He's just not cut out to be a dad the way some other men are. It's not your fault, it's not Kip's fault, it's just the way Roy is."

Kip wiped his eyes on his sleeve, sniffling. "I don't care, if he wants another kid then he can have one. We don't need him."

"I know this hurts, but everything will be okay. After all, we're together, and we have Samantha and her babies. We're a family, even if your dad doesn't live here. Maybe he isn't the best dad in the world, but at least he called you to tell you instead of letting you find out by accident."

I gave them a bracing smile, feeling like a total fraud. If I could, I'd make sure Roy's equipment could never father another child. He refused to take care of the ones he already had; he didn't deserve to have any more.

As their distress faded, I pointed to dinner. "That looks so good. I'm starved, and macaroni and cheese is just what I wanted."

Randa gave me a faint smile. "Really?"

"It was Randa's idea," Kip said. "After Dad called, she said maybe we should make dinner for you. So I went over to Mr. Ledbetter's and asked him for some flowers."

I flashed Randa a silent "thank-you" over the top of Kip's head. She knew perfectly well that his favorite meal was mac 'n cheese.

"Well, it was a brilliant idea," I said. "Now, let's wash up and eat." After a few more sniffs, they ran off to wash up and I finished getting dinner on the table. It really did smell good, I thought, my stomach rumbling.

Thank heavens for one immediate crisis over. I was relieved to see that, as upset as they were, Kip and Randa's appetites remained intact. After we ate, I shooed them out of the kitchen. Since they'd cooked, the least I could do was clean up the substantial pile of pots and pans in the sink. Randa took off for the roof, Kip took off for his room.

I'd no sooner finished rinsing the dishes and filling the dishwasher when the doorbell rang. Who could that be? I wasn't expecting company. Wiping my hands on a tea towel, I hurried to the front door and swung it open.

"Uh . . . hi, Emerald. I just got back in town and I really want to talk to you. May I come in?" Speechless, I stepped aside as Andrew, my ex-boyfriend who had dumped me for a starlet, walked through the door, carrying a bouquet of yellow roses.

"Andrew? What the hell are you doing here?" Rude? Of course, but after he'd dumped me earlier in the year, he was nuts if he thought I'd roll out the welcome mat.

Still as gorgeous as ever, with his long black ponytail

draping down the back of his suede jacket, he flashed those wolf eyes at me, but there was no spark for me this time. Whatever hold he'd had on me was gone.

"I don't expect the red carpet treatment, but I thought maybe we could talk. Do you mind?" He handed me the flowers.

Mind? Hell yes, I minded, but I wasn't about to let him know that. He'd dropped me like a dirty diaper right at a time when I felt terribly vulnerable. I wasn't ready to forgive him. I set the roses on the foyer table and jerked my thumb toward the living room, where he took a seat on the sofa.

I crossed my arms and stood next to my desk where I paid bills and kept my ledgers. "So you're back in town. To stay?"

He shrugged. "Yeah, so it seems. I was in Seattle for a month, but then decided I wanted to come home."

"What happened to Hollywood and Zia Danes?" There. I said her name without crumbling. Feeling proud of myself, I straightened my shoulders.

He winced, then shook his head. "The movie's on indefinite hold, and Zia . . ." He stared at his feet. "Zia told me to get lost."

So he'd been tossed out like a pair of old shoes. The studio had scrapped the movie and Zia Danes had scrapped Andrew. I repressed an urge to shout "hallelujah." Nanna had always reminded me that it wasn't polite to gloat when I had the upper hand.

"Gee, that's too bad. What will you do now?"

He blushed. "Go back to what I'm really good at—writing. Learn from my mistakes. Listen . . . I've been doing a lot of thinking. I treated you like dirt. I really screwed up." He gave me a long, expectant look.

Wait a minute. He wasn't stupid enough to think he could waltz back in and resume where we left off? I took a deep breath, then let it out slowly. "Yeah, you screwed up big time. But I've moved on, so if you're looking for some sort of forgiveness, leave it at this: I'm happy now."

He jumped up and held out his hand. "Em, please—hear me out."

I kept my arms crossed, ignoring the gesture. "No, Andrew."

Wincing, he shoved his hands in his pockets and began to pace. "I know I made a huge mistake, and I'm sorry. But things can be different. Give me another chance? I've changed. You'll see!"

I shook my head. "No, Andrew. Joe and I have been together since early May. We're happy and the kids adore him—"

"Stop, please! Don't say anything yet. Just promise me that you'll think about us, about what it would mean?"

"I don't need to think about it, Andrew. I love Joe—"

Ignoring me, Andrew headed into the foyer, stopping to turn as he opened the door. "You were angry at me, and rightly so. But Emerald, please, don't shut out the possibility just yet. I'll prove that I've changed! It may take months, but I'll make you realize just how sorry I am about what I did."

Stupefied, I stared as the door closed softly behind him. As he pulled out of the driveway, I decided to postpone my call to Roy. I couldn't handle two exes in the same evening. I turned off the light and headed upstairs for my bathtub, where I emptied the last of my Opium bath gel into the water, crawled into the suds, and tried to forget that once again, I seemed to be on the Universe's private little roller coaster ride.

Chapter 12

❖

BY THE TIME Murray came to pick me up on Wednesday evening, I'd roughed out a plan. I packed up Maeve's—or rather, my—crystal ball, a packet of sea salt, and a bottle of Florida water.

When I showed Mur what I'd chosen to bring, she held up a black pouch. "I brought some of White Deer's spirit cleansing powder." Her aunt, White Deer, was a Native American medicine woman. Several tribal members didn't approve of the way she mixed traditions, but White Deer never let anybody's opinion bother her.

Before I climbed into the cab of the truck, I showed the crystal ball to Murray and told her about Maeve. "I wasn't going to accept it, but the cards said go ahead. She really seemed to want me to have this."

"May I touch it?"

I nodded, and Murray lightly grazed the surface of the crystal with her fingers. "This was made for you, Em. It has your energy written all over it. I think Maeve may end up being more of a friend than you realize now. She seems quite . . . efficient."

Laughing, I agreed, and tucked the orb back in the box, shoved everything into the truck, and fastened my seat belt. "Okay, let's head out." As she stepped on the gas, I casually said, "Guess who ended up at my front door last night?"

She glanced at me. "Roy?"

"No, but you're close. He's having a baby, by the way—or rather Tyra is. Roy must be thrilled to pieces. Another little interference to cope with."

Murray cleared her throat. "His karma will catch up to him, Em. Wait and see. So who was at your door?"

"Andrew." And we were off and running on that subject. By the time we drove past Miner's Lake and turned onto Klickavail Road, we had dissected what was wrong with the male population in general, and were on to planning Miranda's birthday. We'd just agreed to order a cake baked in the shape of Saturn, complete with rings, from Davida's Choco-hol Bakery when the road narrowed. We passed over Goldbar Creek and turned right at the "Y" in the road.

The one-lane road was rutted, compact hard dirt. I could only imagine how hellish it would be to traverse after a rainstorm. The road was so narrow that tree branches whipped against the truck windows as we passed, and if two cars were to meet head on, one of the drivers would have to reverse until he was able to back into one of the turnouts scattered along the shoulder.

A glance at the sky told me that we'd still have enough light to work by for an hour or so. "When we're done, we should head back to Highway 9 from the north end of the valley."

Murray agreed. "Sounds good to me. I don't want to get stuck out here in the dark," she added, echoing my thoughts.

We emerged from the forest onto a rough road of sorts, pitted and overgrown, that led through Klickavail Valley. As Jimbo had outlined, the open meadow stretched to our left. Dotting the vale were all sorts of structures, from shanties to trailers to old converted school buses . . . the biker's enclave. Power lines drooped between a row of makeshift poles; the line of roughly hewn trees that led to a main power pole standing near a three-story house at the end of the dirt road.

"That house—think it belongs to whoever owns the land?"

Murray nodded. "Yeah, it's owned by some cousin of Clyde's. Clyde runs the enclave. Their power bill must be huge, but I guess Puget Sound Energy doesn't care, as long as it gets paid every month."

At that point, we turned to the right, where a dense thicket of trees buttressed the base of Klickavail Mountain, and headed toward the copse. Nestled among the scrub and the forest windbreak, the cliff side rose above us, towering and dark. A foothill to the Cascades, Klickavail Mountain was a baby compared to its older siblings like Mount Baker, but from our vantage point, the butte was imposing and stark.

"I think we should finish the ritual first before attempting to ferret any information out of the bikers." Murray nodded over her shoulder toward the encampment, which was now behind us. In the rearview mirror, I could see a few figures emerging from the trailers, looking in our direction.

I was starting to have second thoughts. Maybe this wasn't such a good idea. We were out here, in the middle of a group of outlaw bikers, looking to banish a monster that we weren't even sure existed.

With a snort, I said, "You know what? We remind me of some lame-brained wannabe heroines out of an old fifties B-grade horror flick. *The Valley of Gwangi* or something equally bad."

She laughed. "Yeah, I remember that old clunker. Well, we promised Jimmy we'd do this, so let's just get it over with."

The grass thinned as we bounced along the valley floor. Murray twisted the wheel, avoiding a delightful array of objects, including a scattering of fist-sized pebbles left over from the alluvial flow deposited by the glaciers as they had marched their way through the valley. Five minutes later, we had passed through the dense windbreak dividing the meadow from the mountain, and entered yet another narrow strip of grassland girding the base of the cliff.

She put the truck in park. "I guess this is as good a place as any."

I opened the door, cautiously dropping to the ground. Didn't want to fall and break my neck because of loose stones underfoot or anything stupid like that. I glanced around at the terrain. "You think there are any rattlers around here?"

Murray shook her head, swinging out of the cab to land lightly on her feet. "Nope. They don't cross the Cascades from eastern Washington, thank heavens. Meeting one of those babies would be just a little too much adventure for me, though they really aren't aggressive unless you invade their territory. Actually," she paused, musing, "I've thought of getting a rattler for my collection but I think Sid and Nancy would be jealous."

Sid and Nancy would probably try to eat the thing, I thought. Murray's boas were lovely creatures, but a rattlesnake? Was she out of her ever-loving mind? "Big bad, Mur. Don't do it unless you want me to never darken your door again." I looked around, kicking loose stones out of my way as I made my way to the back of the truck.

Murray joined me. She put her hands on her hips and looked around. "So now what do we do? After all, you are running this show."

I had worked out a rudimentary plan, but as I looked around, I realized that it just wouldn't wash. We were in the wild, and my kitchen folk magic was far too domesticated for this. I unwrapped the crystal ball, which I'd smudged with sage and cedar smoke to clear out as much energy as I could. Lingering energy prints from Maeve's mother surrounded the crystal, but they were just tracks from the past, nothing more, and they wouldn't interfere with my using it.

A rock about thirty yards away from the truck provided an excellent seat, and I settled myself on it, cradling the crystal ball in my hands. "Let me see what we're dealing with out here," I said.

I closed my eyes and allowed myself to drift into a trance. *Downward, inward* . . . following the spiral of energy, flowing on the currents that zinged through the air from deep in the heart of the forest. The trees swayed gently in a light breeze that drifted across the valley. They were thirsty, yearning for the autumn rains that would saturate the area. *Drift lower.* Searching inward, even as my consciousness expanded out to encompass the area. The rowdiness of the biker enclave hovered on the edge of my awareness, but I turned my attention away from them and focused on probing the roots of the mountain, the deep byways of the forest.

And then, I felt it. A resonating heartbeat, buried far below the ground, into the heart of the mountain. The energy was ancient beyond counting, far older than the human race. As I waited, watching, a skull rose up in my mind's eye, human and yet not human; some slumbering creature that had been buried for eons. I could feel it turning my way, questioning, probing my thoughts. Startled, I pulled out, yanking myself to consciousness again. Murray was watching me, a wary expression on her face.

"What is it?" She squatted near the rock, resting on her heels.

"I'm not sure, but the energy here is very old. So old that I think it pre-dates humanity." Disoriented, I rubbed my temples. The beginnings of a headache were starting to whisper in the muscles of my neck. "Whatever it is, it knows we're here. You were right, Murray. These mountains contain primal spirits and I'm not sure what we can, or even *should,* do out here." I held up my hand. My fingers were trembling. "It's not evil, not like Mr. Big & Ugly was. But whatever the source, it's more powerful than anything I've ever felt before."

Murray studied the ground. "Do you think it's the Klakatat Monster?"

Was it the monster? Or was it something else? I thought about it for a moment before answering. "Maybe. I've got nothing to go on, though. I can't be sure. This felt . . . big. Big as in overpowering. Big as in spread out. Big as in rooted in the very land itself. If it was the creature, wouldn't it be been focused into one area?" I struggled, trying to explain a feeling that was—for all intents and purposes—inexplicable. "I saw a skull, but the image felt like more of a representation than any actual bone that's buried around here."

Murray sucked on her lip. "The Klakatat Monster isn't just some beast from a fairytale. It's more than a bogeyman, more than the local legends that have built up around it." She squatted next to me, squinting as a ray of waning light fell across her face. "I called White Deer last night and asked her opinion on all of this."

"What did she say?"

"She warned me to be careful. She said that there are warrior spirits connected with the land here, that they protect the monster and the sacred mountains. They don't like people all that much."

I sighed. Land spirits pretty much didn't like people anywhere, especially in areas that had been developed quickly and without thought. "Well, we did promise Jimbo that we'd try some sort of protection spell, so let's just ask that people be allowed to walk under a safe umbrella when they're in the woods."

As I stood up, about to sprinkle the Florida water, a noise startled us. Somebody was coming through the brush near the cliff side. I tucked my bag of goodies behind the rock. Murray stood alert, eyes focused on the huckleberry bushes, her hand tucked under her jacket. I knew she was ready on the trigger in case we needed her weapon.

A big, burly man burst through the foliage. His beard was long and unkempt, and his hair looked like it had been hacked off at shoulder length by a maverick hairstylist.

"What you women doin' here?" He coughed and, as he stepped closer, I could tell he hadn't had a bath in days. He smelled foul, like a dirty cat box. His face was masked with a layer of compacted grime, and when he looked us over, his eyes narrowed as he first focused on my face, then Murray's.

"None of your business." Somehow, the words had just shot out of my mouth, bypassing my brain. Oh yeah, that's the ticket, all right. Why be diplomatic when I could be belligerent instead?

He tilted his head and grinned, yellowed teeth showing between his moustache and beard. "Spitfire, huh? Listen, girlies, you get on home now. This isn't any place for a couple of women. Dangerous out here. I know, I live around these parts."

Must be one of the bikers, or one of the scattered folk that made their homes out in the mountains. There were some pretty odd types out in these woods, and they didn't all ride Harleys.

"Who are you? What's your name?" I wasn't about to continue talking to him until he told me who he was. Murray gave me one of her looks, pursing her lips as if she'd bitten into something sour. If we'd been standing closer, she probably would have kicked me.

He gave us another once-over. "Bear. Folks just call me Bear. What are you doing out here?"

Murray broke in. "We're hunting for monsters."

A light flashed in his eyes and he snorted. "Monsters? Or *a monster*? You wouldn't be snooping around looking for that critter the news folk have been talking about, now would you? Dangerous to stir up the mountain. Hear tell one of our boys got hisself killed not long ago doing just that."

Word traveled fast. There were probably television sets and satellite dishes all over the enclave. I had no doubt that Jimbo's friends were living pretty cushy inside the rough looking exteriors of their homes.

Murray stepped forward, straightening her shoulders. "We're out here to perform a ritual ceremony to ward off the monster. My people know more about this than you do, so don't bother trying any scare tactics. If you've got something to hide, then quit worrying. We're not interested in what might be growing in the brush. We're just here to take care of matters on a spiritual level."

It took me a moment to figure out what she was talking about, but then it dawned on me that he might be one of those supposed drug runners the police suspected of living out here and that she was trying to put him at ease.

"Well." He let out a big sigh. "Guess I won't bother you folks. But don't go messing around in the backwoods. Just consider this a friendly warning." He turned and headed back the way he'd came. "Oh ladies," he shot over his shoulder, "give the monster my regards, would you? If you get a chance before he slices your gizzards out." And then, with a loud cackle, Bear vanished into the woods and we were alone again.

I looked at Murray. "You as nervous as I am?"

She nodded slowly. "What did you make of that? Of him?"

What indeed? "He had some sort of accent, did you hear it? And his energy is slimy. I really don't want to be around here after dark; let's get moving."

I placed the crystal ball in the center of the grass, resting it on a black velvet cloth and sprinkled a ring of sea salt around the orb, leaving enough room for me to sit down beside it. Then I sent a splash of Florida water in each of the four directions.

Murray stood by my side as I raised my hands over my

head. Nanna had taught me a simple invocation for honoring the spirits. "Spirits of the land, spirits of the waters, spirits of the air, spirits of the sun, spirits of the moon, ancestors and honored guests, be with us, stand by our side, strengthen us with courage, let our hearts beat with compassion, as we focus our will."

The breeze, which had been starting to gust, died down. The sun slowly inched toward the horizon, and an echoing silence fell over the narrow strip of meadow in which we stood. I took a long, slow breath and a rush of cool air filled my lungs as a hawk screeched overhead, circled twice, then flew toward the north.

"The messenger," Murray murmured. "You've been heard. Maybe it's okay to do this. So what's next?"

I motioned for her to stand facing me, just outside of the ring of salt. "I want you to channel the energy I'm going to raise. Guide it so that it flows over the cliffs and the meadow." I picked up the crystal ball and then lowered myself to the ground, crossing my legs with the quartz resting in my lap. I put my hands on the globe as Murray took up her stance, arms spread wide to the sky.

One . . . two . . . three deep breaths. Lower into trance. Let the worries of the day drift away. Focus. Look for the energy of the land. Look for the heart of this meadow, of this valley.

And there it was. A glowing core deep under the earth, a brilliant globe of light, the color of sunshine and leaves, the color of golden corn and rich blueberries. As color met color, swirling into a vortex and then out again, the energy resounded with an ancient pulse, older than any human who ever set foot in the valley, older than the fox and the stag and the bear who had once roamed this land freely, older than the ice age that had covered the forests and ravines, leaving behind rivers of rock in their wake.

The energy went back, way back, it belonged to the volcanoes that had helped create this region, to the Thunderbird who lived high on the barren mountaintops, to the first grasses and trees that had sprung from the newly formed soil. I rode the tide of time as the eons unfolded before me, basking in the magnitude of years this valley had seen.

Any words I might say seemed superficial. We were dust specks, we were motes in the eyes of the universe. I took a deep breath and reached out, coaxing a tendril of the energy closer. The coiling vine of earth mana reached out.

Zap!

The shockwave hit me like a sledgehammer, knocking me over backward.

"Shit!" Dazed, I blinked to clear my vision as Murray knelt by my side.

"You okay?" She rested her hand under my shoulder, helping me to sit up. "Em . . . talk to me, tell me you're okay?"

I shook my head. "I feel like I just got hit by lightning."

"You did." She wasn't laughing.

"Say what?"

"You got struck by a tiny lightning bolt that came out of the ground. It hit you right in the forehead. I saw it. It was green."

Right in my third eye. Delightful. So the valley had decided to use me for target practice? I struggled to my feet, grateful for Murray's support. Other than a ringing in my ears and the sneaking suspicion that I now knew what it felt like to be popped into a toaster, everything seemed to be functioning right.

She reached out gingerly and tapped my forehead with her finger. I winced as she touched the raw skin. "It's like you were burned. You'd better put some antibiotic ointment on that or it might get infected."

I closed my eyes, wavering a little. Hot diggity-dog. Not only had the energy zapped me a good one, but it had left a calling card.

"Enough." I shook my head. "I'm not thrilled about being fried like an egg. Come on, let's get out of here." I picked up my crystal ball, which had made it through the experience unscathed, and started for the truck. Murray scooped up her bag of incense and was starting to follow when a noise reverberated through the long, narrow strip of grassland. It wasn't coming from the trees, but from the cliff side.

Holy hell, what now? I stopped in my tracks, looking from side to side, trying to see where the noise was coming from. *Boom, boom, boom.* Like drumming, or footsteps so heavy that they shook the ground. Earthquake?

"What's that?" I glanced at Murray, who had hurriedly joined me.

She shook her head. "Dunno," she whispered back.

Nervous, but unwilling to go out on the astral to see if I could pick up anything, I started for the truck again, with Murray by my side. We were about twenty yards away when mist began coiling up from the ground in front of us. Uh oh. Not a good sign. Mist usually formed in the autumn, or in the early morning, it didn't just vent up from the ground like steam. Unless the volcano was planning to put on a little show, and I didn't think that it was about to erupt. Not this time.

"Mur, we need to make tracks." Still a little woozy from my encounter with the green lightning, I looked around to see if there was another way we could reach the truck without going through the mist.

"You're right, but somehow I don't think they're going to let us."

They? I looked over to where she was pointing. Emerging from the mists were walking shadows—black silhouettes, and they were headed our way. I twisted around, only to see more mist and shadows behind us. They were hemming us in, forming a circle to surround us.

"What do we do?" I backed up against Murray, who was staring open mouthed at the figures.

"I know who they are," she whispered. "They're the Warriors of the Mountain!"

Warriors of the Mountain? That couldn't be good. "Uh . . . does that mean we stirred up the Klakatat Monster?" Had my attempt to reach out and touch the energy sparked off some sort of other-worldly defense mechanism?

She edged closer as they continued to ring us in. "I don't know, but I suggest we do something, and we'd better make it quick."

"Yeah, I don't want to stick around to find out what they have in store for intruders." I glanced from side to side, desperately trying to come up with a way out of this one. Those walking silhouettes probably packed a punch that would make my little lightning-bolt experience seem like a bee sting.

The shadows began to move in. With no discernable features of any kind, they reminded me of puppets, cut from an ebony board. I noticed that one of them seemed to be faltering a little, as if it couldn't fully materialize.

"There!" I pointed to the gap in the ring of spirits and, clutching my crystal ball to my chest, raced for it, with Murray right on my heels.

We hit the half-empty space in the circle at a dead heat and as we plunged through, the spirit that was having trouble materializing vanished. The Warrior to the left managed to clutch my shoulder, and even though I shook it off and kept on running, my body temperature plummeted, leaving me feeling like I was slogging through icy slush. We broke through the circle and aimed for the truck. The Warriors of the Mountain turned as one and silently gave chase.

"Your door's unlocked, isn't it?" Murray wasn't even panting, while I felt like my lungs were about to explode.

"I think so," I said, falling a few steps behind as I regretted every doughnut I'd eaten over the past month. We reached the pickup, splitting ranks as Mur headed to the driver's side, and I, to the passenger door. I yanked the handle. Thank heaven it was unlocked. As I scrambled in, Mur gunned the engine and threw it into reverse. She wheeled that baby around as easily as if she was handling a Porsche, and we jolted our way back through the windbreak, out into the main part of the valley.

I turned to look out the rear window. Nothing followed, though I could see a pair of red eyes staring at us from the thick undergrowth. Sighing, I fell against the back of the seat.

Murray headed straight for the road near the house. "I'm sorry, Em, but I have no desire whatsoever to stop and question the bikers."

"Not a problem, just get us out of here."

She turned onto the road that would lead us back to Highway 9. The last rays of sunlight vanished as we drove along. I shuddered, thinking what might have happened if we'd tried this in the moonlight. Though I couldn't be sure, I'd lay odds that the Warriors of the Mountain grew stronger after the sun went down. I sure wouldn't want to meet one of them in a dark alley. My forehead twinged and I rubbed the sides of my temples.

"Mur, the Warriors of the Mountain. What do the legends say about them?"

She shook her head. "They're known all over the world by different names. They protect the land and its creatures of the land from intrusion. Some people call them demons. Yet other cultures consider them sacred servants of the mountains, rivers, and valleys they guard. Essentially, they protect areas against human intrusion."

"Well, they do a damned good job of it, that's all I have to say." I thought about Jimbo's insistence that Scar had been killed by some creature out there. If the Warriors of the Mountain existed, then I had little doubt the Klakatat Monster also lived in the mountain. I still believed that Scar's attacker had been all too human, but we would have to walk softly now that we knew there were indeed strong spirits out here.

"There are ghost stories about this area that date back to

when people first arrived in the region," she continued, her voice still shaking. "I even remember hearing tales about how my ancestors wouldn't go near Klickavail Valley. The medicine men warned them away. Now I see why."

A shiver raced up my spine. "Some places just aren't meant for human exploration."

Murray made another turn and we were on Highway 9. We'd be home within fifteen minutes. "I'm worried about the bikers, Em. Sure, they're trouble, but there are some powerful forces in that valley. Maybe one of the boys stirred up some of those old energies. If so, then everybody near the area could be in danger." She sighed and I knew she was thinking of Jimbo.

We rode the rest of the way home in silence. We were no longer dealing with just a murder mystery. The otherworld had stepped in and we had big red targets painted on our auras. Murray dropped me off at the shop and I jumped in my car and started up the engine, eager to get home to Kip and Miranda.

Chiqetaw was a wonderful place to live, but I was only now beginning to realize that this unobtrusive little town seemed to be built over a psychic powerhouse. I flipped on the overhead light and took a peek in the rearview mirror. Yep, a nasty welt graced my forehead, right over my third eye. Praying it would fade with time, I stepped on the gas. I needed a quiet night at home in front of the television, with a bag of burgers and fries, and one of the cats planted firmly on my lap.

Chapter 13

❖

TO KEEP THE kids from asking questions I wasn't
ready to answer, I pulled my bangs over the reddened
skin of my forehead before entering the house. Klickavail
Valley was beginning to scare me more for its bogeyman
denizens than for the bikers that made it their home. Compared to the Warriors of the Mountain, Jimbo and his buddies were fluff bunnies, all sweet-and-sunshine.

Miranda had left me a note that she'd brought home
leftovers for me from Mrs. Trask's house, and that she was
upstairs in her room, reading. After a quick "hello" back
and forth on the stairs, I ambled into the kitchen. The Tup-
perware container contained sliced roast beef, along with a
substantial serving of garlic mashed potatoes and gravy.
Arranging the food on a plate, I popped it in the microwave and, while nuking my dinner, I hunted in the
downstairs bathroom for the antibiotic ointment. I ran a
thin layer over the welt, hoping the redness would fade
soon.

The microwave beeped and I cautiously extracted my
plate, using a potholder to avoid getting burned on the glass.

As I slid into my chair, I took a long whiff of the flecks of rosemary, marjoram, sage, and oregano swimming in the rich gravy. I closed my eyes as a mouthful of mashed potatoes slid down my throat. Yum. Heaven on a fork.

The phone rang. I wiped my lips on a napkin and answered. It was Murray. "Hey, what's up?"

She snorted. "I just filled Jimmy in on our little adventure. He was not amused. And he never heard of that guy, Bear."

"Really? I thought he knew just about everybody out there."

"The guy's probably new. People come and go from the enclave all the time, and nobody keeps track of everyone who comes through. I was thinking, though, we could go back this weekend and talk to the men like we'd planned to."

"As long as we go before dark." I had no desire for a reprise of our little adventure.

"Hell, yes! You're not catching me out there at night again!"

We said goodnight and I hung up, wondering why she was so gung ho. Murray usually went through channels; she was a by-the-book woman whenever possible. However, the fact that she was snuggling with Jimbo might just up the ante. The loyalty factor, Harl and I'd dubbed it when talking about all the crazy—and not so crazy—things that women would do for their boyfriends, lovers, and husbands.

After finishing off Ida's delicious meal, I trudged up to my bathroom, soaked for a good hour in a tub full of bubbles, and tumbled into bed, dead tired. At least all I had to do the next day was sell china and gossip with my customers.

CINNAMON AND I were rearranging a display of new teas that we'd just set up the week before when the bells over the door tinkled and I turned to see Murray, with Kip in tow. One look at her face told me that he was in some sort of trouble. I left Cinnamon to finish up and motioned them into my office.

Murray closed the door behind her and jerked her thumb toward one of the chairs. Kip slid into the seat as she took up her stance behind him, her hands on her hips.

"Kip has something he wants to tell you."

I sat down behind my desk. "Okay, let's hear it."

My son's gaze was glued to the floor as he mumbled. "I tried to sell monster fur."

"Monster fur? What are you talking about?" I looked at Murray for help.

She cleared her throat. "Emerald, I caught your son on the street corner, hawking some dilapidated-looking dreadlocks that he and his buddy Sly were calling Klakatat Monster fur. They were charging a buck for a small swatch."

Oh God! I stifled a laugh and gave him the look that I reserved for serious breaches of behavior. "Kip, maybe you should explain yourself?"

He bit his lip. "Umm, we said you got it up in Klickavail Valley and that you said it was fur from that monster."

Shit! I burst into a coughing fit. My son was committing fraud and he was doing so under the shelter of my name! That damned Sly, he had to be behind this.

"Tell me, please, how in the world did you get the idea that this would be okay?" My desire to laugh vanished as I thought about the potential for disaster. Not only was Kip playing on the wrong side of the law, but what if someone like Cathy Sutton got wind of this? Time to put the breaks on, before this crap got out of hand.

Kip shrugged. "This mornin' Sly and I wanted to go buy comic books, but we didn't have any money and I didn't want to get into my piggy bank. We got to joking about the monster, and then Rasta came in . . . I dunno whose idea it was, really, but Sly got the scissors and we cut a bunch of hair off."

Rasta was Sly's dog. Oh man, his mother would be pissed out of her mind. I didn't know what breed it was, but the dog was bizarre, with long grey hair that trailed almost to the ground. Looked like it had dreadlocks.

"You cut off the dog's hair and sold it as monster fur?"

With a flutter of his long lashes, Kip nodded. "Yes, ma'am."

He knew he was in trouble when he started calling me ma'am. I rubbed my forehead. The welt had faded, leaving only a pale red mark, but now a headache leaped up to take its place. "Just out of curiosity, how much hair did you cut off this dog?"

Again, a shrug. "We figured it's summer, Rasta's prob'ly hot. We didn't hurt him, Mom! Honest!"

Yep. They'd shaved the dog bald. Now we'd all get to see what that poor thing looked like under all that hair. Shuddering, I turned to Murray. Time for good cop–bad cop. Unfortunately, since I was his mother, I always played "bad cop." "So what now? Think you'd better book him?"

She hooked her thumbs through her belt loops as she towered over him, staring down with a gaze that could pierce steel. "I don't know. First let's see how bad things really are. Kipling, did you actually sell any fur?"

Kip's lower lip wavered and he flashed me a look of panic. "N-n-n-not much. Just some to Suzy Warnoff and her cousin, Tyler. We charged them a buck each."

Thank heavens for that. Right after we were done here, I'd call Farrah, Suzy's mother and one of my regular customers, and tell her what happened.

I slowly stood up and leaned across my desk, staring at my son. "So, not only did you lie to them, but you lied in order to take their money. That's stealing. I didn't raise you to be a thief, and by God, you're not going to end up one while you live under my roof."

He pressed himself against the back of his chair. "I

didn't think of it that way! I didn't mean to hurt any-body . . . it just . . . Sly thought it would be cool and we were laughing and joking around and . . . somehow we just . . . did it."

I walked around the desk. "Perhaps next time you'll think before you do something like this. You know, it seems to me that you and Sly have been in trouble a lot this past year." I turned to Murray. "What's happening to Sly?"

She shrugged. "His mother wasn't home. I'll have a talk with her later."

About right. Sly's mother paid as much attention to her kids as she would a fence post. "Well, what should we do about Kipling?"

"Hmm. Maybe rather than jail, he should serve a little time down at the Bread & Butter House, helping out peo-ple who don't have any money to spend on things like monster fur?"

I flashed her a grateful smile. "Good idea."

"Aw Mom!" The whiny-monster reared its head.

"Enough! It'll do you good to see what life's like for people who don't have enough money to eat, let alone buy comic books. I'll call them and make arrangements. In fact, I'll probably go along myself. And Kip, since you took Suzy's money, you need to dig out your piggy bank."

That caught his attention. My parsimonious son hoarded every penny he got. I was proud of his ability to save up money for the things he really wanted, but he needed to remember this lesson.

"What?" He sounded about ready to choke.

"Since you aren't going to jail, you'll have to pay a fine. After you give Suzy and Tyler their money back, you can donate half of what you have left to the homeless shelter. Will that be enough, Detective Murray?"

Mur let him squirm for a minute. "Okay. But Kip, if I ever catch you up to a stupid stunt like that again, I'll run you in. Got it?"

He nodded, biting his lip.

I walked Murray to the front door and we stood outside of the shop. "I can't believe he did that. What am I going to do? I've already grounded him for the stunt he pulled in December. The way things are going, it will be a wonder if he makes it to twenty-one without ending up in juvey . . . or worse."

She laughed. "Oh come on, Em. He's a kid and kids do stupid things. I doubt that the thought that he might be doing something wrong ever entered his mind. But I would curtail how much time you let him spend with Sly. I know you feel sorry for the kid. I do, too. But Sly's headed for trouble and you don't want him taking Kip with him."

"Yeah, you're right." I shook my head. "Man, I hope this doesn't get around."

With a cockeyed grin, she headed for the door. "I've got to get back to work. I happened to be driving by when I saw those two on the street corner with a big sign proclaiming that they had Klakatat Monster fur. Spelled it wrong, too."

I waved her off and returned to my office. Kip hadn't budged an inch. I sat down beside him and tapped his knee. "You're grounded from seeing Sly anymore except during school—"

"But that means I won't see him till next month!"

"Hold on buster. Don't you interrupt me again. We'll talk about this when I get home. I want you to go straight home and stay there. And no Internet, and no phone calls to friends, and you can't have anybody come over to play. Now scoot, and I'm going to call in fifteen minutes to make sure you got there."

Without another word, he took off out of the store. I watched as he grabbed his bike and pedaled off in a mad rush. He would have just enough time to get home before I picked up the phone, and he knew it.

I turned back to Cinnamon, who was working the early lunch rush. Lana came bursting through the door, breathless. As she tied her apron around her waist, I picked up a stack of inventory sheets and headed for my office. Maybe I could get something done before the next crisis diverted my attention.

I WAS ALMOST through with the week's paperwork when Cinnamon stuck her head in the door. "Harlow's here to see you, Emerald."

Shoving the stack of completed forms and reports away, I pushed myself out of my chair and stretched. My body ached and I realized that I was actually looking forward to Saturday's yoga class. I was tired of feeling blah and sluggish.

Harlow was waiting at the counter. She wiggled her index finger at me.

"Hey, what's up?" I gave her a quick hug. "Sorely needing to evict that kid, I see."

She snickered. "Uh huh. Well, I'm hoping she holds off until James gets home. He called and said that he finally got his reservation confirmed and he'll be flying into SeaTac next Thursday."

"One week left, then. Wonderful!" Everybody who knew Harlow's husband had worried about him the whole time he'd been in Africa on a photo-shoot. He'd had a few close run-ins, and I had no doubt his photo spread would be astounding.

She gave me a gentle smile. "I had to get out of the house. I couldn't stand being cooped up any more, and when this baby gets her butt in gear and shows up, I won't have much freedom to come gallivanting into town."

I led her into the tearoom, where I filled her in on Kip's short-lived crime spree.

She snorted lemonade through her nose. "Ouch! That hurt. I tell you, that boy will be the death of you yet. How will I ever cope with being a parent, Em? I'm just a big old kid myself!"

"Like I'm not?"

"Ha! Good point." Pointing to the sandwich shelf, she asked if I would fetch her a turkey on sourdough. I snagged a couple, handing her one.

"So what else is going on? You have the nursery ready yet?"

Biting into the sandwich, she nodded. "Um hmm. All decorated and decked out. Say . . . Em . . . I need to tell you something." She sounded serious.

"What's up?"

"Andrew's back in town." She winced. She'd introduced us and was still apologizing, even though I told her to can it.

I smiled. "I know. He came over to the house night before last."

Her eyes bugged out of her head. "What on earth did you do? What did he say? What did he want? Did you throw him out on his ass?"

Good old Harlow, she loved to dish and this time, I was happy to pile it on for her. "I guess his movie deal fell through and Zia Danes dumped him. He came back all nice and penitent and begging for another chance."

She stiffened. "Oh, Em, you didn't—"

"Of course I didn't! What do you take me for? I told him that Joe was my boyfriend, and he rushed out the door, begging me not to make up my mind yet. He's going to have to accept that there's not a chance in hell that I'd ever take him back."

Harl shook her head. "He realizes what he's lost and now he's trying to get it back. Do you think you can ever be friends again? Would you want to?"

I thought about her question for a moment. "You know, I honestly believe that we'd make good friends, if he can just accept that I've moved on. Things just weren't right for us to be lovers, but everything worked out for the best. At least for me," I added, grinning. "I think his ego's stung by the fact that I found somebody else, more than him really wanting me back."

"Give him a little time. Once he sees you with Joe . . . I think he'll understand. Speaking of Joe, have you told him about this?"

Tell Joe? Was she kidding? I flashed her a skeptical look over my sandwich. "Um, somehow I don't believe that he will appreciate this situation in the way that you do."

Harl shrugged. "Maybe not, but he has to know. Joe won't trust you if you don't tell him about Andrew's visit."

Cripes. She was right. I'd given her the same advice when she'd found out she was pregnant, and was afraid to tell her husband. But man, oh man, I didn't relish the conversation that I knew would emerge from my revelation. Joe thought Andrew was scum. With a sigh, I promised that I'd talk to him as soon as possible. "Now that that's over, let me tell you about the adventure Murray and I had last night . . ." And I was off and running, with Harl hanging on every word.

AFTER AN EARLY dinner, Kip settled himself at the computer while Miranda went out for a bike ride. I picked up the remote, then stopped as the phone rang. It was Sly. Kip jerked around as I firmly informed the little con artist that my son would not be allowed to see him until school started. Glaring at me, Kip stomped upstairs to his room, where I heard him banging his stuff around. Tough. He had to learn how to accept the consequences of his actions.

The phone rang again before I could sit down. This time it was Murray. "Hey chick! Got some news you might want to hear. Yet another chapter in the Klakatat Monster saga."

Oh boy, just what I needed. "What's going down now?"

"I just got a call from Jimmy. He was out in the valley this evening, talking to the boys, when Cathy showed up with George. They were nosing around to see who—if anybody—knew anything about the Klakatat Monster. I guess George went into a swoon and started shouting about how he could sense some sort of psychic turbulence and that there would be another murder."

"Oh jeez." That sounded about right. "So what happened?"

She cleared her throat. "Clyde messed up George something awful. Gave him a black eye. I guess he got fed up with their yakking and told them to leave. When George got cocky, Clyde hit him. Jimmy heard Cathy scream and intervened. He managed to give the pair time to get out of sight; guess he didn't want any more bloodshed after what happened to Scar. But Clyde warned Jimmy that if he caught those two out there again, there would be hell to pay."

What a mess. This monster business was certainly riling up a lot of people. Not only that, but Cathy and George had just gone and managed to destroy any chance we had of getting information from the bikers out there. Nobody would be willing to talk to us now. And to top it off, everybody seemed to be ignoring the fact that a man had died. A flesh-and-blood man, not just some "monster victim."

"Did they leave? Cathy and George, I mean."

I heard the sound of a soda opening. Murray took a sip and then said, "I suppose. Don't really know. I wish that I could go out there and ask around in my capacity as a detective, but thanks to Coughlan closing the case, I can't rely on my badge for this one. Word would get back to him and I'd be sacked."

After we chatted a little more, I meandered into the kitchen and brewed myself a cup of lemon-lime tea. Had George really sensed another murder in the offing? I hoped not, but couldn't ignore the uneasy feeling that he might actually have keyed in on something. I wandered back into the living room, sipping my tea, and stared at the étagère. The crystal ball was sitting front and center, shining softly in the lamplight.

Maybe if George had picked up on something, I could,

too? I set my tea on the desk and unlocked the cabinet. As I withdrew the heavy sphere, my intuition kept telling me, "don't get involved, don't get involved" but the fact remained that I *was* involved, and growing more curious by the moment. Scar had been murdered, that was one thing that George and I agreed on. And I wanted to expose who did it; not only to soothe my own curiosity, but to make things right.

I crossed my legs and rested the ball on my lap, more than a little nervous considering what had happened the last time "ol' Crystal" here had hooked me up to the astral realm. "Okay, let's get one thing straight," I told the sphere. "I am not a semi-conductor for juice from the other side. Got it?"

The orb remained silent. I took that as a "yes."

"Okay then, let's rock 'n roll."

As I tuned in, a sweeping sensation raced through me. I let myself go with the flow as my astral body shot out of my material form. Woohoo—could that baby make me fly! When it felt like I'd come to rest, I warily opened my inner sight and glanced around. Okay . . . misty clouds, no real landscape. Yep, I was on the astral plane. What next?

Nothing big and nasty emerged from the fog to take a bite out of me, but it only took me a moment to figure out that I hadn't the faintest idea of where I was or what I was doing there. As I prepared to break trance and head back to my body, the mist quivered and a strange light began to glow, shooting lightning bolts across the tops of the vaporous clouds.

Something was on the way in. I turned to hightail it back to my body as a wave of energy knocked me forward. As I glanced over my shoulder, I saw the same skull I'd seen the night before, but now it was huge, hovering over my head. I scrambled to my feet as it slowly turned, searching my energy. As the eyes zeroed in on me, a dark shadow crept from behind the skull, standing in front of it in a protective stance, arms raised to keep me from passing.

That was fine by me. Yessiree! Not getting any closer!

"You were in the valley." A voice echoed through the mists from the shade.

"I—I . . ." Stammering, I looked around wildly, wondering if this thing was going to try to make me its lunch.

"There is an intruder in the valley. Make him leave."

Huh? An intruder? Make him leave? Make *who* leave?

"Help us protect the lore-keeper. Help us protect our secrets." And then the shadow vanished and I knew, in my very core, that it had been one of the Warriors of the Mountain. As the skull slowly faded back into the mists, I found myself catapulted back into my body. I fell back against the cushions, shivering.

"Holy hell, that tears it."

The Warriors of the Mountain knew how to find me. They must have tracked my energy signature. And, apparently, they had decided I was just the person to help them protect their lore-keeper, whoever that might be. Woo hoo—Emerald O'Brien, bodyguard for the denizens of the netherworld! Oh yeah, that would look good on my résumé. More confused than ever, I replaced the crystal ball in the étagère and stared at the silent television. I had the queasy feeling that I'd soon find the answers to my questions, and more.

I just hoped I didn't end up finding them the hard way.

Chapter 14

❖

AS I FIXED breakfast for the kids, I was so preoccupied that I almost burned the pancakes. The smell of smoke startled me out of my reverie and I flipped the hotcake onto the stack sitting next to the range. A little crisped, but hey, Nanna always said that a little charcoal was good for the digestion.

Kip sidled into the kitchen. He silently placed a jar full of coins and dollar bills on the counter next to me. I glanced at the money.

"I take it that's half of your savings?"

He winced. Yep, that was my son, a mercenary little goober if ever I met one. "Yes ma'am. And an extra dollar for Suzy and one for Tyler."

I motioned for him to sit down, then flipped through the phone book until I found the number for The Bread & Butter House. As I dialed, Kip watched me, his lower lip jutting out. A woman answered the phone and I told her that we were interested in volunteering for a few weeks during September or October.

"Okay, we're set for the first three Sundays in October."

I hung up the phone and placed his jar of money on one of the shelves high in the cupboard. No use leaving it around within temptation's reach.

"Mom, what happens to people who don't have any money or lose their jobs?" Kip began setting the table, unasked.

I wiped up a drip of batter that had fallen on the counter. "I suppose it depends on where they live. Some people ask for help from their families or the government. Other people end up losing their homes and have to rely on shelters, like the Bread & Butter House. And there are some folks who live on the streets and beg for help."

He considered this for a moment. "In some countries, little kids die because they don't get enough to eat. I saw it on an ad on TV."

I put my hands on his shoulders and gave him a kiss on the forehead. "Yes, honey," I said gently. "In some countries, children die from starvation. Kip, life can be very hard, and we should never begrudge helping those in need."

"If we give money to the Bread & Butter House, then we're helping people who are hungry, right?" A spark flared in his eye. He was making the connection.

I nodded. "We sure are. And people who are homeless can stay there for awhile." The local chapter of the Interfaith Coalition Against Hunger—ICAH—had turned a rambling, old Victorian on Sepia Street into a homeless shelter and a food bank. There weren't many people in Chiqetaw who needed a free meal, but we banded together to make sure that help was there for anybody who needed it.

"I'll be back in a minute." Kip raced up the stairs. When he returned, he had the rest of his money. "I want to help them—the hungry kids."

I gulped down the lump rising in my throat. My son was growing up. Even though I knew he'd eventually regret giving away all his money, right now he needed to make the gesture, and I'd find a way to reward him without being obvious. "I'm so proud of you, Kip. And there are people you may never know who will be so grateful for what you're doing. Now, why don't you feed the cats and then wash up for breakfast? We're having pancakes today, at least we will if I don't burn them all."

As I flipped the last of the hotcakes onto the warming plate, Randa wandered in. She retrieved the butter and syrup from the refrigerator and placed them on the table. The phone rang and I winced when I heard the voice on the other end of the line.

"Emerald? Why didn't you return my call?"

Oh joy. Roy, the cretin. Hugging the phone to my ear with my shoulder, I transferred the pancakes to the table and motioned for the kids to dig in. "I've been busy the past few days. I own a business, remember?"

He snorted. "Right. You're the tea lady. Big whoop." Before I could say another word, he blurted out, "Did Kip give you the news? Tyra's pregnant."

I squelched the urge to pass on my condolences, more to the kid than either one of them. "Yeah, he did. Congratulations. When's she due?"

"February third. The doctor said she's small-hipped and may have to have a C-section. Tyra's upset. She doesn't want a scar."

No scars, huh? That sounded about right, even if a scar meant an easier delivery. "Well, if the C-section is safer, then she shouldn't worry about it."

Roy cleared his throat. "*Some* people care about their looks, Emerald."

I knew right then that it wasn't Tyra who was concerned about a scar. Roy was worried his little trophy wife would be damaged. Impatiently, I asked, "So, what else is up? You have any time to see Kip and Miranda before summer's over?"

"That's why I was calling, actually. I'm making a business trip to Bellingham on the twenty-seventh. I'll book a room and I want you to bring them over the next day."

Amazing! The invisible father was actually uncloaking for a day. I glanced at the calendar. The twenty-eighth was a Thursday. I'd have to take off work but that was okay. We'd dodged the bullet of Labor Day, when the kids and I made our annual pilgrimage to Murray's family fish fry over on the Quinault Reservation. We all looked forward to the holiday and I wouldn't have been very happy if we had to cancel.

"I'll put it on the calendar. Call me with your hotel and room number, and I'll bring them over." Roy wasn't setting foot in or near my house. I'd happily drive the kids a hundred miles to see him, if it kept him out of my private life.

I waited, but he didn't say anything else. Drumming my fingers on the counter, I asked, "Is there something more you want to talk about?"

Roy snorted. "Just can't wait to get me off the phone, can you? By the way, I hear you've got yourself a boyfriend. I hope you aren't exposing the kids to any *unsavory* influences."

Oh jeez! He'd found out about Joe. I focused on the silent mantra that I always used when talking to Roy. *Calm, calm, calm, remain calm, he's just an idiot, he's just a jerk.* This time, it didn't work. After counting to ten, I exploded. "Unsavory influences? I'm not the one who had sex in Miranda's bed with my lover right when my daughter was due home from school!"

Oh God! Me and my big mouth. I cringed as Randa and Kip jerked their heads up, staring at me. How could I have been so stupid? I motioned for them to finish their breakfasts. Randa toyed with her pancakes and I knew she was fighting away the tears that still spilled out every time she remembered walking in on Roy while he was screwing Tyra, right on her little wicker bed. I'd burned that bed, along with Roy's suits and underwear, right on the front lawn.

Roy was silent for a moment. When he spoke, his voice

was unusually restrained. "You're never going to let me off the hook for that, are you?"

He had me there. I'd never let him forget. Randa had to live with the memory and so should he. However, that little fiasco had guaranteed me custody of the children. Roy hadn't even bothered to fight the order, glad to have us all out of his hair. He didn't like losing control, but neither did he want us around. Since this was the first time in over a year that he'd expressed any interested in seeing the kids, I figured that somebody must have shamed him into calling.

I slipped into the pantry and lowered my voice. "Roy, let me tell you one thing. You better not disappoint them. You may have a new baby on the way, but you fathered two children who are already on this earth and by God, you'd better start taking responsibility or I'm taking you back to court to terminate your visitation rights."

After a moment, he broke the silence. "I'll have my secretary call you to make arrangements for my visit. Oh, and Emerald—a piece of advice. Don't get too serious over this guy. Once he figures out what a bitch you are, he'll wise up and get out." The phone went dead in my ear; Roy usually didn't bother with niceties like "good-byes."

I returned to the kitchen and replaced the receiver. "Your father will be in Bellingham on the twenty-eighth and wants to see you guys. I'll drive you over."

Kip perked up; he so very much wanted his father's approval, even while he struggled to deal with feelings of abandonment and betrayal.

Randa just stared at her plate. "I don't want to go."

I winced. If only I could grant her wish. "I know you don't, baby. It's only one day, though, and the court said he has the right to see you. Afterward we'll go out and do something special, okay?"

She nodded, silent. The rest of breakfast was a quiet affair. As I took off for the shop, the kids began to whisper while clearing the table. I wished I could have been a fly on the wall for that conversation.

I HAD NO more than reached the shop at a few minutes after nine, when Jimbo and Murray pounded on the door. Murray was her usual stoic self, but Jimbo had a look on his face that could melt stone. Cinnamon glanced at them quizzically, then at me.

"Finish writing up the menu for the day, would you?" I told her. "Then you can do a little dusting and make sure the plates and napkins are out." I hurried over to Murray and led them into the tearoom.

Jimbo swung his leg over the chair opposite me and leaned in close. "Clyde's disappeared," he said, his voice low. "I got a call this morning from Terry-T, his right-hand man. He told me that Clyde was supposed to gather everybody together for a meeting this morning, but then he didn't show up. Terry-T searched his trailer . . . nada. What with what happened to Scar, the boys are worried. They don't want to call the cops, though."

Well, hell. Another missing biker. "Do you think . . . could Clyde and Scar have known each other back in— where was it? Grand Rapids? Could there be a connection to what went down back there?"

Jimbo shook his head. "Nope. Clyde lived in southern California most of his life until he joined the navy. That's where I met him. We kept in touch when we got out, and when the boys started congregating in Klickavail Valley, I told him about it and he rode on up. We've never been really good friends, but I know his past and it doesn't include any state east of Montana."

"So what are you going to do?"

Murray spoke up. "We wanted you to come with us. We're going to search the meadow while it's daylight."

Oh joy. My desire to head out to Klickavail Valley again was pretty much nil, but last night's adventure in astral land had left me little choice. Not only was I involved, but I'd been asked for help and I knew better than to turn away from the request. The Warriors of the Mountain knew how to find me if I tried to ditch them. And then there was Scar. It was too late for him, but if Clyde was in danger, we might be able to intervene before it was too late.

"Okay, I finished up most of the paperwork on my desk yesterday. Let me tell Cinnamon I'm taking off."

I instructed Cinnamon to open at ten as usual. "I have to head out for a few hours; something important has come up. I'll take my cell phone in case of an emergency."

We piled into my Mountaineer. As I drove along the road at a good clip, I asked Murray, "How did you get out of work today?"

She gave me a big grin. "Apparently, Coughlan got drunk yesterday and fell off the deck onto his woodpile. He broke his leg in three places and it looks like he's going to have to have surgery. I'm free from his prying eyes for a couple of weeks, and the guys in the division aren't all that thrilled with the wage freeze, so they won't tell."

The freeze on city employees' salaries had been a subject for hot debate lately, and the paper was filled with Op-Ed pieces on the move. Thanks to reduced revenue from ill-advised tax cuts and rollbacks, Chiqetaw was feeling the pinch just as much as the entire state of Washington. Budget crunches were trickling down everywhere.

"Hmm . . . I'd say 'too bad' but it's hard to feel sorry for the man. He's such an ass. Hey, I've got a story for you." I filled them in on last night's sudden jolt onto the astral.

Jimbo let out a grunt. "O'Brien, you better watch your step. You may be a hoodoo woman like my granny, but you're not invincible."

Murray gave me a worried glance. "He's right, Em. These spirits aren't from our world. They've never been human and now they want *you* to help *them*? I dunno. Could they be setting you up?"

Could it be a setup? In my unusually addled state the

night before, that thought hadn't even crossed my mind. Wonderful. Something new to worry about.

"Yeah, I guess it could be, but you know, I just don't get the sense that they're trying to fool me. They meant business." As I turned the thought over in my mind, I knew for a fact that they wanted my help. The energy had been clear, if a little spooky.

"Watch your back, Em. I mean it."

We fell silent as I followed Murray's tire tracks, which were still visible from Wednesday night. We eased into the meadow and turned right, in the opposite direction of the enclave, toward the tree line. As we jolted along the rocky path that led through the copse buttressing the mountainside, Murray patted her pocket, checking her gun.

"If Clyde is out there hurt, we may be his only hope. I just pray that the Warriors won't be there to greet us, because bullets won't affect them."

"We should be okay." I glanced at the clock. Not quite ten. "I think they come out during the night."

Just then, we entered the thin strip of meadow girding Klickavail Mountain. I stopped the car and we waited, looking at one another. After a moment, I took matters in hand and clambered out onto the grass. Murray and Jimbo joined me. The air was still, with only the whisper of a breeze. The drone of the bees and chirping of birds reverberated through the area, echoing with a torpid resonance.

Fighting the urge to jump back in the car, I cautiously rounded the fender and looked to my left, then to my right. No sign of the Warriors. Maybe they only came out if somebody mucked with the psychic energy field around here. Maybe they only came out in the dark. Maybe they really did want me to help them. Banking on luck, I hoped my balance was enough to prevent an overdraft.

I took a deep breath. "Now what?" Everybody jumped when I spoke, even though I'd kept my voice low.

Murray glanced at Jimbo, then at me. "We search."

As a unit, we moved toward the mountain. Jimbo and

Murray stepped back, letting me lead so that I could open up and try to pinpoint Clyde's energy. Reluctantly, I let myself slide into trance, slowly dipping below the clear edge of consciousness. The droning of the bees became louder, and the hovering waves of heat intensified. Suddenly, I found myself heading toward a thicket of huckleberries and fern that covered a large boulder the locals called Turtle Rock. Mur and Jimbo followed close behind.

I let my feet follow the draw of the energy, skirting around a dense patch of brambles that jutted out from the woods, into the grassy meadow. Cautious, feeling like I was nearing something very cold, very dark, very—oh jeez! Up ahead, on the other side of the thicket, a biker was sprawled on the ground, his tank top covered with blood. And right beside him sat George, looking sick as a dog and totally out of it.

"Here!" I rushed forward. The biker wasn't moving. George stared at me, bewildered, as I dropped to the ground by the body. I didn't have to be a doctor to see that the man was dead.

"Clyde!" Jimbo hurried over to my side and grabbed the man's wrist, trying desperately to feel for a pulse. He sat back, dazed.

Murray immediately pulled out her cell phone and began searching for a vantage point that would give her a clear signal. Jimbo glared at George, his eyes flashing. George cringed, but didn't move. I scooted over next to the young man. He was sporting a purplish black eye and a few bruises, and he looked like he'd been through the wringer. Dried vomit covered his shirt, but I could see no other immediate visible damage. I looked around for his glasses, but couldn't find them.

"Are you okay? Do you need help?"

He tried to fasten his gaze on my face, then blankly shook his head. I was about to ask him what happened when Murray tapped me on the shoulder.

"Em, can I speak to you over there? Jimmy, there's

nothing you can do. Clyde's dead. Stay where you are please, so you don't disturb the crime scene." She led me aside, and when we were out of earshot said, "Did you ask George what happened?"

I shook my head. "I was about to when you came up. Why?"

She looked uncomfortable. "The M.E. is on his way. I need to question George. Officially, he's going to be a suspect, and I don't want anybody else bothering him until I decide whether I need to haul him in on a murder charge."

George, a suspect? I stared at her, unbelieving. "You're kidding? You think that *George* killed Clyde? I can believe that Clyde could kill George, but look at that dude. He's a wimp. And look at Clyde." The biker had been wearing a tank top and jeans, but no jacket. Even in death, it was easy to see how much time he'd put into sculpting his arms into formidable shape. "Compared to George, Clyde was a giant."

"Remember the story of David and Goliath, Em." Murray let her gaze trail over the scene. "This is so bizarre. You know, I got a good look at Scar's body. Clyde's injuries are suspiciously similar."

"What? Now you're saying George might have killed Scar, too?" My mind refused to accept the thought that George could have overpowered even one seasoned biker, let alone two. Maybe a grandma, or a paperboy, but the rough-and-tumble twins? There had to be another explanation. But then, reason countered, why else would George be sitting by Clyde's corpse?

Murray leaned against a nearby stump. "Em, Clyde is dead, and who should be sitting right next to the body? George. I'm not saying he did it, but I have to consider him a suspect. If he's innocent, why didn't he go for help? We have to consider the possibility that he killed Clyde and then, realizing what he did, went into shock. And remember—we found him out at Miner's Lake, near Scar's body. He could have already known Scar was there."

True, very true. And Murray was right, out-of-character acts could send a person into shock. So could some forms of psychosis, and if anybody seemed on the edge right now, it was George. I glanced back at him, he was casting looks at the dead biker to his left and at the very alive and angry biker to his right. "You'd better call off Jimbo or he's likely to throttle the guy."

Mur gave me a bleak smile. "Thanks. Would you go out to the main meadow? Keep a watch out for Deacon and Sandy? Show them the way here when they arrive. Meanwhile, I'll go rein in Jimmy."

Her cell phone rang and she flipped it open. After a few, brief words, she snapped it shut, looking stoic. "That was Chief Bonner. It appears that I'm now in charge of the investigation. Coughlan went into surgery for his broken leg this morning and he just had a heart attack on the table. They're going to have to perform a triple bypass, and the doctors say his prognosis doesn't look good."

"Holy hell. What next?"

Shaking her head, Murray pulled out her notebook, and headed over toward George. I trudged back through the patch of woods that led to the main valley, trying to fit all the pieces together. Scar had been killed, even if Coughlan insisted on labeling his death as accidental. Now Clyde was dead. Surely, there had to be some connection between the two deaths?

And just how did George fit into all this? True, Jimbo had seen him get into a fistfight with Clyde, but had he known Scar? Coincidences happened, but something told me that everything going on here was interconnected. I just couldn't see the threads yet.

I plunged out of the thicket right as the squad car pulled up. A line of bikers stretched across the entrance to their enclave, watching as the police arrived. Though their expressions were shaded from where I stood, their energy hailed loud and clear. Not happy. And they'd be even more unhappy when they found out their leader was dead. Of course, one of them might already know. One of them might just be the murderer.

Deacon Wilson was driving the cruiser, with Sandy Whitmeyer riding shotgun. I led them back through the thicket, where Murray filled them in on what was going down. Deacon glanced at Clyde's body. "Stryker will be here in awhile. He's having brunch with his country club buddies."

Murray nodded. "That figures. Okay, get George on his feet, if you would. Sandy, start looking around the scene for evidence."

Deacon helped George to his feet, steadying the young man as he swayed and almost toppled over. George muttered something incoherent as Sandy bent over where he'd been sitting. Abruptly, he straightened and snapped on a pair of latex gloves, then took a picture of something lying in the grass before he picked it up. "Detective? I found a knife," Sandy said, holding up the object he'd found. The blade was covered with a reddish substance. Blood. I knew it was blood.

Deacon frisked George and pulled out a plastic bag filled with tablets out of his left pocket. "Add to that a bag of roofies, and it looks like there's blood on his jacket." He said something to George, then helped him take off his jacket. I could see red splotches on the hem and one elbow as Deacon carefully folded it and placed it in the paper evidence bag. Uh oh, that couldn't be good.

"Roofies?" I whispered to Jimbo, who was standing next to me. "What are those?"

He leaned close enough to whisper in my ear. "Rohypnol. Roofies. Commonly known as the date rape drug. Some of the boys . . . well . . . some of them aren't all that choosy when it comes to how they make their money."

I shuddered. I'd heard of roofies, all right, but never knew their name until now. I dreaded the day Randa started dating. There were so many dangers in the world.

Murray handed the camera to Sandy and looked at the

knife, then at the bag of pills. "Bag these and mark them." She asked George for his wallet and, still looking thoroughly confused, he handed it to her. Money spilled out onto the grass as he pulled the tri-fold out of his pocket.

"I think it's about time to put Mr. Pleasant here under arrest. Read him his rights, Deacon, and make sure he understands them." She slipped on a new pair of gloves and began picking up the money that had scattered onto the ground. "Sandy, count with me."

After they'd sorted through all the bills, Murray jotted down a note in her book and the cash went into yet another bag. "About a thousand dollars here," she said. I motioned to her and we moved aside.

"You really think George did it?"

She shrugged. "That's not up to me to decide. But Em, the fact that they got into a fight last night and Clyde blackened George's eye . . . well, it looks bad. He's got a lot of answers to come up with, and so far, he's barely said a word."

"What about one of the other bikers? Now that you're heading up the case, you can question them."

With a curt nod, she said, "Don't worry. We'll question them, all right. But Em, face it. A bloody knife? Blood on George's jacket, and a bag of pills? Toss in a thousand bucks, which is just about what those drugs are worth? I'm looking at this and the pieces are starting to add up."

I stared at her. She'd shifted into that professional Murray-as-cop status I knew so well. Resigned, knowing she was following procedure like she should, I flashed her a tight smile. Just because my intuition was screaming that George was innocent, didn't mean it was true.

"What do you think happened?" I asked.

She shrugged, motioning for Deacon to take George out to the squad car. "Looks to me like a drug deal gone sour. The kid decided he didn't want to pay for them after all, so he killed Clyde and planned to take off with the roofies."

"What's wrong with George, though? He seems really sick. Why would he have stuck around if he killed Clyde?"

Mur gave me a gentle smile. "Emerald, I thought you could tell. George is hopped up higher than a hot-air balloon. He's stoned out of his mind and I'm surprised he didn't OD, he's so high. Of course, they'll do a drug test at the station, but ten to one, he's had his fingers in the candy jar. There could be a dozen reasons why he's still out here—I'm sure we'll find out eventually."

Stoned? Of course, it would explain George's strange behavior, but a niggling suspicion of doubt worked away at my brain. Yes, George was annoying, and yes, he was a downright nuisance, but I had my doubts that he was a hardcore drug user. Then again, logic countered, you never could tell with some people. At any rate, there wasn't much more to do here except wander around, waiting for the medical examiner.

Murray had Sandy take statements from Jimbo and me, but we couldn't add much to her official report since she'd been with us when the body was found. We finished up by the time Stryker arrived. As they clicked away with their cameras, I felt my stomach lurch and excused myself. I hightailed it to the bushes, where I said hello to my breakfast again. With my mouth tasting like sour coffee, I poked around in my truck for a bottle of water and then popped a couple of breath mints. Jimbo gave me the first smile I'd seen since we found Clyde.

"Can't handle the rough stuff, can you? Just like a broad."

I glared at him. "Next time you need somebody to go ghost hunting, look elsewhere, would you? I've found just about all the dead bodies I care to, thank you muchly." I stared at the technicians who were working up their report. "I wonder if Bear might know anything about what happened. He was out in this part of the meadow the other night when Murray and I came out here and he says he lives out here in the woods."

Jimbo looked mystified. "I still can't figure out which one of the guys you're talking about. Here comes Anna."

Murray wandered over. "Clyde's wallet is missing," she told us. "He's not wearing a jacket, either, and though the days have been hot, it gets chilly out here at night."

"I think George's glasses are missing, too," I said.

She jotted another note in her book. "Are they? I didn't realize he wore glasses. Listen guys, we've got a lot of work to do here, so why don't you head back to town? I'll ride in with Stryker."

Jimbo gave her a long look, and I knew it was the best good-bye they could manage with other people watching them. As he and I headed back to my Mountaineer and we pulled out of the woodland, I gave a last look backward. An inescapable feeling that we were being watched rushed over me. I glanced from side to side, but could see no sign of anyone—human or spirit—observing us. Glad to be leaving, I started the car and we headed out of the woods.

Chapter 15

✥

I MANAGED TO get back to work by one-thirty. After brushing my teeth and changing into the spare outfit I always kept in my office, I kept myself busy until Joe came in at around three. He held out his arms and I rushed into them, eager for the warmth of his embrace. He stroked my hair, then kissed me soundly. I motioned him into my office.

"We found another dead biker," I blurted out when we were alone.

He coughed, eyeing me warily. "This ought to be interesting."

After I gave him a rundown on my morning, he shook his head. "Emerald, you get into the weirdest predicaments. What's next on the list?"

"You mean you aren't going to tell me to stop poking my nose into dangerous business?" I didn't know whether to be flattered or indignant. Up until now, Joe had pointedly emphasized my need to develop a suitable sense of self-preservation.

He laughed. "Ha! First you complain because you say

I'm too protective. Now you think I'm not being protective enough. That about the size of it?"

Sheepishly, I nodded. "I guess it does sound a little stupid."

"Would you back out of this if I asked you to?"

I shook my head. "No, probably not."

"Then why should I waste my breath? Nope, I'm just going to beg you to be careful. I love you, and don't want to lose you." After another short but sweet kiss, we headed out to the tearoom. Joe piled cookies on a saucer while I decided I'd better have some lunch. After leaving my breakfast out in the meadow, I was starving. I chose a tuna fish sandwich.

As I unwrapped my sandwich, Joe said, "I agree with you on one thing, though. George isn't a killer, especially when we're talking about one of those bikers. He's a weenie, he doesn't have the backbone for it."

"I know, but then again a number of murderers don't seem to fit the stereotype. Look at Ted Bundy. He was charming, from what everybody says. And yet, he turned out to be a monster." I bit into my sandwich.

Joe shrugged. "Yeah, but your intuition tells you that George didn't do it. One thing I've learned over the past few months is that you're usually right on the money. I trust your hunches." He paused to wolf down a Russian tea cake. "By the way, I think I saw Andrew on the street the other day." He said it so casually that I let down my guard.

"Uh huh, he showed up on my doorstep Tuesday night."

Joe's face clouded over. "He was at your house? What did he want?"

Oops, the green-eyed monster had struck. I cleared my throat. "Uh . . . he just wanted to say hello."

"You're lying."

Anytime I tried to gloss over something, Joe seemed to pick up on it. I leaned back, trying to sound casual. "Joe, nothing happened. Andrew came in, we talked and about five minutes later, he left. End of story."

"If nothing happened, then tell me what he said." Joe stared at his plate, looking more upset than I expected him to be.

"Don't you have to go to work?" I glanced at the clock.

He leaned over the table and took my hand in his. "Not until you give me a straight answer."

I bit my lip. Harlow was right. I had to tell him the truth. "All right. Andrew's fling with the starlet went bad. She dumped him, so he came crawling back to ask me for a second chance. I told him that you were my boyfriend now and I was happy with you. He didn't want to hear what I had to say and he left. End of story."

Joe exhaled. "Really? You told him about me?"

"What do you think I'd do? Fall back into his arms? Give me some credit, Files. You're my man. I'm not letting you off the hook."

"Honey, I just don't like him hanging around your house." He shifted uncomfortably. "Especially if he's nosing around you."

Joe had said the same thing about Jimbo, to start. Now they got along fine. "Andrew isn't a bad person, just a lousy boyfriend. But I promise that I won't invite him into my house unless somebody else is there. Okay?"

He hesitated, then nodded. "That works for me. But if he lays one finger on you, I swear, I'll pop him a good one and he won't ever see it coming."

"If I don't smack him first," I said, grinning. "Okay, it's a deal. Now, you get yourself to work, they need you there. I've got stuff to do."

Stuff to do, the understatement of the week. Two murders, a rogue bunch of warrior spirits guarding a mountain, an elusive monster on the prowl, a shop that needed tending, and two children clamoring for my attention. Yep, that was enough to keep me busy for a while.

• • •

THE NEXT MORNING, Miranda toyed with her eggs. "Mom, you remember that tonight we're supposed to go watch the Perseids, don't you?" I could tell she was hoping that I'd say yes, and for once, my memory hadn't failed me.

I popped a bite of toast in my mouth, hustling to finish breakfast so we could get down to the shop and clean, since it was once again Saturday morning. I swear, sometimes I just wanted to let the cobwebs take over. Maybe during Halloween I'd give myself a break and invite the dust bunnies to decorate for me.

"I wouldn't miss it for the world, hon. Rest assured, your brother and I will be there. Now, please hurry so we can get going." I rinsed my dish and stuck it in the dishwasher. "After we finish cleaning, I want you and Kip to go look for school clothes. We'll shop next week, but I'd like you to have some idea ahead of time of what you want to buy." I gulped my espresso, then burped. Shit. Heartburn. Just what I needed.

"I'm glad it's almost fall, I'm really getting tired of shorts. All my school clothes are too tight, though," she said, a wistful tone in her voice.

"I suppose you're going to want all blacks and grays again?" I winced, sensing that at any minute my miniature Donna Karan was about to resurface.

A smirk flickered across her face. "Uh huh. And white blouses. I can't button any of the ones I own since . . ." She blushed and ducked her head.

"Since you got boobs, huh?" I winked at her. She nodded back, suddenly shy. "Honey, growing up, developing a figure, this is all just part of being a woman. You look great. Just right for being in ninth grade, so don't worry yourself over it." I sighed. "If you want to wear black and white and gray, I'm not going to stop you. But do you think you could buy a few bright things? Maybe you could choose some pretty blouses? You look so good in jewel tones."

She carried her dish to the sink. After a pause, she shrugged. "Okay. I do like blue and green. Are you ready to go?"

"Plate in the dishwasher, please." I shook through my purse, making sure I had everything I needed for the day. Randa rinsed her dish, then piled it in with the rest. "Thank you. Run a load through when you get home, would you? And don't forget to add detergent this time."

"Okay." She blushed again. "And I know—no dishwashing liquid." Earlier in the summer, Randa had made the same mistake I had when I got my first dishwasher. We ran out of detergent for the machine, and she decided that dishwashing liquid would do the job just as well. It had taken us hours to mop up the suds that had foamed out to cover the floor.

"Good girl. Now, please go call Kip while I grab my shoes." She ran off to fetch her brother.

I slipped on a pair of canvas-topped slides. Though I was wearing my grunge clothes, I'd packed a broomstick skirt and tank top to change into after we finished cleaning. Snagging my keys, I hurried through the living room. Randa was already out by the car. Kip was stomping down the stairs, one by one. He was still mad at me about Sly. I nodded him out the door.

"Hurry up. We're going to be late." I armed the security alarm and locked the door, then ran down the steps. Across the street, Horvald was watering his roses. He waved as we hopped in the car, clicked our seat belts, and headed for the store.

After shaking down all the dust bunnies, I gave the kids the green light to take off. Kip hung around for another half-hour, ogling Lana as she worked. She gave me a wink, then asked him very sweetly if he'd mind helping her arrange the dishes in the tearoom. He jumped at the opportunity. Oh yeah, he had a big-time crush on her, all right. It had lasted all spring and summer, but I was hoping that once school started up, he'd transfer it to some lucky little girl in fourth grade.

After a little while, he got bored and I sent him home to finish his chores. I was about to retreat to my office to put in an order with the Adams & Adams Tea Company when Cathy Sutton rushed in. I glanced frantically at my office door, wondering if I could make it before she saw me, but no such luck. She spotted me and was on my tail like white on rice. For once, her cameraman Royal was nowhere in sight.

"Emerald, I need your help."

Something was different about her. The plastic mannequin smile had disappeared. This was the first time I'd seen Cathy without her usual bravado and polished demeanor. She was wearing a rumpled pantsuit, and dark circles under her eyes told me that she hadn't slept.

I held up my hand to forestall her. "I'm not going to give you an interview, so you might as well just turn around and leave."

She shook her head so vehemently that I thought she was going to break her neck. "I'm not here to interview you. I'm not here about the station at all. Please, I really need to talk to you. I know we don't get along but . . . I need a favor. Please listen to me. The police won't hear me out."

My curiosity aroused, I motioned her into the tearoom; having no intention of inviting her into my office. When we were seated, I asked, "What do you want?"

She blinked those big, wide eyes twice. They really were a lovely shade of blue. "The police have arrested George for murder, but he's innocent!"

"I know, I was there—"

Impatiently, she cut me off. "You don't understand. He's my cousin. I got him the job at the station and he was working for me."

"Your cousin?" So nepotism was still alive and thriving. "I still don't see what that has to do with me."

"He idolizes you."

"Not likely, after the jackass-way he acted. I kicked him out." I leaned back in my chair.

"Emerald . . . oh God, this sounds so horrible. You're going to hate me." She paled, covering her face with her hands.

A knot began to form in the pit of my stomach. What the hell had she done to me now? "Go on, I'm listening."

"Emerald, I know you don't like me, and you aren't going to like what I have to tell you, but please, keep an open mind. Don't judge me too quickly." She gave me a beseeching look and, growing impatient, I gestured for her to continue. She cleared her throat.

"Well, it's like this. George is my cousin and he's always looked up to me. Then, last December, he heard about you on the news. When he found out I know you, he begged me to introduce him. He seemed so eager to meet you, and I just . . . well, I was angry because you're always such a bitch to me. I guess that I planted the idea that you might be a fraud."

It took a moment for what she said to sink in.

"You what?" Realizing I'd shouted, I lowered my voice and clutched the edge of the tabletop. So that's why he'd gotten so snarky when I rejected his overtures—not only had I hurt his ego, but it must have seemed a confirmation of Cathy's suggestion. "You were jealous, so you convinced your cousin that I'm a con artist? What the hell is going on, Cathy? What did I ever do to you?"

She grimaced. "Nothing."

I locked her gaze, forcing her to look at me. "I ought to kick your ass to hell and back. First you set me up, and then you come asking for help? I can't believe you, Sutton. I've never once lied to my customers, never once hurt you, and yet you try to trash my reputation? You're pathetic!"

Cathy buried her head in her hands. "I know, I know," she said. "And I'm so sorry, but Emerald, I need your help.

George is innocent. You wouldn't let him go to jail just because you're mad at me, would you?"

The old guilt-trip. I could smell it a mile away. "I've got news for you, babe. *George is already in jail.*" But as much as I wanted to smack her upside the head, I agreed with her on one thing. Whatever else he may have done, I didn't believe that George killed Clyde. I ground my teeth together. "And just what do you think I can do? I'm not a cop, and contrary to what your cousin believes, I don't have any delusions of grandeur. I'm not Wonder Woman."

She sniffed, mopping her eyes with a lace handkerchief. Her mascara was streaked, and her fire-engine-red lipstick had migrated outside of her lip liner. Talk about Marilyn Manson in drag. Actually, he looked better than she did right now.

Struggling to compose herself, she said, "George and I were out in the valley two days ago. I guess you know about the fight he had with Clyde?"

I nodded. "Word gets around."

"George asked me to go with him. Regardless of how angry he was at you, somehow you managed to convince him that the monster exists. We went over to the biker enclave to ask a few questions. After a few minutes, George started acting really strange. He said he was having a vision, that he could see a man getting murdered. At first, I thought he was talking nonsense, but he grew more and more agitated. That's when Clyde hit him."

No wonder, I thought. The bikers wouldn't have any patience for a pair of airheads like Cathy and George. "What happened after the fight?"

Cathy shrugged. "We hunted around a bit. I had to get back to the station for the broadcast, but George didn't want to go, so I left him there. He called me a little later and told me that he'd gone prowling through the woods—that he'd found an old shack and an entrance to a cave. He marked the path with some torn strips off of some canvas that he found in the shack, and said he was going to explore a little bit more. I warned him not to go into the cave alone. That's the last I heard from him till he called me from jail yesterday. By then, he couldn't remember anything very clearly."

He'd actually found one of the caverns? "Go on."

She dabbed at her eyes again. "The next thing I know, Clyde was dead, and George was arrested for murder. George never takes drugs, Emerald, but they tested him and he was high as a kite."

"You said he was having visions? Is this common? It can be a sign of drug intoxication."

"I know it can, but . . ." With a deep sigh, she said, "He's always had these abilities, but nobody in the family ever wanted to talk about it. My aunt and uncle are pretty conservative and they never let him bring up the subject around them. He talks to me about it, since nobody else will listen. Or at least, he did, until he heard about you."

A flare of jealousy rose around her like a mist, then wafted away. I chose to ignore it—she was so painfully lacking in self-awareness. So, apparently George really did have second sight, and that might mean there was something to his visions.

"Emerald, he insists the monster is real. I believe him. That's got to be the answer—the Klakatat Monster, whatever it is, killed Clyde and somehow George got involved." Cathy wasn't playing the ditz today, but I could tell she was grasping at straws. I didn't like her any better, but at least she was being as honest as someone like her could ever hope to be.

"Is there anything else I should know?"

She thought for a moment, then shrugged. "George can't remember anything from Thursday night. This morning I talked to Detective Murray. She said that the tests showed so much Rohypnol in his system that he should be thankful he isn't dead. Apparently, when the drug interacts with alcohol, the effects are a lot worse, and his blood alcohol level was three times the legal limit for drunkenness.

She said the only thing that saved him was vomiting—he got enough of it out of his system before it killed him. But I'm telling you, he doesn't drink more than a beer or two, and he doesn't do drugs. He sure isn't stupid enough to mix the two."

I frowned. Even though I didn't like the pipsqueak, I knew something was horribly off-kilter. But how could we prove it? "What do you want me to do?"

She took a deep breath, held it for a moment, then slowly exhaled and straightened her shoulders. "I want you to go out there with me to look for the cave. Maybe we can find some sort of evidence to prove he's innocent. The police say he was in the meadow all night. The coroner set Clyde's death around eight hours before you found him, so George was somewhere out there during the time that Clyde was murdered. If we don't find something to prove otherwise, they'll convict him."

I stared at her. How nutso could she get? She actually believed I was going to gallivant out to the valley and hike through a cave with her, hunting for evidence? "Maybe you should ask somebody else, Cathy."

She stared at the table, blushing. "No! It's got to be you."

"Why me? Why not someone from your station? What's so all-fired important about having me there with you?"

Verging on the edge of panic, she stumbled over her words. "I'm scared. There's a monster running loose out there. I was only having George spy on you because . . . because I missed having him look up to me. I'll feel safe with you along. You've solved several murders and you seem to be a good-luck magnet."

Good-luck magnet? Was she out of her mind? I narrowed my eyes. Nope. She was still holding something back. "I'm not buying it, Cathy. If you don't spill the rest, I won't help you."

The floodgates opened then and she burst into tears.

"Okay, okay. I need your help because nobody at the station will even listen to me. They all hate me, and they can't stand George. He may be a pain in the butt sometimes, but he's my cousin and I love him. Nobody there cares whether he lives or he dies."

Bingo! "What about your friends? Can't they help you?"

She blinked through her tears. "Friends? What friends? I don't have any friends, Emerald." With a moan, she rested her head on her hands. "You were the only person I could think of to ask."

Oh jeez, not this. Why should I help her when she'd been such an ass? But George's face kept popping up in my mind. Misguided and arrogant? Yes. Testosterone-laden little twerp? Yes. Murderer? No.

With a sigh, I caved. "I know I'm going to regret this—"

"Oh thank you! Thank you!" She clapped, but I held up one hand.

"Hold on! I will help you, but on one condition: I'm going to ask Murray and Jimbo to come along. Murray's in charge of the investigation; she'll be fair and give George every chance. If neither one can make it, then you can forget it."

She nodded, contrite. "I won't cause trouble."

"It will have to be tomorrow morning. There's no way I can get away any earlier than that." I had to clear some of the paperwork off my desk and Miranda's meteor-shower party was tonight. I wasn't about to miss that for anybody or anything. George wouldn't be hauled into court until Monday, so he was safe until then. A night or two in jail wouldn't hurt the kid and might just teach him a little humility.

She stood up. "Thank you," she said, barely above a whisper. "I'm sorry to bother you. I'm sorry that I told George you were a fraud. I'm sorry about a lot of things."

I had the feeling she'd be sorry just as long as it took us to prove George was innocent. The old Cathy Sutton was way too entrenched to hide out under this chagrined façade forever. "Whatever. Meet me here tomorrow morning at seven A.M. We might as well get this show on the road as soon as possible."

With that, she nodded and took off. As I watched her retreating back, the air seemed to grow thick. Shivering, I pulled out my deck and focused, asking what would happen if I let Cathy go off exploring those caves by herself. I drew a card and turned it over. The dancing skeleton of Death stared back at me, and I knew—with absolute certainty—that if she waltzed out into those woods alone, Cathy wouldn't make it back alive. Even though I didn't like her, I couldn't live with her death on my conscience.

WHEN I CALLED Murray to find out if she could go along, she wasn't at home. I tried her office number and she picked up on the second ring. As I spilled out what Cathy had told me, I could hear her pencil tapping against her desk.

"Em, I'd love to go, but things have gone wacko here. There were complications during Coughlan's surgery. They don't know if he's going to pull through. In the interim, Chief Bonner has appointed me as the acting head of detectives. There's so much work to do that I can't possibly get away tomorrow morning." She lowered her voice. "Coughlan's files are a mess. The man never organized anything, and it's going to take me days just to sort out what's on his desk."

Disappointed, I leaned back against my chair. Well, at least one good thing was coming out of this: Murray was getting the recognition she deserved. "Acting head of detectives? Congratulations!"

"Not all of the guys are happy about it. I'm going to have to watch my back, tell you that."

"Hey, you've put up with a lot. Bonner was right to appoint you to the position."

"Maybe, but even though Coughlan is scum, he doesn't deserve this."

I drummed on the desk with my fingertips. "Well, can't you at least send somebody out with us to check the cave? Cathy said George marked the path."

"Em, I can and will do that, but it's not going to be until Tuesday or Wednesday." I heard the shuffle of papers. "We're running short-staffed right now. Two men are out with the flu, and the chief just told me that we're going to have to make even more budget cuts. I'd have to pay somebody overtime to go out there this weekend and I just can't justify it unless there's an emergency. If Cathy wants to go now, I can't stop her, though I wish she wouldn't. Why don't you tell her to go by herself?"

I stared at my desk, soberly thinking about my decision. "Mur, I don't believe that George killed Clyde. And there's something else." I told her about the tarot card. "If Cathy goes alone, she's going to die. You and I both know that the Death card usually means some life-altering transformation, but this time . . . it means what it says. I can feel it, deep down in my gut. I know I'm right."

Murray lowered her voice. "Em, if that's true, then there's real danger out there. Don't go unless you can get Jimbo or Joe to go with you. Please?"

"Don't worry—I'll give you that one."

"Good. On the same subject, you'll be happy to know that because of Clyde's death, I'm reopening Scar's case. We're exhuming the body and I've called in the M.E. from Bellingham to give us a second opinion Since both Scar and Clyde lived in Klickavail Valley, I figure that there's got to be some link between the two. Monday, I'll be able to send a couple of the boys out to start asking questions. I talked to Chief Bonner and, even though he wasn't thrilled about the idea, he gave me the go-ahead."

"Well, that's good news. What do you think will happen to Stryker if they find out he overlooked evidence?"

With a grunt, she said, "You're talking opening a can of

worms the size of Seattle. The whole M.E.'s office would fall under investigation, as well as Coughlan's involvement. It might jeopardize the rulings of a number of already closed cases. But regarding George . . . Em . . . you have to face facts. We found him right next to Clyde's body. We found him near Scar's body. And even though Scar was already dead, George still could have known he was out there."

Hell. George might end up facing a double-murder charge. I wished I knew why I was so positive he was innocent. I just couldn't shake the feeling that the kid was in the wrong place at the wrong time. "Do you really believe he killed Clyde? And Scar?"

She paused just a beat too long. "I don't know. He doesn't seem like the type, but Em, I've met murderers who were baby-faced young men. They seemed like sweet kids, until you peeled off their veneer. I can't assume George is innocent. Nor will I assume he's guilty. I can only go by what we find."

"Yeah, I understand. Okay, I'll call Jimbo and Joe. You going to make it to yoga class this evening?"

"Nope. As I said, I'm stuck here and probably won't get home before midnight. You go though, and tell Tina why I can't be there."

I promised I would, then hung up. When I rang Jimbo, he was out. I left a message at the beep asking him to call me as soon as he could, then rang the fire station. The dispatcher answered and put me through to Joe, who promptly informed me that he was scheduled to drill his men on rescue techniques during a controlled burn on Sunday morning.

"Em, I don't want you going out there. Listen to your intuition!"

"My intuition tells me that Cathy is the one in danger."

He changed tactics. "Then maybe you should listen to reason instead."

I almost laughed. "Oh Joe, I'm scared, don't worry

about that. I promise, I'll be careful, but I have to go check it out. I'm going to persuade Jimbo to go, even if I have to hogtie him to the top of my car. We should be safe with him tagging along."

"Safe from the monster or safe from killing each other?"

"Funny man, you're such a funny man." I blew a kiss to him over the phone and hung up. The rest of the afternoon passed quietly, but I had the feeling it was only the calm before the storm.

Chapter 16

❧

$\mathscr{Y}$OGA CLASS WENT surprisingly well, and I wasn't nearly as sore this time as I had been the first. When Tina showed me how to use a strap to prevent me from straining my back while practicing the asanas, the exercises went much easier than I thought they would. By the end of class, I actually felt like I'd had a massage. Woohoo! I told her I'd be back the next week and raced home, where I jumped in the shower and changed just in time to drive us out to Perry Field, where Miranda's astronomy club was meeting to watch the Perseids.

The Chiqetaw Stargazers Society was primarily composed of a handful of older men and women in their retirement years, three or four earnest young nerds in their twenties, and two members under eighteen—Randa and her friend Lori. All of the older members looked out for the two girls, especially Naomi French, who made sure that the talk remained PG-rated at the most, and that the two girls didn't get overlooked in the discussions. Twice a year, they drove over to Bellingham to meet with another group of amateur astronomers, and I allowed Randa to go as long as Naomi went.

The group welcomed us with a hearty hail of greetings. I had stopped on the way at the QVC to pick up a box of doughnuts and now offered them around. Randa beamed at me. Even at her age, she knew that the quickest way to win favor was by placating the sweet tooth. Several of the members came up to tell me what a polite and intelligent girl my daughter was. She blushed, but looked pleased. I unfurled our blanket and we settled down to await the celestial light show. Kip, trying desperately to hold onto his tiff, planted himself a few yards away, on a makeshift bench that had been created out of a fallen log. After a few minutes of his self-imposed isolation, he crept back to join us on the blanket.

Randa sat up her telescope and tested it out. "Okay, it's ready. Have you got the binoculars?"

I held up the pair that were hanging around my neck. "Check!"

She nodded, a satisfied look on her face. "Good. We'll start watching in about half an hour. The club needs to go through the minutes from the last meeting and stuff like that. If you want to wait here, you can."

"Sounds like a plan to me," I said. She joined the others who were gathered around a picnic table while Kip and I sat on the blanket.

Set on the outskirts of town, Perry Field was six blocks away from Lincoln Elementary, the school Kip attended. The land—a good five-acre plot—had been deeded to the city by Wilber Perry, an old eccentric who had frightened all the kids with his threats to keep the baseballs they hit into his yard, and to call the cops whenever they ran through his vegetable garden. He'd died the year before we arrived in Chiqetaw, and the city had found itself the proud owner of the five-acre parcel. It hadn't taken much to turn Wilber's house into a meeting hall that could be rented out for weddings and other events, and the land itself was primed and ready for turning into a park. Outfitted with jungle gyms, swing sets, and picnic tables, Perry Field had become the perfect place for birthday parties and impromptu meetings.

A number of other meteor-watchers had decided that the park would be prime sky-watching territory; blankets and figures shaded by the dusk lay scattered across the field. The city had acquiesced to the Chiqetaw Stargazers Society's request and doused the streetlights scattered throughout the park for the next two evenings to give us prime viewing.

I leaned back on my elbows, staring at the sky. In Seattle this would have been impossible; there was too much light pollution. But here, the velvet dark surrounded us, the stars spread in a glittering panorama over our heads. I took a deep breath and let it out slowly, relaxing for the first time in awhile. Monsters, murders, these were thoughts for the day, not this evening.

Kip must have been feeling the same way I was, because he scooted closer and stretched out on his back, his hands cradling his head. "Mom, I'm sorry about what happened with Sly. I really didn't mean to steal anybody's money."

I reached down and patted his shoulder. "I know you didn't, bud. You just have to start using that brain of yours a little more. Try to think about the ramifications of your actions—ask yourself what might happen because of what you choose to do. We talked about this in December, remember?"

"Oh boy, do I ever." He nodded fervently, then, out of nowhere, asked. "Mom? Are you and Joe in love?"

Whoa. I hadn't been prepared for that one. How to answer? What with Roy and Tyra having a new baby, the kids felt left out enough as it was. Would my saying "yes" make them feel pushed away even more?

"Well, I think we might be." I looked down at my son. "Does that bother you?"

He popped up then, like a jack-in-the-box, and stared at me intently. "Bother me? Heck no! I like Joe. Hey, if you guys get married, will you have another baby like Dad is? I wouldn't mind having another brother . . . or sister."

Heavens! Now Kip had us married and pregnant. "Slow down, kiddo! Joe and I've never talked about marriage, and I certainly think that if we do get married, we'll have to wait awhile to make a decision about another child. After all, you and Randa are my children, and I would never do anything to make you feel left out."

Kip picked at his shoe. "Dad really doesn't love us, does he?" He sounded so sad that I wanted to scoop him up in my arms, to cover him with kisses and hugs, to wipe away any loneliness or pain he was feeling.

How could I answer his question? How could I, in good conscience, tell my children the truth: Their father didn't care about them. He didn't care about anybody but himself. And when he and Tyra had their new baby, he would lose interest in that child, too. I didn't hold out much hope for his marriage, the odds were just stacked too high, and Roy wasn't a good gambler. Someday he'd start finding fault with Tyra, just the way he had with me.

I searched for the right words. "We've talked about this before, Kip. Your dad isn't cut out to be a father, but he loves you dearly."

"I don't think he does." Kip set his lips in a thin line. "You don't have to lie to me. Randa and I know, we talked about it the other day. That's why I've decided I don't wanna go see him. He never bothers to call us, or to come visit."

I pulled my knees to my chest and rested my chin on them. What now? He was right, he and Randa knew the score as much as I'd tried to shelter them from it. I finally looked over at my son who was waiting for an answer. "Kip, your father has a lot of emotional problems. He mainly cares about himself. It's not your fault, it's not Randa's. It's not mine. Roy never learned how to care about others. However, he is your father, and by law, he has a right to see you. I know you don't want to go, but please, give him another chance. Maybe he's trying to reach out—you never know."

Kip bit his lip, then shrugged. "Yeah, guess so."

Just then, Randa showed up. She sat down on the blanket and accepted the soda I offered her. "We're about ready to begin our official count. Every time I see one, I'll mark it down." She sat back on the blanket, scorecard in hand.

I forced back a sigh. She was so analytical that sometimes it almost broke my heart. I wanted her to enjoy the wonder of her passions, not just to probe and prod data into order. "Do you want our counts, too?"

She thought for a moment, then shook her head. "No, you're not actually members so we couldn't really use them in our tally."

"Where do we look?" Kip asked. At first he'd balked at the excursion, but now he seemed to be getting into the spirit.

"It doesn't matter where you look—they'll be all over the sky." As she launched into an explanation of what meteors were, and what they weren't, I tipped my head up and stared at the canopy of diamonds that stretched from horizon to horizon. The night had grown darker and all of a sudden, a brilliant sparkle of light streaked across the heavens, leaving a glistening trail behind it. Despite myself, I gasped and pointed.

"There's one!"

Randa and Kip swung their faces skyward, just in time to catch a second that went zinging overhead. "Yay!" Kip yelled, clapping his hands. "I'm gonna make a wish."

As he shut his eyes and wished, I caught sight of yet a third, and we were off and running. Dusk drifted toward midnight as the cares of the day vanished amid our shouting and cheers each time we saw another shooting star. The entire field was filled with victory cries, and we lost track of the meteors that went streaking overhead.

At one point, I looked over at Randa. The scorecard that she'd been holding so diligently had dropped to the ground, forgotten, as she watched with a look of sheer delight plastered across her face. I needn't have worried. This was her passion, and all the statistics in the world couldn't keep down her love for the stars. I settled back and we sat there late into the night, watching in wonder as the skies came tumbling down around our shoulders.

I WAS UP at six, still sleepy but feeling extraordinarily relaxed. At least, I was feeling relaxed until I remembered that I had to go cave-hopping with the reporter from hell.

I dug through my closet and came up with an old pair of jeans and a grungy tank top. I'd been meaning to toss them, but they'd be perfect for spelunking; caves were notoriously dirty, and I didn't relish getting covered in whatever cave-goo our expedition might encounter. I tied my sneakers, pulled my hair back into a braid and tucked a bandana around my head. Eschewing makeup, I opted for sunscreen instead.

A hooded fleece jacket would complete the outfit; caves could be icy cold even in the middle of summer. I'd rather lug the jacket along with me than end up shivering all the way through the morning. In the kitchen, I filled a backpack with a couple of water bottles, three peanut butter sandwiches, an apple, and a handful of cookies. On second thought, I added a roll of toilet paper and a thin nylon rope. I also made sure my cell phone battery was fully charged.

Speaking of phones, I punched in Jimbo's number. When we got home from the field last night, I found that he'd left a message, agreeing to go along. At least I wasn't facing a day alone with Ms. Sutton. I caught him mid-breakfast. The static-laced drone of the TV in the background filtered through his mumbled "A-OK."

"I'll meet you where we found Clyde's body," he said. "I'll be there at around seven-thirty."

As I was brewing a quick espresso fix, the kids came running in from out back, their mouths covered with a bright purple stain. "Let me guess, you've been picking berries?" I gave them a quizzical look. "You're up early."

"We thought we'd get busy before it gets too hot," Randa said. The lot next door was overflowing with brambles. I had the feeling they'd be covered head-to-toe with blackberry juice by the time they finished harvesting the fruit.

"That's a good idea. Pick enough and I'll do my best to make us a pie. But be sure to rinse them off when you bring them home. I don't want a lot of bugs crawling around in my kitchen." I gulped down my mocha, swallowed the last bite of my Pop-Tart, and then grabbed a slice of cold pizza. That should hold me until lunch time.

"We'll clean 'em," Kip promised. "Mom, can we have hamburgers for breakfast? Randa said she'll make them for us."

I peeked in the fridge. Sure enough, we had ground beef and buns there. I shrugged. "Why not? Sounds nutritious to me." I pulled out the beef and handed it to Randa, along with the nonstick skillet and a plastic spatula. "Use this to cook them in, honey, so they don't stick."

"Thanks Mom," she said, forming patties and sliding them into the pan. I had the suspicion that she'd actually started to enjoy cooking, even though she still professed to hate it.

"Listen, while I'm gone today, I want you to hang out with Horvald. He said he'll take you out for lunch if I'm not back by then, but I don't expect to be gone longer than noon. I'll take my cell phone, though, so you can get in touch with me if you need to."

Randa smiled "He's nice. I wish he and Mrs. Trask would get married."

"Yuck! Mush." Kip screwed up his face. "Besides, whose house would they live in? They can't get married anyway, they're too old."

Randa watched the burgers sizzle. She buttered the buns and popped them in the toaster oven to brown. "Can too! They'd make a great couple. Feed the cats, stupid, while I fix our breakfast."

"Who you callin' stupid?" Kip stuck his tongue out at her. He dished out breakfast for the cats, who were milling about underfoot. "Why do you want them to get married, anyway?"

"'Cuz they both seem lonely." Randa transferred the hamburger patties to the buns and set them on the table as I emptied the dishwasher. After they finished eating, I herded them across the street, to where Horvald was already hard at work in his dahlia bed.

They waved as I hopped in the car and took off up the road.

Come seven o'clock, I was sitting in my Mountaineer in front of my shop, a triple-shot grandé iced mocha in hand, waiting for Cathy to show up. Six shots and counting so far.

I patted the dashboard. "It's okay, Tenzing. She doesn't bite. If she does, we'll kick her ass." And maybe I could. After yoga class, I'd expected to wake up feeling stiff and achy, but I was actually feeling pretty good. It occurred to me that I should stretch before bed every night. Just to hurry results along.

A glance out the window showed the usual Sunday morning lack of traffic. Chiqetaw was deader than a fence post. The only shops that opened early along Main Street were a couple of restaurants, Starbucks, and the Barnes & Noble bookstore a few blocks away.

A knock on the passenger door startled me out of my thoughts. Cathy was standing there, dressed in a pair of black jeans and a designer T-shirt. I unlocked the door for her and she hopped in, breathless. I noticed she was wearing a pair of black suede loafers, and if I wasn't mistaken, they were Ralph Lauren.

I pointed to her feet. "Are you sure you want to be

wearing those when we go mucking around a cave? It's probably filled with slime and mold."

She glanced at her shoes and shrugged. "They'll be fine. I don't think we're going to find anything that nasty, and if we do, I'll just buy another pair."

Just buy another pair. I'd like to have money like that to throw away. "Fine, whatever. Let's get this show on the road. It's almost seven-thirty."

She clicked her seatbelt shut. "I'm sorry I'm late. I couldn't get my car started." As I eased out of the parking space, she asked, "Where are your friends?"

I shrugged. "Murray and Joe had to work. Jimbo will meet us there."

She shuddered. "I don't like him very much. He's crude."

I glanced at her as I turned onto the road leading out to Klickavail Valley. "Crude or not, he helped me save my son. Sometimes the cover really doesn't reflect the book."

"Well, he hasn't got any manners, that's all I have to say about him."

Manners? Jimbo? Not for someone like Cathy Sutton. He'd told her just where she could stick her microphone a few months earlier and I had the feeling she was still holding a grudge. Time to change the subject.

"So, do you like your job? You always seem so cheerful on TV."

She snorted. "I'm paid to be cheerful. I'd love to work at a station over in New York or down in L.A., but it's impossible to find a good agent when you live in a dump this size." She studied her nails as we lapsed into an uneasy silence.

So Ms. Sutton was a big city girl stuck in a small town. Considering her attitude and disregard for people, she probably would fare better in a large, anonymous city. Then again, I had the feeling she was blaming her lack of promotion and new offers on Bellingham's size, rather than on her own shortcomings.

"So . . ." she said. "Why did you decide to open a china shop?"

I flicked on my right-hand blinker. Not far to go, thank God. "I've always loved china and teapots, so when I left my ex, and decided to go into business, it seemed natural to draw on my passion for inspiration."

"How long were you married?"

I gave her a long glance. Ten to one, Cathy couldn't hold a normal conversation without digging for gossip. "Too long. I was married too long. And you? Have you ever been married?"

She turned to stare out the window. "Yes, actually, I was. When I was twenty."

Well, that was a shock. I couldn't imagine what kind of man could put up with her. "Divorced?"

"He died." She shrugged. "He was twenty-four. One day he went skiing with a friend and they were caught in an avalanche."

Oh jeez! I caught my breath and let it out slowly, feeling terrible for all the uncharitable things I'd been thinking about her. "I'm sorry. I can't imagine how hard that must have been to cope with."

"It wasn't easy. His family didn't think I was good enough for him to begin with." She shrugged. "Anyway, after Tom died, I sued the resort, and used the settlement to go back to school. I graduated with a degree in broadcasting, got hired at KLIK-TV, and thirteen years later, here I still am, in a dead-end job, with a dead-end résumé."

Not sure of what to say, I kept my mouth shut and concentrated on the road. After a few more minutes, we pulled into Klickavail Valley and I idled the motor. None of the bikers paid much attention to us—they were used to seeing people coming and going through here by now. "Before we get this show going, I'm going to tell you something and you need to remember it."

She looked at me, expectantly.

"There are some freaky things out here, including spirits

that don't like people screwing around in their territory. You do what I say, when I say. Got it?" Chances were good I was wasting my breath, but I might as well try.

She grunted and I took that for a "yes." We eased through the shaded foliage at a snail's pace, then abruptly shot out into the area where Clyde had lost his life. I shivered. There was something wild and untamed out here, a feeling that the forest could close in and swallow us whole. I looked around, but Jimbo was nowhere in sight. He was running late, as usual.

"Where's this shack you were talking about?"

Cathy stared at the terrain, sucking on her lip. After a moment, she pointed left, past the outcropping of brambles and bushes that blocked our view. "On the phone, George told me it's over that way, beyond a huge patch of briars and brambles, a little ways beyond Turtle Rock."

Hmm. Past the area where we'd found Clyde's body. I pulled to a stop and we got out of the car and started walking. "That's where we found Clyde and George." I pointed out the murder scene. Signs of the investigation still littered the ground. A crumpled cigarette pack, a forgotten latex glove, dark splotches of dried blood. Monuments to unexpected death.

Cathy stared at the patch, somber. "I've never seen a dead body."

"I've seen more than I ever wanted to." It seemed like the past year had been steeped in blood. I'd managed to stumble over several murder scenes and by now, I had realized that the memories and images weren't going to fade away. "So, where is this shack?"

She pointed to a place where Klickavail Mountain jutted into the strip of meadow, a tiny bump in the manner of mountains, but large enough to obscure our view. In fact, it looked as if the meadow ended there; the forest crowded in around the base of the slope. "There. It should be in the forest over there."

Hmm. Jimbo wasn't here yet, but I didn't want to drag

this out. Maybe if I left a message for him on my windshield, telling him where we were going, then Cathy and I could at least take a look at the shack while we waited for him. I told her to come with me and hurried back to the Mountaineer, where I dug around in the back and hauled out my pack, slipping the straps over my arm. "I suppose you didn't bring so much as a bottle of water for yourself, or even a flashlight?"

She blanched. "Oh. I thought you were bringing those things."

Good God, either the woman really did believe I could read minds or she expected to be waited on hand and foot. I plastered a huge note on the windshield, and then took another gander at the road, hoping to see Jimbo's truck. No such luck. "All right, show me this shack. We should be safe for now."

We trekked back past Turtle Rock and rounded the curve, trudging through the verdant foliage that girded the gigantic boulder. Once we reached the tree line, it only took a few moments to locate the cabin. Weathered and worn, it couldn't possibly be inhabited.

"The cave is back in the woods, beyond the shack," Cathy said. "George told me that he marked the path with torn pieces of a canvas sheet. That's when he said he was going back to explore further," she added glumly.

I headed over toward the building. The outer walls were gray with age, and if it had been painted, the paint had long since flaked away. I fingered the wood. Rough, splintered. Nope, this didn't look like a house, even for someone roughing it. *Shack* was the only word that fit.

"Whose place is this? Do you know?"

She shrugged. "I have no idea, but it looks abandoned, doesn't it?"

I cautiously ascended the three sagging stairs that led to an even more precarious porch, and sidled up to the door. There was no sign of anyone around, in fact, no sign that anybody had lived here for a long time. If there had ever been glass in the windows, it was so much dust by now. The floor listed under my feet, and I held my breath as I pushed open the door.

Light streamed in from the cracks in the walls and the windows. The cabin was bare-bones, with a rusty old cot pressed against one wall and a rickety table in middle of the room. A couple of stools were drawn up to the table, and there was a dilapidated dresser pushed up against the opposite wall. The drawers were open, and empty, save for the remnants of the canvas that George had found. All of the furniture looked makeshift. The nail heads were rusting, and it was obvious that the mildew had eaten through a good share of the wood. Nothing indicated that this cabin might play home for anybody except the bugs.

"Well, this is a dead end." I turned to Cathy.

She huddled near the doorway. "This place gives me the creeps. Let's go look at the cave."

"No way, not without Jimbo."

"Oh come on," she wheedled. "Leave him another note. Tell him to follow the path George left—the canvas ribbons will show up easy enough for him to see. I promise, I won't ask you to go into the cave until he gets there. Or . . ." she said, eyeing me speculatively, "we can sit here and play twenty questions until he shows up."

That was enough to get me moving. Talking to Cathy in the car had been agony enough. I followed her back into the sunlight. Jimbo would show up soon and he could easily catch up to us. If anybody knew these woods, he did. But any way you sliced it, I didn't like this. However, I didn't have all day to waste, so I maneuvered around till I found a signal for my cell phone and punched in his number. His answering machine beeped, but he didn't pick up.

"He must be on his way; I can't get him at home." I hesitated another minute, then decided that we might as well start back through the woods. The Warriors of the Mountain seemed to only come out near dark, and it was far from evening. If we waited by the entrance of the cave, we'd be safe enough. I dashed off another note and stuck it prominently on the door of the shack.

"He'll show by the time we're there. Let's head out." We swung around back of the shack and sure enough, there in the bushes glimmered a moldy white ribbon. Maybe this wouldn't be so hard after all, I thought as I plunged into the bushes, Cathy close on my heels.

Chapter 17

❧

ABOUT THIRTY YARDS behind the shack, the forest curved to meet the mountain, a blending of vegetation and rock, of the ephemeral springing from the bones of the earth. We paused, hunting for the second ribbon. Cathy spotted it, pointing out the strip of cloth tied around a huckleberry bush. The foliage was dense, and I found it difficult to believe Cathy would willingly crawl through the branches and fronds.

"You're actually prepared to wade through this?"

She eyed the vegetation, looking apprehensive. "I didn't know it would be so thick. But I want to see that cave. George was there, and I want to know what happened."

"The cops will be out here poking around in the next day or so. You could just wait for them."

Raising one eyebrow, she gave me an incredulous look. "I don't trust the cops anymore than you trust the media."

"This time I side with the cops," I muttered. Cathy was up to something, I was sure of it. While she really did seem to care about her cousin, it was hard for me to believe that she didn't have an ulterior motive sneaking around in that bleach-blonde brain of hers. "Are you sure you're not just looking for more dirt for some news story?"

She planted herself in front of me. "Listen Emerald, you have a tidy little life. You've got your shop and your local celebrity status and your kids and your boyfriend and your house. Me? I've got squat. I have a lousy job at a cut-rate television station. I make half of what I could in a different city. Would I like to get a good story out of this? Sure, if that happens to be part of the fallout. But this is my cousin's life we're talking about. He's sitting in jail right now, facing a charge for a murder he didn't commit. We're out here to help George. I thought that's what mattered to you."

I sighed. Cathy would never be anything more than a two-bit anchorwoman, and she'd probably be stuck in Bellingham till the day she died. However, as much as I hated to admit it, she seemed sincere and she was right about George. He might be a little weasel, but I'd be a pathetic excuse for a human being if I sat around and let him get railroaded for a crime he didn't commit.

"Either you come with me, or I go on alone." Cathy pointed toward the strip of cloth. "One way or another, I'm going to find that cave."

Once again, the image of the Death card flashed in my mind and a feeling of dread swept over me. Cathy was heading to her doom if she went into those woods alone. I could either go with her, try to stop whatever was lying in wait, or I could stand back and watch her walk right into the hand of fate. Did the fact that I disliked her mean that she deserved to die?

"Let me take the lead," I said gruffly. She swung in behind me and, with a deep breath, I plunged into the overgrowth, past the ribbon. As I fought my way through the ferns and berries and salal, the smell of deep woods filtered into my lungs and it hit me that we really were isolated. A scream from here probably wouldn't reach the bikers in the encampment. Great. If we did run into an emergency, we were on our own, at least until Jimbo high-tailed his butt over here.

"What's wrong?" Cathy bumped up against me, knocking me against a cedar that stood directly in my path. The makeshift trail wound around the tree, hugging the fragrant trunk.

I rubbed my arm where the bark had scratched me. "I don't like this. I still think we should wait for Jimbo."

"We'll wait outside the cave and if he doesn't show up, we'll come back. I promise I won't ask you to go in there without him."

Not sure how much a promise from her really meant, I sighed. "All right, but at the first sign of trouble, we turn around."

As we stumbled over leaf and branch, I saw another marker tied to a branch up ahead. Okay, so George had come this far. I turned in that direction. The ground was growing spongy, with moss-covered rocks littering the path. One slip could mean a twisted ankle. I held up my hand for Cathy to stop.

"We need a couple of sturdy walking sticks to help us maneuver around these rocks without breaking our necks." I looked around; there were plenty of windfalls here and it was easy to come up with a couple of broken limbs from one of the downed firs. I sat down on a fallen log and motioned for Cathy to join me. She gingerly settled onto the moss-and-mushroom-covered log.

"Strip some of this bark off, at least enough to make sure the wood inside isn't rotten. That will give you a better handhold, too."

I began peeling away the wet bark. If the branches were too dry, we wouldn't have been able to do this, but even in the midst of a warm and sunny summer, the inner sanctum of western Washington's forests were usually moist. A sour smell drifted up. Yep, mildew, but not deep enough to rot through the core yet. I tapped the branch on the ground, and then leaned on it. Good. Sturdy enough to support my weight. I sat back down, waiting for Cathy to finish.

"Damn it, I'm going to break a nail," she said.

"Better than breaking your leg."

She glanced at me, but didn't answer. After a few minutes, she'd managed to strip off enough bark to give herself a firm grip. I motioned for her to shadow me as we followed the ribbons, picking our way through the pebbles and rocks and broken branches that littered the ground. The entire world seemed to be composed of a kaleidoscope of leaves and fern fronds and overhanging branches. At our current vantage point, we couldn't see the shack or the meadow, and I was grateful that I'd brought my cell phone. I plunged out from a dense stand of fern and vine maple and found myself standing face-to-face with Klickavail Mountain.

To our right, up a graduated slope on the mountainside, a ragged ribbon marked a thicket of mountain ash. The trees sported a tinge of color edging the unending green of the leaves—the first hints of autumn. Dense clusters of red berries dangled from the branches like ornaments. We picked our way up the slope until the cliff face of Klickavail Mountain soared directly in front of us. To our right, shaded by dense undergrowth, a hole had been gouged into the side of the mountain.

I hesitantly moved toward the opening. "George's cave?" I asked, pushing back the branches so we could see better.

The entrance was uniform, about seven feet tall, and its gentle gradient sloped downhill. The ground in front of the opening was covered with moss and mulch, springy to the touch.

Cathy eyed the entrance nervously. "On the phone, George said he saw bats circling around here. Do you think they're in there?"

I strained to remember what Murray had tried to teach me about bats one lazy evening when we'd been discussing favorite critters. "Maybe, though it seems a little early for them to go into hibernation. They swarm during August, though, usually for mating. Maybe they roost here in the winter? I think Murray said they hibernate."

"Hibernate? Bats hibernate? You just know about all sorts of creepy things, don't you?"

"I didn't come here to be insulted. Do you want my help or not?"

Cathy sighed. "Yeah, yeah . . . sorry. Well, let's go." She started to push past me toward the cave entrance, but I stopped her.

"You promised to wait for Jimbo." I knelt down and slid the backpack off my shoulders, fishing out the flashlight, as well as my cell phone which I flipped open. I managed to get enough of a signal to punch in Jimbo's number, but there was no answer. Where the hell was he? I clipped the phone on my belt.

As I was fastening my pack, I noticed several splintered pieces of wood poking up through the mossy carpet. I tugged at one, finally encouraging it to slide out of its spongy womb. Déjà vu. I stared at the splintered wood, trying to conjure up just what it reminded me of.

"Hmm . . . what does this look like to you?"

"Paul Bunyan's toothpick?" She snickered and, my train of thought disrupted, I tossed the foot-long sliver aside.

"Did anyone ever tell you just how helpful you are, Cathy?"

She let out an impatient sigh. "I'm tired of waiting."

"So am I, but we aren't going in until Jimbo gets here."

Just then, a low growl emanated from within the stand of mountain ash. I whirled, my skin crawling as the sound echoed through the trees.

"What's that?" Cathy straightened, her eyes growing wild.

I shook my head. "I don't know. Could be a bear, or cougar, or maybe . . ." I didn't want to scare her but there was another possibility that was creeping through my mind and I really hoped I was wrong.

"Just say it—you know you're thinking it. Maybe that thing is the Klakatat Monster!" Cathy frantically looked around for an escape. Just then, a loud shriek reverberated out of the tree stand and the bushes began to rustle. Something was headed our way.

"Oh shit, what's that?" Cathy began to back up toward the cave.

"Stop—if you run and it's a cougar, it'll come right for you!"

But my words evaporated as a muster of crows, startled by the noise, launched out of the trees. There must have been fifty of them, at least, and their wings glistened in the light as they swooped in Cathy's direction. She just had time to scream before they were sweeping past, cawing wildly. Flailing to keep them away from her head, she plunged into the mine.

"Cathy! Wait!" Even as I shouted, she disappeared into the gloom.

Oh hell, now what was I going to do? The rustling sound paused and I had the distinct feeling something was watching me. Cougar, bear, or monster, the choices weren't pretty. I stood stock still, remembering that bears couldn't see very well. As I'd warned Cathy, cougars would chase a running target quicker than one who held its ground. I had no idea what the Klakatat Monster might do, and I hoped to hell that I wasn't about to find out.

I slipped my cell phone out of my pocket and punched in Jimbo's number again. Still no answer. I tried calling Murray, but she was away from her desk, too. The signal wavered, but I managed to leave messages for both of them. Cautiously, I eyed the mouth of the cave again, hoping Cathy would emerge before whatever was in the bushes decided to show itself.

Taking precise, even steps, keeping my back toward the cave, I edged closer to the side of the mountain. If my voyeur was sneaking around to come up from me on the other side, I wanted to be able to see it when it came out of hiding. As I debated what to do next, a woman's scream ricocheted out of the cavern. Oh shit!

I sidled over to the entrance and called out, "Cathy? Cathy? Are you all right?" No answer. I tried again. "Cathy!" Still nothing. What should I do? She could be dying for all I knew. She might have cut herself, might be bleeding to death. Or maybe there was something in there that was bent on hurting her?

The bushes rustled again and a low growl echoed out of the trees. I made the only choice I could and headed for the cave. Once I was standing just inside the entrance, I fumbled for my flashlight. Yep, the floor sloped down at an angle, though not as steep as I'd feared. Taking a deep breath, I plunged ahead, light held low to the ground. If there were bats hanging around topside, they wouldn't appreciate an eyeful of light in the middle of their slumber.

The cavern turned out to be a tunnel. I flashed the light to the sides, not knowing what to expect. The rock wasn't glowing with phosphorescence like it had in *Journey to the Center of the Earth,* and it wasn't covered with a mass of creepy-crawlers like in *Indiana Jones and the Temple of Doom.* There were a few bugs here and there that I could see in the halo of my flashlight, but I wasn't in danger of falling into a mass of scuttling centipedes, at least.

"Cathy?" I called softly. Caves and rock slides went hand in hand, especially here in the Pacific Northwest where the mountains were always on the move. No answer. If she was screwing with me, I'd smack her a good one after we got out of here alive.

I cautiously tapped my way along, holding the light in one hand, my walking stick in the other, and tossing an occasional glance behind me to make sure I wasn't being followed. The tunnel was narrow, and at first the air was dry, but as I slowly descended farther into the passageway, it began to take on the faint tang of trapped moisture. At least fifty yards long, the channel seemed to swallow me up like a giant worm as I inched my way along. Finally, I came to the end, where it opened into a larger chamber. I stopped to assess my position.

As I strained to hear something—anything—I glanced at the wall. What the—? I leaned in close to examine a square wooden beam that was leaning against the bedrock. It looked like a girder of some sort. Now how had that gotten in here? Oh wait—oh no! Not good. Not good *at all.*

The rock was covered with angular surfaces, as if bits here and there had been chiseled away. I took another look at the wooden beam and began to hyperventilate. Oh shit, we weren't in a cave! We were in an old adit—a mining tunnel. The supporting timbers at the mouth of the tunnel had probably rotted away or were hauled off for firewood or something. That sliver of wood I'd found at the entrance had probably been part of one of those beams.

Breathe deep. Breathe deep. Just find Cathy and get the hell out of here. Everybody who lived near the mountains knew how dangerous abandoned mine shafts were. And adits, the passages leading into the mines, were just as deadly. The deserted tunnels were often shored up with untreated wood that had rotted away over the years. Being near the Cascades meant that the rocks surrounding the mines were easily destabilized thanks to the multitude of tiny earthquakes that rumbled through the volcanic range on a regular basis.

"Cathy?" I stepped just inside the larger chamber and almost stumbled into a sinkhole. "Shit!"

"Emerald, is that you?" A faint voice echoed from below. I shone my light down the hole and sure enough, there was Cathy, about ten feet below me.

"Cathy, are you okay?" Thinking that the ground here might be unstable, I sprawled face down, like kids were taught to do who went ice skating on ponds. "Can you get out of there?"

Her voice was muffled, for some reason it wasn't echoing

out of the chamber. "If I had something to hold on to, I could walk my way up the walls."

I slipped off my pack, thanking my foresight, and pulled out the rope, then belayed it around my waist. "I'm dropping a rope to you, but I can't support you completely." I flickered the light down to her and she caught hold of the end of the rope. "I'm going to have to set the light down," I called to her. "I can't guide the rope and hold it at the same time. You have to come up in the dark."

"Let me know when." Her voice was definitely muted. The tunnel had formed some sort of sound vortex, like a black hole.

I made sure I had the rope firmly cinched, then braced myself in a sitting position, doing my best to dig my heels into the floor. "Get up here now."

Cathy's weight startled me. For such a petite woman, she was pretty hefty. But I was even more surprised by her dexterity. I wouldn't have thought her capable of it, but she was actually walking up the walls, pressing her back against one side of the hole with her feet against the other. Within just a few moments, she'd scaled the sinkhole and was climbing over the side.

I let go of the rope and grabbed her arm, pulling her to safe ground. "Can you stand up? Are you okay?" Please, oh please, don't let her be hurt. I didn't have the strength to drag her all the way back to the car.

She coughed and pushed herself to her knees. "Yeah, I'm just covered in crap . . . mold, I guess. And I'm bruised up, but at least I didn't break any bones. I didn't see the hole and went down so fast I didn't have time to tense up."

I flashed the light on her face and she blinked. A few scratches, a lot of dirt. Nothing major. "Cathy, we have to get out of here pronto. We're in an old mining tunnel."

"Oh hell." The look on her face told me I wouldn't be getting any argument from her on this one. As we scrambled to our feet, a faint rumbling reverberated through the shaft as the floor began to vibrate. Uh oh, I knew what that was.

I pushed her back into the tunnel. "Cave-in! Run!"

We raced for the entrance, but before we could make it even halfway, the rumbling turned to thunder as a cloud of dust and debris plummeted down from the ceiling. I swung her around.

"Back into the other chamber! And don't fall in that sinkhole again!"

As we stumbled through the archway, we covered our faces, trying to protect our lungs from the dust cloud that boiled through the passage. I skidded to a halt and pressed my back against the wall, eyes closed tightly, not caring what might be lurking around. Please, oh please, let the debris stop falling. If only I'd been able to recognize the abandoned mine for what it was, I never would have set foot in the tunnel. I'd have waited for help. Jimbo would have known what it was right away. Damn it, why had he been late? Why did Cathy have to run into the cave instead of away from it?

As the rumbling slowly died, all we could hear was a trickle of pebbles as they finished their freefall to the tunnel floor.

Cathy shuddered next to me. "Are we trapped?" She sounded on the verge of panic but she was managing to keep it together, I gave her that much.

Petrified I might set off another cave-in, I motioned for her to stay where she was and cautiously peeked around the corner. My flashlight couldn't possibly show us how bad it was, so I turned it off and looked for any sign of sunlight coming in from the mouth of the tunnel.

There—faint and near the ceiling—a shaft of light. It penetrated the darkness like a ray of hope, but the area around the mouth was terribly unstable. One wrong move, one more loud noise, might send the rest of the mine down on our heads. I doubted that we could clear away enough rubble to escape without bringing even more down to bury us.

"We've got air, but I don't think we can go back that way. It's too risky." I whispered.

"Your cell phone! Call for help."

I shushed her. "Lower your voice, damn it. You have to speak softly. It was probably your scream that got us into this mess. Cave-ins are like avalanches—any vibration or noise can trigger them." I unclipped my cell phone from my belt but had the feeling we were out of luck. I punched the On button and waited. Yep. As I thought, nothing.

"I can't raise a signal down here." Furious, I whirled on her, keeping my voice low. "The only good thing about this situation is that whatever was stalking us outside can't get in through the mouth of the tunnel. Now you listen and listen good. I told you this before and you ignored me. From now on, you either do exactly as I say, or I'll leave you behind. Got it?"

She nodded, lips set in a firm line.

"Okay then. Stay behind me, walk softly and in my footsteps, and no matter what happens, keep your mouth shut." I took off my bandana and tied the end to one of my belt loops, then handed her the other end. "Hold onto that and don't let go."

I shifted my backpack to a more comfortable position, then, cautiously, we began slowly skirting our way around the edge of the chamber. Using my walking stick, I gently probed the floor before I took each step and flashed the light from side to side. I had the feeling this chamber might have been a natural cave that had been excavated by the miners who had come through here. Who knew what manner of metal or gems they were seeking? The hills were full of secrets and thousands of prospectors had spent their lives searching for that one elusive mother lode that would make them rich. Most had died without ever finding a thing.

As we edged around the perimeter of the room, I tried

to gauge its size. Rock formations and outcroppings in the center made it difficult to see the other side. Though far from huge, I gauged that it might be a good fifty yards in diameter; but couldn't make an accurate estimate using the one flashlight I had with me. We'd circled nearly halfway around when the beam of light showed a glimpse of three archways exiting out of the cavern, one to the left, one opposite the tunnel through which we'd entered, and the third, to the right. So the mine went on into the mountain.

But what to do? Go deeper into the caves and lose our way? It seemed safer to wait near the mouth of the tunnel. Jimbo was on his way. He'd find my notes and come looking. And I'd left messages for both him and Murray. I turned to Cathy, who stood wide-eyed, waiting for me to speak. The gloom and isolation seemed to be squelching her natural tendencies, for which I was grateful. Maybe we'd get out of this alive after all.

"We should take a brief look at all three of those passageways," I whispered. "We won't go into them. I'm only going to peek around the corner and see what's there."

She nodded. The passage to our left was shored up by a trio of beams, one to each side, the third holding sway against the rock ceiling. While I had my doubts about their strength, for they looked like they'd been there a long time, they were probably better than no support at all. I cautiously poked my head into the tunnel.

It seemed fairly level from what I could make out in the beam of my flashlight, and extended both to the left and to the right. No big boulders, no cave-ins. The air in the tunnel wasn't fresh, but neither was it dank, so it probably wasn't blocked at the other end. To the left, an object lying on the ground about three yards into the tunnel caught my attention. It didn't look like a rock.

I turned back to Cathy. "Stay here. Don't move a muscle. I'll be right back."

She let go of the end of the bandana and leaned against

the wall, sliding down to rest her chin on her knees. I could feel her energy—all her bravado had vanished with the cave-in.

I stepped into the passageway, carefully picking my way up to whatever it was I'd seen. As I got closer, I realized that it looked like a cloth of some sort. Using my walking stick, I gingerly prodded the object, and was rewarded by seeing something that looked suspiciously eight-legged and big scuttle away. Oh hell, a spider. With my luck it was probably a mutant and would soon summon thousands of its creepy little friends and come back to eat us alive. After all, we were now in prime position to become the dubious eye-candy of some cheesy horror flick.

I prodded the cloth again but nothing else moved, so I propped my stick against the wall and leaned over to pick the thing up with the tips of two fingers. The material felt like nylon. Miners didn't have nylon, at least not back when this mine appeared to have been excavated. So where had it come from, and what was it? After shaking it to make sure that there weren't any other creepy-crawlies embedded within the folds, I spread it out on the ground and flashed the light over it. A windbreaker. And it didn't look that old, nor was it covered with dust. Whoever owned it had been in here recently.

With a glance at the roof to make sure the rock still looked stable, I rummaged through the pockets to see if I could find anything identification. A wallet! I pulled it out and stared at the black leather case. It was studded along the edges with brass rivets. There was something familiar about it, though I couldn't put my finger on what that was. Something about . . . not the case itself, but the energy surrounding it. I flipped it open and found myself staring at Clyde's driver's license, along with a receipt for gas dated the day of his death. Shit. Clyde had been in this cave, probably right before he'd been murdered. I stared down the darkened tunnel. Was he headed somewhere? Had he been following the monster?

I shivered. Scar had also been in a cave before his death; the bat guano on his shirt attested to that. And I'd be willing to bet anything this was the cave he'd been in. What was the connection that had drawn both men to this place, and why? About to turn back, my toe kicked against something and sent it skittering against the wall. Probably a rock, but I'd better make sure. I flashed the light down at my feet. Wire frames and broken glass stared up at me. Glasses. And I immediately knew whose. George's glasses. Right next to Clyde's missing windbreaker and license.

Had George and Clyde gotten into another fight? In the cave, perhaps? Maybe my intuition had gone haywire this time and Murray was right. Maybe George was a murderer—he'd been carrying drugs and a thousand bucks on him and they were probably Clyde's. So many loose threads, and nothing to tie them together with yet.

Confused, I picked up the glasses and tucked them into the pocket of Clyde's jacket, then headed back to Cathy. She was still in the same position that I'd left her in. I decided to keep my mouth shut about what I'd found. I didn't need her going ballistic. She glanced at the jacket, then at me.

"Found it on the floor of the tunnel in there. Somebody was here recently—" A noise to our right stopped me in mid-sentence. The sound of footsteps, and heavy breathing. Oh shit, somebody . . . or something . . . was in here with us! I handed Cathy the jacket. "Hold onto that and get ready to run," I hissed and tightened my grip on my walking stick. It was the only weapon available.

Just then, from the right hand entrance that we hadn't yet explored, a figure emerged out of the darkness. By the pale light of my flashlight, I could only make out that it was tall and stocky. The silhouette slowly advanced. I sucked in a deep breath, trembling as I slowly backed away, Cathy creeping behind me. The Warriors of the Mountain? The Klakatat Monster? Visions of Scar and

Clyde floated before my eyes and I got ready to run, expecting the creature to lunge forward, to tear me to shreds at any moment.

And then, just when the silence was ready to set me to screaming, the creature stepped out of the shadow and into the full beam, and I saw that it wasn't the monster. It wasn't one of the Warriors. We were facing a man with an overgrown beard and long, stringy hair. Relief coursing through my body, I let out my breath as I recognized him. Bear! The man who had interrupted Murray and me out in the meadow. Cathy and I were saved!

Chapter 18

❦

BEAR STRODE TOWARD us, a cloudy look on his face.

"Thank heaven you found us—" I started to say, but stopped when I saw his expression. He looked a lot more intimidating than he had out in the meadow. Maybe Murray had been right, maybe he had a pot farm or something hidden back in these woods and thought we'd stumbled over it.

"I told you womenfolk to quit messing around out in these parts," he said. "What you doing in here?" A shift in energy rippled through the cavern, and he seemed to grow larger, more menacing.

Cathy spoke up, nervously twisting her hands. "There was some animal outside chasing us and we ran in the cave. The tunnel collapsed and now we're lost. Is there another way out besides the main entrance? Emerald's cell phone doesn't work in here."

I stared at her. It was obvious that Bear was upset we were here; he didn't need to know that we were stranded and alone. The woman wasn't all that bright, but did she have to pick now to prove it?

Bear shone his dim flashlight in my eyes, illuminating his own face in the process. The look on his face chilled me to the bone. This man was big, and I had the feeling he could be mean in a way that Jimbo had never been, even at his most obnoxious. "Lost, are you? And nobody looking for you?" His energy flared, and a picture of slime-mold and slugs flashed through my mind.

I shuddered. "Jimbo, our friend, is on his way. Maybe you know him—he's a regular visitor up here in the biker's enclave. Big guy, does a lot of hunting and trapping out here. He should be here any moment. There must be another way out if you got in here. If you could point us in that direction, we'll probably run into him out in the meadow."

Bear chuckled. "So, you were told to stay out of this area and you didn't listen. Now you get yourself lost and you want my help." He turned to Cathy. "Why are you *really* here?"

I interrupted before Cathy could speak. "Just looking for the monster again. We were on our way out when the cave-in happened."

His eyes narrowed and he turned back to me. "I don't trust you. Just what have you been up to? What have you got there?" He pointed to the windbreaker that I was holding. "Why don't you show old Bear what you found?"

And then I knew, in the pit of my stomach, that he was going to hurt us. I whirled, grabbed Cathy by the hand, and pulled her back toward the passage in which I'd found the jacket. "Move it!" Once we were in the tunnel, we might stand a fighting chance of losing him, or of finding a way out.

Bear sprang forward as we stumbled out of his reach. Cathy whimpered as I forced her along, but to my relief, she offered no resistance. No time for hysterics, no time for tears. We needed to run, and run fast. I put myself on autopilot, letting my inner guidance take over. It was the only help we could count on for now.

Once in the tunnel, I turned right, following gut instinct. The gradient of the floor shifted, leading us upward. Maybe this was a good sign. Maybe this would lead us to another entrance onto the mountain? A glance back showed me the feeble beam bobbing from Bear's flashlight as he raced along behind us. Damn it! If only we had a few minutes head start.

"Oh Nanna," I whispered as I ran. "If you can hear me now, then help me! Please help me."

A thud echoed in the corridor, and Bear swore up a blue streak. I tossed a quick look over my shoulder; there was only inky blackness behind us. Either he'd dropped his light, or his batteries had run dry. I dragged Cathy along, jogging as fast as I could without falling over my own feet.

As we stumbled along the pebble-studded passage, I could hear Bear struggling to follow us. He could probably see our light, but if we managed to gain enough ground, he wouldn't be able to see anything and maybe one of the rocks littering the tunnel would trip him up. *Trip him up.* Hmm. I whirled around and tossed my walking stick in the middle of the path, then sped up the slope at a dead run. So awash in her fear that I could have sensed her a mile away, Cathy struggled to keep up.

I was panting by the time we rounded a bend in the passageway.

There, ahead to the left, a faint light filtered out of an opening in the rock wall. As I ran toward the light, a figure shimmered into view, leaning against the archway. There—thanks be to all the heavens—stood the spirit of my Nanna, haloed in gold. Dressed in the Bavarian dress we'd buried her in, with her ever-present apron, she gave me a big smile, then pointed behind her, into the chamber.

Cathy skidded to a halt. "Who—is she?" she managed to gasp out.

"My grandmother. Congratulations, you've just seen a ghost. Now, come on! Hurry!" I yanked on her hand. Just then, we heard a groan and a loud curse from a ways behind us. I had the suspicion that Bear had discovered my walking stick. The hard way.

We ducked into the opening, and found ourselves in a small, natural cavern; a sinkhole, really. A shaft of light streamed in from above through a hole in the roof. A ladder was propped up against the hole.

I shoved Cathy over to the ladder. "Get going."

As she scrambled up the rungs, I took a quick look around. The cave was obviously being used as a hidey-hole. There was a bed on the floor, made of blankets and sleeping bags, and a propane camping stove. Boxes and bags littered the room, as well as a pile of clothing and a basket full of potatoes and apples.

Cathy was halfway up the ladder by now, so I began my ascent, clambering up. As she rolled out onto the ground, I followed suit. A jolt of inspiration hit me and I grabbed the top rung of the ladder.

"Help me pull it up!"

She took hold of the other side and together we managed to drag the ladder out of the cave and drop it on the ground next to the sinkhole. Bear wouldn't be following us this way, not unless he managed to get all those boxes stacked, and by then we'd be gone. Unless he knew of yet another exit.

We were standing on a slope. Below, to the left, the patch of mountain ash glistened like green gold in the sunlight. A little farther left, I could see a dusty path leading down the slope; it appeared to head directly into the strip of meadow where I'd parked the car. We had to get down there before Bear was on our tail again.

"We don't have time to rest," I told Cathy. "There could be other passages leading out and we want to get our butts away from here before Bear pops up again. My guess is that this mountain is riddled with tunnels and he probably knows them all."

I pulled off my pack and stuffed Clyde's jacket in it, then shouldered the rucksack again. Murray would want to see this, and I'd be damned if I let Bear get away with attacking us. I'd be filing a report on him for attempted assault.

As we navigated our way down the mountainside, we saw no sign of the biker following us. I kept a close watch over my shoulder, but we managed to hit the meadow not far from where I'd parked the Mountaineer. I unlocked the doors, tossed my pack in the back, and climbed wearily into the driver's seat. Cathy said very little as she fastened her seat belt. I turned on the ignition, grateful for the comforting sound of the engine, then wheeled around and headed out of Klickavail Valley as fast as I could. When I found Jimbo, I'd wail on his head for spacing out on us.

WE WERE WELL along the highway before I felt comfortable in pulling over to the shoulder and punching in Jimbo's number. Still no answer. It was past eleven and, worried, I called Murray at work. She wasn't at her desk, so I left a message telling her that we'd had some trouble and asking her to call me when she could. Next, I tried Joe at work. He was there, and I gave him a full rundown on what had happened and how we'd escaped. "I can't get hold of Murray or Jimbo and I'm worried about them."

He exploded. "You're worried about them? Emerald O'Brien, you could have gotten yourself killed! Running into a mine shaft? What were you thinking?"

All too aware that Cathy was sitting right next to me, I said, "What was I supposed to do? Leave her in there when I thought she might be dying? You would have done the same thing I did and you know it! Besides, I didn't know it was a mine shaft until after I had already headed down the tunnel."

Joe inhaled sharply. "Yeah, yeah, I know. What did you say this guy's name was?"

"All I know is that he goes by the name of Bear." It felt good to have somebody worry about me. When I'd been with Roy, his concern was always focused on his own well-being. "Can you meet me at my house in twenty minutes?"

"Probably not, but I'll try to be there by three. And Em—" He paused.

"Yes?"

"I love you. And don't you forget it." *Click.* He hung up.

I stared at the phone, a rush of warmth rising in my chest. He loved me. He really, truly loved me. Feeling as if I could take on a whole slew of Klakatat monsters, I flipped the phone shut, shifted into gear, and headed back to town.

As the forest disappeared behind us, I took a deep breath and let it out, slow and easy, then glanced over at Cathy. She was gazing out of the window, and she looked a mess. She must have felt my stare, because she turned to face me and, with the most sincerity I'd ever heard out of her, said, "You saved my life. Thank you, Emerald. I never meant to put us in danger. I was so scared that I wasn't thinking."

"Forget it," I said. "Next time, don't be so all-fired up to rush into a dangerous situation. That's one experience I don't want to repeat."

Her eyes flickered. "Trust me, I'm never setting foot in another cave."

"Technically, we entered an abandoned mine tunnel, though there were natural caves back there that the miners appear to have broken into."

"Technical-schmecnical. I don't care what you call it, I'm never going underground again." Another moment and tell-tale signs of the old Cathy emerged. "So, is this what you do for fun? Get lost in caves, hang out with ghosts and creepy bikers?"

My frustration, which had been building up all morning, broke free, flooding out like a tidal wave on steroids. "Remember, *you're* the one who wanted to go out there.

You could have gone alone, but I'll wager twenty to one that you wouldn't have come out alive. And why on earth did you tell Bear that we were lost and alone? Are you blind? Couldn't you see that he was dangerous? You come in my shop, invade my privacy, plaster me on television without my permission. You sic your goober of a cousin on me and then when he gets in trouble, you come whining for me to help you. Just what do you expect out of me, Cathy? Because I'd really like to know!"

The reservoir dry, I focused on the road, watching as the pavement passed silently beneath the car.

Cathy didn't answer for a few minutes, and when she did, the controlled, perpetually-on reporter was back. "You could have said 'no' so don't blame me for what happened. I didn't know it was an old mining tunnel. And I never met this Bear. How was I to know he was dangerous?"

"Not your fault? You're the one who ran into the cave after I told you not to! You're the one who shrieked and brought down the roof. You're the one who fell into a sinkhole and told Bear that we were alone!" I took the turn onto Main Street at a sharp angle, heading straight for the shop, where I screeched into my parking space. I jumped out and stomped over to her side, where I yanked open the passenger door.

"Out, now! And don't bother me again, or I swear I'll hex you up one side and down the other! You're a power-hungry bimbo!"

Cathy leaped out and faced me, nose to nose. "At least I'm not some dippy tea shop owner, who thinks she can predict the future. How did you pull that little trick with your 'Nanna'?" She jabbed me in the chest with her finger.

I stared at her for a moment, then reached out and gave her a little shove. "You're a lousy reporter. You stink so bad that it's no wonder why L.A. or New York doesn't want you. You should count your blessings they let you keep the job you have."

She stared at me for a moment, open-mouthed. "I can't

believe you said that! I'm not a bad reporter, I'm good—really good! They just don't know talent when they see it. I've got bigger balls than Dan Rather and Walter Cronkite combined!"

As she stood there, wild-eyed, hands on her hips, makeup smeared, hair sticking out in all directions, covered with leaves, twigs and mold, a well of laughter rose up from the pit of my stomach. Then I caught sight of myself in the shop's reflection. I looked just as bad. The dam cracked and I dropped to the curb, hee-hawing so loud that I snorted.

"Oh jeez, can you believe us? I'm just glad nobody's standing around yelling 'Cat-fight! Cat-fight!' "

Cathy sputtered. "You sound like a hyena," she said, but the next thing I knew, she was sitting next to me, laughing so hard she was crying.

After a few minutes, I gasped, trying to catch my breath. "What's next? Pistols at fifty paces?"

"Anything, just as long as we don't have to go back to that goddamn cave." She wiped her eyes on her sleeve, wincing as she brushed against the scratch on her head. "Oh God, I needed to blow off some steam." She flashed me a tentative smile, which I hesitantly returned. "You know, the truth is that I've never had such a scary morning in my life. It was kind of exciting, though."

I'd had a few that were worse, but I let it go. "Yeah, it was pretty dicey. I'm glad we got out of there alive. How's your head feeling?"

"Like I nosedived into a brick wall." She took a deep breath, then let it out slowly. "Look, I'm sorry about the dippy comment. And the one about your grandmother's spirit. I know what I saw. She was there. But you have to understand, that's the first time I've ever seen a ghost. Does your grandmother help you a lot? She looked like she was really concerned."

"Yeah, she drops in every now and then. My Nanna was a wonderful and wise woman." I thought for a moment, then decided that if Cathy could be big enough to apologize, so could I. "I'm sorry I called you a lousy reporter."

She stood up, heading toward her car, then turned back to say, "You're right. I know it. Hell, I try hard enough, but I know I'm never going anywhere. But hey, that's life, I guess. Thanks for helping me out. Let me know what you find out about that jacket. I just wish we could have found something to prove George didn't kill Clyde."

"Me, too." I thought of the glasses in my pack and prayed that they would be George's salvation, but I had a sinking feeling that maybe, just maybe, they would be his undoing. Hoping I was wrong, I waved as Cathy took off. I turned back to my shop. Thank God it was Sunday and I didn't have to work. Lana had opened up on time, I saw, and was waiting on Mrs. Bartleby. I didn't bother poking my head in to say hello and just crawled back into my car. As I pulled away from the curb, it occurred to me that Cathy and I had actually managed a civil good-bye. Well, Nanna always told me that miracles could happen. Maybe she was right.

WHEN I REACHED home, I found Harlow leaning against the porch railing, talking to the kids. I hugged her as I asked Randa if Jimbo or Murray had called.

"Nope, not that we know of, but we haven't been home long—just since Harlow got here. Mr. Ledbetter said it would be okay. Eww . . . you stink bad!"

I opened the door and kicked off my mucky shoes as I headed toward the phone.

"Is something wrong, Em?" Harl asked.

I nodded. "Yeah, big time. Would you mind fixing the kids something to eat while I try Murray again?"

"Sure." She herded them into the kitchen.

I picked up the phone and punched in Murray's number yet again. This time, she answered.

"Em, there's been an accident," she said, before I could say a word. "Jimmy was hurt early this morning."

I pushed my bangs off my face. Jimbo was hurt? My voice trembling, I asked, "Oh my God. What happened? Is he okay?" Visions of his bike colliding with a semi ran rampant through my mind and I steeled myself for the worst.

"He got up on the damned roof to straighten his TV antenna and fell off. He busted up his ribs so bad he couldn't stand up. He also managed to land on a rake and tore open his thigh. One of his neighbors found him when he came over to ask Jimmy to make Roo stop barking."

Relieved, I slumped against the wall. "Is he going to be all right?"

"Yeah," Murray said, sighing. "We were at the hospital all morning, and we just got back to my house. Jimmy's not at all happy about the situation and he wants to go home, but I won't let him. He needs to rest and if he goes back to his house, he'll hobble around trying to get stuff done."

"Jeez, well at least he's going to be okay!" I felt like a louse for being so mad at him. Now I couldn't shake the image of Jimbo lying there, waiting for help while Roo howled by his side. I wished I'd dropped by his place first, before we went into the valley.

"How about you? What happened this morning? Your message was pretty cryptic. Jimmy felt bad about letting you down."

I grunted. "Cathy and I had big trouble out there. I really need to talk to you about it. Any chance you could come over? I've got a couple of things to give to the police, too. I found Clyde's jacket and wallet, and George's glasses."

Murray sucked in a breath. "Woof. Okay, let me pack up Jimmy so he doesn't get any ideas about wandering off on his own. See you in a few minutes."

I hung up and filled Harl and the kids in on Jimbo's

accident, trying to circumnavigate my own encounters that morning. Kip and Randa didn't need to worry about me anymore than they already did.

"There have been a lot of weird things going on the past year, you know?" Harl had made a pot of tea and she pressed a cup in my hands.

I gratefully breathed in the soothing scent of mint, needing to calm my jangled nerves. "You can say that again. Harl, this area is some sort of psychic powerhouse and I don't think that anybody is going to pull the switch in the near future. Since I seem to be a magnet for *weird,* maybe that's why I get caught up in all these bizarre happenings."

"Uh huh, sounds about right to me." She peeked into the teapot. "We're empty. I'll make some more tea."

She put the kettle on while I asked the kids to give us some privacy. They ran off to the backyard and I took the opportunity to tell Harlow everything that had happened.

"Em, that would have scared the piss out of me." She winced and shifted in her chair. After a few seconds, she relaxed.

"What's wrong?" I asked.

"Nothing. I've been having mild labor pains for a few days. Just gearing up for the real event, I guess. My doctor said that there's nothing to worry about, that I'll know when it's time. And it could be any day now."

"Oh babe, your doctor is right. You'll know when it's for real."

The doorbell rang and Murray stumbled through the door, Jimbo leaning on her shoulder. He groaned as she helped him into a chair.

"Say, O'Brien, I'm sorry I didn't show up this morning." He grimaced, clutching at his side. "I don't think I would have been much help."

"So where are the things you found in the cave?" Murray asked.

"In the car, in my pack." I grabbed my keys and was

headed toward the door when the phone rang. It was Roger White, from the fire station. Every possible tragedy in the book raced through my mind. "Is it Joe, is he okay?"

"That's what I was calling to ask you. He took off like a bat out of hell over half an hour ago and we need him here. I thought he'd be at your place."

"No, in fact, he said he couldn't be here until around three. Did you try his aunt?"

"Yes, and she hasn't seen him since yesterday. He's not at his apartment, either. I was hoping you'd know where he is."

A shudder of apprehension rippled up my spine. Joe wasn't at the station, he wasn't at Margaret's, and he wasn't at his apartment. And then, I knew where he'd gone.

"I'll call you back, okay?" I hung up and whirled around. "Mur, Joe's gone after Bear. He was so upset when I told him what happened out there and now he's headed for that old mine and he's going to get himself hurt."

Murray stared at me. "Oh shit. We have to stop him. Between the lunatic hiding in the caves, the creature lurking in the bushes, and the Warriors of the Mountain, Joe's in real danger."

Jimbo, who by now was fully engaged in using his finger to follow the tracers produced by his pain pills, piped up. "I'll go," he said, trying to push himself to his feet.

"No you won't." Murray steadied him, keeping him from taking a nose-dive onto the floor. "I'll call for backup and then Emerald and I will head on out there and stop Joe before he gets himself in trouble. And you," she added, "will rest." She led him to the sofa as Harlow watched her with interest.

"Murray's right, Jimbo. You stay here." I grabbed an afghan and covered him with it. Grumbling, but too wiped to do anything about it, Jimbo sprawled out on the sofa and was snoring within less than a minute.

Murray brushed the bangs out of his eyes. "You stupid

galoot. You're going to get yourself killed one of these days."

"Murray—?" Harlow asked, her voice soft, but Murray ignored her and turned back to me.

"Let me give Deacon a buzz and then we'll take off."

I grabbed my jacket while she put in a terse call. "Harl, can you stay with the kids and Jimbo? I don't want to leave any of them alone."

She nodded. "Finally, part of the action again, even if it is only to baby-sit a banged-up biker and two precocious kids."

Murray jerked her thumb toward the door. "Deacon will meet us out there in twenty minutes. Let's take my truck, it's got better clearance."

I grabbed up my pack, which still had Clyde's jacket in it, and we headed out the door. As we pulled out of the driveway, I glanced at Murray. "Joe was so mad when I told him about Bear. I guess he decided to take matters into his own hands."

She flashed me a knowing look. "He's in love, doll. And men do the strangest things for the women they love." As we drove into the growing dusk, I knew she was right, and I knew that Joe and I were headed for a shift in our relationship. I prayed it would be a good one.

Chapter 19

❖

B Y THE TIME we got to Klickavail Valley, Deacon was waiting for us. He was standing next to Joe's pickup, which was parked in the shade beneath a huge fir tree. "Sorry Emerald, but Joe's nowhere in sight," Deacon said as I ran over to him, with Murray right behind me. I gave him a feeble smile and checked the truck but both doors were locked.

As I pressed my face to the window on the driver's side, not sure what I was hoping to find, Murray rested a hand on my shoulder. "See anything?"

I peered through the glass. Joe's baseball bat, which he kept on the floor of the passenger's side, was missing. "Oh hell. His bat's gone and I don't think he's off playing baseball with the biker boys. He's gone after Bear."

Murray nodded. "Okay, then. You need to show us where the caves are. We have to get a move on. Dusk falls early in these mountains, and we sure don't want to be still hunting for him out here after dark." She checked her gun, then snagged an industrial-strength flashlight out of the back of her truck. Deacon handed her a roll of pale, greenish-looking tape.

"Here's the tape you asked for, Murray."

"Tape?" I asked.

She nodded. "Just shine the flashlight on it for a little bit and it will glow in the dark for over an hour. I thought we might be able to use it to mark our way in case the tunnels get confusing, so I asked Deacon to snag a roll on his way up here."

Impressed by her forethought, I opened my pack and handed her Clyde's jacket and George's glasses. She examined them briefly, then gave them to Deacon to lock in the squad car while she brought him up to speed.

When she finished, he nodded and said, "While I was waiting, I talked to one of the bikers—a guy named Terry-T. Apparently, the boys are scared shitless about this patch of land. Not only have they heard weird things over on this side of the windbreak, but a few of the guys mentioned seeing shadows where there shouldn't be shadows, and movements in the bushes like some big animal was roaming this part. Cougar, maybe, but they said it was bigger than that. Clyde's death appears to have left a real mark on the enclave. A few of the men have actually hit the road."

"Oh wonderful. Well, I hope our murderer wasn't among them." Murray shaded her eyes and glanced around the narrow strip of meadow. "I wonder how long Joe's been out here."

"Joe must have taken off shortly after I told him what happened." I struggled to remember about what time that had been. "He probably left the fire station fifteen . . . maybe twenty minutes after I phoned him, so I'd say about ninety minutes."

"Long enough to get himself into trouble, then. Okay babe," Murray motioned for me to take the lead. "Let's book."

I led them past the outcropping and bramble patch directly toward the slope leading up to the sinkhole. Since the cave-in had effectively blocked the main adit, our best course was to hike up to the shaft through which Cathy and

I'd made our escape from Bear. Frustrated, I started up the mountainside.

Damn it, why did Joe have to go and play the hero? Images of him lying somewhere in a pool of blood swirled in my mind. George might stand accused of murdering Clyde, but I knew damned well that he didn't do it and I was terrified that whoever—or whatever—had killed the two bikers was now stalking Joe. Or maybe, it had already found him. On one hand, we had the Klakatat Monster, who had warrior-spirits protecting him. On the other, we had Bear, who—well, I didn't know his story but he obviously didn't want to be disturbed and I had the feeling he'd go to any lengths to protect his privacy.

As the slope became steeper, my heart raced along, adrenaline fueling my muscles as I forced my way up the side of the mountain. Going down had been much easier, by the time we reached the top, I was panting. I crouched, resting my hands on my knees as I struggled to catch my breath. Neither Murray nor Deacon had broken a sweat.

With a cough, I straightened up, pointing ahead to a huckleberry bush. "There, to the right of that bush. That's where Cathy and I escaped. Bear must have found another way out. The ladder's gone."

"Or Joe found it," Murray said. "He'd have to use an alternate route, since the cave-in blocked the main adit. You told him everything, right? Including where you escaped and how you got out?"

With a sinking feeling, I nodded. "Yeah, everything."

Murray took a long look around us. "There's no sign that anybody's watching us. Can you sense anything?"

I dreaded opening myself up to the energies out here on the mountain, but it was the most expedient way, and both Murray and I knew it. Deacon cleared his throat and stepped back, studiously watching the trees that dotted the slope. I closed my eyes and concentrated on the breeze as it played against my skin. As it lulled me into trance I sank to the ground, but nothing triggered an alarm. A rabbit was hiding behind a nearby fern, and I sensed a deer farther in, among the trees, but otherwise—nada. The area on the surface of the slope was clear.

"Nothing." I squinted up at Murray. "There's no one topside. Mur, I'm going to go out on the astral and peek in the caves."

She glanced over at Deacon, who was doing a good job of pretending to be otherwise occupied. I could sense that he was . . . not exactly skeptical, but wary. "Are you sure? Remember what happened the last time?"

I still had a faint mark on my forehead where the last psychic blast had nailed me, but there was too much at stake for me to chicken out. Joe's life might be in my hands, and I couldn't turn away.

"Yeah, I'm sure. Shake me out of it if things get too weird." I closed my eyes again and sent my consciousness down, delving into the tunnels, deep into the earth to see if I could pick up movement or life. The energy on the slope was older than that of the meadow, and the energy in the tunnels older than both.

Dense and stubborn, the waves of earth-mana ran sleepy. Haste would not waken the dreamers here, but only persistence—like tickles of water that constantly eroded away the surface layers of the rock millimeter by millimeter, that filtered in through the tunnels and trapdoors to wash ashore the treasures and mysteries secreted in this mountain.

Flowing on the astral currents, I reached out, searching for Joe.

And then—somewhere beneath the tons of rock and dirt, a flutter caught my attention. Joe! The shimmering spark that fueled his spirit beckoned to me. Living and warm, but fuzzy, as if he might be asleep or unconscious. A rush of relief washed over me. He was alive!

I couldn't pinpoint where he was in relation to where we were standing, but when I thought about the configuration of the maze Cathy and I'd ran through, I figured it had to be somewhere to the left of the main cavern, near where I'd found the jacket. I was about to bring myself out of trance when I sensed something else, something close to Joe. I homed in on it. Big . . . ancient and definitely not human.

As I tuned into this new energy, a chaotic tangle of emotions flooded my mind—hunger, confusion, weariness. And then, once again, the image of the skull floated before me, only this time a sense of urgency emanated from it. Words that were not words formed in my mind, and I knew that it was asking me for help. Floundering, I struggled to sort out the vortex of emotions before snapping out of the trance.

"What is it?" Murray dropped to my side.

"Joe, he's down there, but so is something else and it's not Bear and it's not one of the Warriors of the Mountain." I gazed into her eyes, knowing all too well what I'd stumbled on.

Murray read me loud and clear. "The Klakatat Monster?"

I glanced at Deacon, then lowered my voice so he couldn't hear. "Yeah, I think so. And I can tell you right now that it's not happy. It seems to need help, though for the life of me, I don't know what I can do for it. Something weird is going on down there and we have to get Joe out before it's too late." I pushed myself to my feet. "The ladder's gone from up top, but is there another way we can get down through this chute?" As I headed toward the sinkhole, Murray grabbed my arm, holding me back.

"Let me check," she said. Murray edged toward the shaft, dropping to her hands and knees as she neared the opening. She drew her gun as she approached, cautiously peering over the side. She motioned me over. "The ladder is back in place," she said. "The question being: Is Bear down there waiting?"

"I didn't sense him in the area, but don't wager a bet on

my impressions. They don't come with a money-back guarantee."

Deacon joined us. "If there is somebody down there, chances are they've heard us by now. I'll go down while you cover me. We're not going to find an easier way in, not without scouring this mountain."

After a moment, she nodded and pulled back. Deacon slid his legs over the edge and, with gun in one hand, used his other hand to steady himself on the ladder as he disappeared into the dark hole. After a jittery thirty seconds, we heard, "All clear."

Murray agilely swung onto the ladder and, quick as a mountain goat, descended into the black cave. I waited until she was clear, then hesitantly slipped onto the rungs. As I scurried down to join them, memories of Cathy's and my frantic race out of this cavern flooded back. I dreaded facing the dark tunnels again, but the image of Joe loomed large in my mind and I pushed away my fears.

The chamber was as I'd last seen it—though the boxes were closed, and the sleeping bags were rolled tight. A backpack sat atop one of the boxes, and Murray poked through it. She pulled out a piece of paper, along with a handful of cash.

"Well, what do we have here?" Poking around in the stuffed backpack, she pulled out bundle after bundle of stacked bills. "Holy crap, look at this—there must be seventy or eighty thousand dollars here! And what's this?" She examined the paper. "It appears to be a copy of a recent court order, releasing somebody named Ian Hannigan from jail." She handed it to Deacon. "That name sounds familiar. Where have I heard it?"

It sounded familiar to me, too. "Wasn't it on the news not long ago? I can't remember where but . . ."

"Could be. I can't seem to place it though. Okay, Deacon, head topside and get down to the squad car. Call the station and find out everything you can about this guy, then hightail it back here."

"Should I just use my cell phone?" he asked.

Murray shook her head. "Use the radio—it's too easy for people to tap into cell phones and I don't want anybody listening in on this." She pulled out the roll of glow-in-the-dark tape. "I had a feeling this might be handy. I'll use strips of it to mark our path, so keep your eyes peeled when you get back. And Deacon—step on it?"

We watched as he shimmied up the ladder. When he'd disappeared out the mouth of the sinkhole, I turned to Murray. "We have to get to Joe," I pleaded. "I think he might be hurt."

Murray nodded. "I'd really like to go through this stuff, but we'll come back for it. Which way do we go?"

I led her down the tunnel through which Cathy and I had escaped, stopping along the way as my walking stick, kicked to the side of the passage, came into view. I retrieved it, feeling more confident now that I had some sort of weapon in my hands.

Mur's flashlight cut a swath through the darkness, accentuating the shadows that played against the wall as we crept through the tunnel. Time seemed to be going much slower than it had my first time through, and I began to appreciate just how long this passage actually was. Every few yards, Mur stopped to tear off a strip of tape and slap it against the rocky walls. She shone her flashlight on it for a few seconds, and then we moved on. Once, I thought I could hear the faint fall of footsteps echoing somewhere up ahead, but it could have been water dripping or rocks trickling off the roof of the cavern.

"Did you hear that?" I whispered, leaning closer to Murray.

She sucked in a deep breath. "I'm hearing a lot of things—whispers and voices and footfalls. These tunnels have a lot of history bound up in them and I'm not sure I really want to know all of it."

As we moved farther into the mine, the energy began to thicken until it felt like we were walking through pea soup.

We crept closer together, and even Murray's strength seemed to diminish as the power of the caverns took hold. Just another foot, I told myself. We'll just go another foot and maybe Joe will be there. But I knew he wasn't. Joe was somewhere down the tunnel from us, past where I'd found Clyde's jacket.

Finally, we came to an opening on the left. I recognized it—it led into the main cavern where Bear had first appeared. I pointed it out to her. "Joe isn't in there. He's farther along this tunnel. Whatever else is down there, I dunno."

She nodded and, silently led off again, with footsteps that barely seemed to graze the passage floor. I used my walking stick to steady myself as we picked our way through a scattering of loose rocks and pebbles that littered the tunnel floor. At one point, Murray held up her hand.

"Be careful, there's another fissure directly ahead. It's small, but I think the lip is thin. If you get too close, you'd probably break through and who knows how deep it is to the bottom." She shone her light on the shaft that fractured the surface of the floor, and carefully marked it with the tape so that Deacon wouldn't chance falling in. The last thing we needed was a repeat of Cathy's fiasco, especially with a fissure as deep as this one seemed to be.

As we skirted the cavity, testing each step as we went, I paused, listening to the sound of water trickling along far below in the darkness. Images of vile creatures hiding in the depths raced through my mind, courtesy of J.R.R. Tolkien and Sir Arthur Conan Doyle and Edgar Rice Burroughs. Shuddering, I caught up to Murray. The corridor turned sharply to the left.

Mur peeked around the edge. "Are we on the right track?"

I leaned against my walking stick, resting my weight on it as I let myself spiral down again, searching for Joe, searching for signs of life. There—ahead—he was nearby. I was starting to pull out when a surge of energy hit me. I reeled, as did Murray. Whatever it was had caught her in its wave, too.

She flashed her light around, searching for the source. As she turned to look behind us, I cautiously stepped around the corner, sensing that whatever it was, was there, waiting for me. In full-living silhouette, one of the Warriors of the Mountain faced me, near enough to touch. I inhaled sharply. Just then, Murray rounded the bend. I heard her stumble back with a gasp.

"You are walking on sacred ground." The words reverberated through the tunnel, but whether they'd been spoken aloud or were just echoing in my mind, I didn't know.

Shaking, I forced myself to stand my ground. "What do you want from me?"

The shadow-shape flared ever so slightly, and once again, I heard the thundering voice. "Clear this place of the intruder's presence."

Intruder? Who was he talking about? Joe?

The spirit must have been peeking in my mind because he said, "The man reeking of death and destruction who woke up the mountain with his anger and greed. We must protect the lore-keeper from him, but we cannot touch him. He doesn't hear us. We need your help."

The lore-keeper. *The lore-keeper of the mountain*—of course! Everything made perfect sense to me now. And then, before I could say another word, the shadow vanished and everything came into focus again. Breathing heavily, I leaned against the tunnel wall. "Shit. Did you catch any of that?"

Murray shone her flashlight at me. "Yeah, I heard it all right, but I can tell you right now, the roof would be tumbling now down if he had been speaking aloud. Who's the lore-keeper?"

"Don't you know?" I asked her, surprised that she hadn't made the connection. "The Klakatat Monster . . . he must be the creature that embodies this mountain—he's like an elemental, directly from the earth. A shaman or

seer. Don't you see—he's not dangerous, but the Warriors
of the Mountain are, and they're his protectors. They told
me as much in my vision, but I didn't realize that's who
they were talking about."

She studied my face for a moment, then said, "I'm sorry
I doubted your vision the other day. The spirit said the intruder was the 'man reeking of anger.' He's got to be talking about Bear. But why don't they just get rid of him?"

I'd been wondering the same thing myself, but then
everything crystallized. "Murray, want to make a bet that
Bear is head-blind? I'll bet that he doesn't realize the
Klakatat Monster is real, but that he's playing off of the
legend because people are so scared. Head-blind or not,
Bear's stirred up plenty of trouble."

"You could be right," Mur said. "Just because he
doesn't know it really exists, doesn't mean he's above
using the legend for his own ends, and it doesn't mean he's
not a catalyst to waking the creature."

I squinted, rubbing my forehead. "I'll go you one further. I think that the Warriors of the Mountain can only hurt
people who can sense them. Even though they can mani-
fest in our world, they primarily exist on the astral. And not
everyone can perceive that energy. The Warrior just said
they can't touch him. Now, I can be hurt by them, and so
can you—but only because we have the ability to tune into
them."

She nodded slowly. "That makes sense. And since the
Klakatat Monster is a lore-keeper, an oracle and not a warrior, he doesn't have the ability to protect himself. But
Bear can hurt him because the creature is still part of this
world—more so than his guardians, living between two
realms, two dimensions." She paused, thinking. "If Bear
somehow manages to see the creature, he could shoot it.
And I have no doubt that he would."

"You're right," I said slowly. "Ten to one, the Klakatat
Monster's spirit wanders the Dream-Time that all the native cultures and aborigines talk about, while its body rests

and sleeps here under the mountain. From the Dream-Time, it watches the world go by, and remembers. But, if somebody wakes it up . . ."

Murray took over. "Then what's happening in the world starts to affect it. Like becoming part of the action instead of just watching a movie. And once that happens, it becomes enmeshed in events that it's not supposed to be participating in. And my guess is that being awake both confuses and hurts the creature. Especially when somebody like Bear is perpetuating a good share of violence right here in its home." She smiled sadly. "It's hard enough being psychic as a human. Can you imagine being a hundred times more sensitive than we are?"

I sighed. "I'll tell you right now, that 'monster' has never killed anybody, regardless of the reputation that local legend's given him. He's not capable of violence. That's why the Warriors are worried. They can't protect him from someone whose head-blind, like Bear, and he can't protect himself. This probably doesn't happen often. And when it does . . ."

Murray nodded. "We'd better get moving."

"Yeah, I want to find Joe and get him out of here before there's any more trouble."

We'd gone about another fifty yards when she stopped. The tunnel ended at an archway, opening into another chamber. Nearby, lay a pile of rocks, but they looked as though they'd been stacked, rather than falling haphazardly.

We cautiously approached. Murray examined the edges of the arch while I began poring over the pyramid of rocks. "This is natural stone," she said. "It wasn't chipped out. The tunnel was excavated, but it looks like the miners broke into a cave here. There aren't any signs of activity—"

"Mur—" I broke in, as I knelt by the rock pile, my stomach flip-flopping. "We aren't exactly alone."

She whirled around. "What do you mean? Did the spirit come back?"

I flashed the light on the bottom layer of rocks. In the dim beam, we could see ivory fingers thrusting out from the stones. I hesitantly reached toward it. Smooth bone. "Oh boy. Somebody was here before us, all right, and they decided to stick around."

Murray sucked in a deep breath. "Shit, another body." She leaned down and took a closer look. "Skeleton. Been here awhile, probably, from the look of things. See? There's the head of a mining pick over there. The handle must have rotted away. I'll bet this is one of our miners who originally came down here."

"This is either a grave, or an extremely effective method of death. What do you think? He had some semblance of psychic ability and the Warriors got him when he delved too close to the Klakatat Monster?" I shuddered as we sidestepped the rocks and headed into the cavern.

"Probably. One way or another, he never found his way out of the mine, that's for sure."

As soon as we passed through the entrance, I gasped, holding my breath. The stench of ammonia overwhelmed me, and rustling sounds fluttered from high up on the ceiling. I exhaled slowly and breathed through my mouth.

A shaft of light penetrated the gloom from a small sinkhole overhead, slicing down to illuminate the center of the chamber. The entire room sparkled. Limestone formations, fragile and delicate, reminded me of sea foam, caught forever in freeze-frame. Near the center, a table-sized rimstone pool rippled in the light, filled with cave pearls and dripping water from the broken shaft overhead.

Speleothems stretched from floor to ceiling, long strands of calcite twisting into thin columns. They were nowhere nearly as grand as the ones in the Carlsbad Caverns, but the tenuous pillars were stark and beautiful, with helectites protruding from the surface. Flowstone covered the farthest wall of the chamber, while a thin ridge to our right led up to a ledge overlooking the chamber.

"Oh my God, it's so beautiful." For a moment, the dazzling sight wiped my mind clear of all thought.

Murray nodded, her eyes dancing. "Em, this is rare for Washington, I can tell you that. There are some limestone caves here, but not many. I doubt if this cavern has ever been mapped by any spelunker or geologist."

I shook out of my reverie and looked for Joe. The ground squished beneath my feet and I frowned. Mud? In here?

"I know Joe's somewhere near here. I can feel him." As I circled the rimstone pool, I caught sight of someone sprawled on the ground behind a small stalagmite. The baseball bat was lying next to him. "Joe! It's Joe!"

As she raced to join me, her light bobbing wildly, Murray slipped and went sprawling in the mud. "Oh hell!"

"What's wrong?"

"This crap we're walking in is a layer of bat guano and pee."

I cringed and tried to keep my mind away from what might be crawling around down there in the bat-poop soup. As she struggled to her feet, her light flickered toward the ceiling and we heard a rush over our heads. I looked up in time to see a colony of bats. Murray hurriedly pointed her light toward the ground in order to keep from spooking them.

As I knelt beside Joe, I could tell he was breathing, though his breath was raspy. He was laying on a dry part of the floor, away from beneath where the bats made their bed. Either he'd tripped and hit his head on the corner of a stone, or he'd been targeted by a falling rock.

I cradled his head in my lap as Murray felt for his pulse. "A little weak," she said, "but he's alive." She pulled out her water bottle and splashed some water onto a bandana that was tied around her neck like a scarf. As she gently washed Joe's face, I tried to wake him up.

"Please, Joe, can you hear me? Wake up, hon. Please wake up!"

His eyes began to flutter and I could feel him struggling for consciousness. I spoke in soft whispers. We had to get him out of here before the Warriors got antsy. And I sure as hell didn't want to be here should Bear show up.

Murray touched me on the shoulder. "Deacon should be here by now," she said. "I'm getting worried. Will you be okay if I take a peek out in the tunnel? I won't go far, but I want to see if he's on his way."

I took the bandana from her and continued to coax Joe back to wakefulness as she hurried over to the cavern entrance and peeked out. As her light faded, leaving my dim one in its place, goose bumps puckered up on my arms. Something . . . or someone . . . was watching us. I scanned the cave, squinting into the darkness. Nada. Nothing in sight, but the feeling was growing stronger.

Joe groaned and began to struggle. I helped him, bracing his back as he rolled to a sitting position and rested his head in his hands.

"Sweetie? Honey? Are you okay?" I kept my voice low, not wanting to disturb the bats or other denizens of the cave.

He coughed, and his cough ricocheted off the walls. Wincing, I tensed, ready to leap up and drag him out of the way should a stalactite or boulder decide to dislodge from the ceiling, but the echo faded away without dislodging any rocks.

"I twisted my ankle. Man, the last thing I remember is slipping in the mud and trying to crawl out of the cave. I guess I blacked out."

Maneuvering the light so that it illuminated his right ankle, I pulled up the leg of his jeans. Yep, black and blue and looking painfully bruised. "You aren't going to be walking out of here on your own," I said.

"Shit. I came out here to play hero and you end up having to save me." He stared at the ground, deflated.

I grunted. "You are a hero to everybody whose life you've saved on the job. But Joe, what the hell did you think you were doing? Bear is dangerous. He's serious trouble. I called Murray. I was going to let the cops handle it." Both angry and relieved, I pulled him into my arms and kissed him, trembling at the thought of how close I'd come to losing him.

He wrapped his arms around me and held me tight. "You're one to talk. I just couldn't stand the thought of that bastard attacking you. Chalk it up to testosterone, if you want."

I snorted, then gently brushed his lips with my finger. "Shush, that doesn't matter now. Murray and Deacon should be back any minute and they'll help me get you out of here."

Just then, a figure burst into the room at a dead run.

Bear! He took one look at us and leveled a gun directly at me. "Don't move or I'll shoot," he said. He motioned to Joe. "You—tough guy. Stay where you are or I'll kill her." With eyes stone-cold sober, he said, "Get your pretty little ass over here. If either one of you tries anything funny, the other one gets a bullet in the brain."

Knowing all too well that he meant every word, I slowly untangled myself from Joe and stood up, wondering what Bear had in store. I had the sinking feeling that this time, he wasn't going to take the chance that we'd escape.

Chapter 20

⁂

D O WHAT HE says, Joe. He killed Scar and Clyde."
I glanced at the cavern door. Where the hell was Murray? What if Bear had surprised her? Was she lying out there somewhere in the tunnels, dead? I took a closer look at his gun. Though I couldn't be sure—I wouldn't know a Colt from an AK-47—it looked suspiciously similar to the one Murray carried.

Bear motioned to me. "Over against that column."

"No!" Joe's voice rang through the cavern, startling the bats topside. *Swooshing,* a flurry of wings filled the air. "Leave Emerald alone—"

"Keep your mouth shut." Bear gestured toward one of the pillars that ran from floor to ceiling. "Emerald, is it? Well, Emerald, you just get your pretty little ass over there in front of that stalagmite." He waited until I picked my way over to the column.

"Bear, you can still get out of here before they catch you. Leave now and you'll have a head start."

"Good try, toots, but no go," he said with a grunt.

As I stared at Bear, his energy flared and I knew for

certain that he'd never let us go free. Scar and Clyde's energy prints were embedded in his aura, they were riding his conscience.

"Why did you kill them?" If I could keep him talking, maybe I could buy us some time.

Bear shot a piercing look at me. "Put it down to settling an old score. And now, sweet-cakes, you better make your peace." He lifted his gun.

"Please—may I say a prayer first?" I ask

Joe let out a strangled noise. "Emerald—" but I stopped him with a look that said, "Follow my lead." He nodded imperceptively and I could see him tense, ready for my next move.

Bear sucked in a deep breath. "Yeah, what the hell, but be quick about it."

Taking a deep breath, I bowed my head slightly, inhaled as deeply as I could, then let out a shriek so loud and so ringing that I could have won an award at a Star Trek convention for the best Klingon death wail.

A stream of rocks cascaded down from the ceiling. Startled, Bear jumped out of the way too late as I hurled my flashlight at him and dove behind the column. The light hit him square in the balls. Score a triple-shot-in-one for the home team! Bear doubled over with a groan, and Joe seized the opportunity to roll behind the boulder he'd been leaning against.

I scrunched myself up behind the stalagmite as several loud *pops* came flying in my direction. Bear and his gun. Maybe he'd use up his ammo before managing to hit us.

The shots reverberated from wall to wall as I held my breath, squeezing my eyes tight. His aim was too high, too far to the left, thank God, and the bullets ricocheted against the wall behind me. Another stream of rocks fountained down the side of the flowstone.

"We're sitting under a time bomb," I shouted, peeking out from the side of the column. Without my flashlight, we had only the muted light filtering in from the ceiling to

illuminate our way. I was pretty sure that Bear couldn't see
me, but I had him directly in my line of sight. "All we need
is one good shock to trigger a major cave-in. If you don't
get out of here and leave us alone, I swear, I'll scream so
hard and so loud that I'll bring the whole freakin' mountain down on our heads. You'll be trapped right along with
us. You know I'll do it!"

Another trickle of rocks responded to the sound of my
voice. Bear wavered. He could probably kill at least one of
us—he still had a couple of bullets in his gun by my count.
But I was banking on his instinct for self-preservation. He
knew the caves here were unstable, and he wasn't stupid. He
had to know that I'd go through with my threat, considering the alternative.

"Drop it, Ian!" A voice startled all of us, echoing from
the entrance of the cavern. "Put down the gun and hold up
your hands."

Murray! She was alive! Sweet, wonderful Murray had
come to save us. At the sound of her voice, Bear made a
dash for the ridge. He raced up the ledge as Murray tried
to navigate the guano-covered floor without slipping.

"He's getting away!" Joe shouted, crawling in front of
the boulder, out of Bear's line of sight.

Caught up in the fray, I grabbed a sharp stone from behind the column and lobbed it toward the ridge, but it fell
short. Bear brought up the gun and I ducked back behind
the stalagmite as another bullet whizzed by, but my dis-
traction had some effect, allowing Murray to make the last
leap to dry stone. She raised her gun, drawing a bead on
Bear.

Standoff, a tableau of hesitation. The silence grew thick
as the seconds stretched out, ticking away.

"Drop your weapon while you have the chance," Mur's
voice echoed eerily in the chamber. "You either drop it
now, or I swear, Ian, I'll shoot you, and I shoot to kill!"

At that moment, a movement from the back of the ridge
caught my eye. I was pretty sure Murray noticed it, too, but

she kept her attention trained on Bear. A low growl rolled out from the shadows, followed by the sound of shuffling as two glowing, topaz eyes sparkled through the murky light. The Klakatat Monster. The lore-keeper.

"Who's there? Who is it?" Bear whirled, looking frantically from side to side. He dropped his gun and it clattered over the side of the ledge.

The lore-keeper grunted and I found myself sucked into a vortex that swept through the cavern; a kaleidoscope of earth and water-mana deep from within the land itself, as ancient as we were young, as wise as we were foolish. Standing here in our presence was the very heart of Klickavail Mountain.

Images filled my mind, and I watched as time rolled backward, past the ice ages marching across the continent, back to the formation of the Cascades, when they still played as children in their volcanic infancy.

On and on the images flickered . . . back to before the ascendance of mankind when we first stood erect and looked around, claiming the land for our own; back to the rise of mammals as wit and cunning took precedence over size and ferocity; back to the reign of the dinosaurs who swept through prehistory on their way to a dust-clouded oblivion. The lore-keeper had been witness to it all and, for one brief instant, he granted me a glimpse into living history.

I took a hesitant step forward as he stared down at me from the shadows, with wizened and gentle eyes. Towering, covered with downy gray fur, he was not human and yet his humanity resounded like a crystal bell singing across a snow-covered plain. He grunted softly and a wave of gratitude settled around my shoulders. Tears sprang to my eyes; I wanted to run and throw myself in his arms, to rest in a dreaming slumber so deep that I might never awake. But then he withdrew his energy and gently backed away. Silently, he disappeared into the darkness along the ridge.

A low rumble shook the cavern, startling me out of my reverie. Bear screamed and flailed wildly as he tried to steady himself. The ground rolled beneath our feet again, and he lost his balance and tumbled down the path to land at Murray's feet. She scrambled forward, handcuffing him before he could regain his senses. When he was restrained, she read him his rights.

Joe leaned against the boulder, his face a mask of amazement. Still in a daze, I handed him my walking stick to lean on, then hurried to Murray's side.

Bear stared up at us, his eyes wide. "What was that? Was it a cave-in?" he asked, acting as if he didn't know what had just happened.

"Nope, but trust me, you're going to wish it was by the time the courts get through with you." Mur roughly yanked him to his feet and then she turned to me. "He shot Deacon," she said.

"What?" Oh man, not Deacon! He was a good guy, with a wife and two kids and a little house.

"It's just a surface wound, but not for lack of trying." Mur sucked in a deep breath, then let it out slowly. "Ian—Bear—here managed to jump him and grab his gun, but apparently, you're not a very good shot, are you? You only grazed Deacon's shoulder and Deac was smart enough to play dead until you were gone." She turned to me. "I helped Deacon back through the tunnels and up the ladder. That's why I was gone so long."

"You're sure he'll be okay?" I glared at Bear. Too bad there were laws against smacking prisoners upside the head for things like this.

"Yeah. I told him to radio for backup and an ambulance. He'll be fine once we get him patched up at the hospital. So . . ." Murray nodded up at the ridge, her voice softening. "We really saw it."

I inhaled sharply. "Oh Mur, it's so much more than we ever thought. We can't say anything to anybody. We can't let people know it really exists."

"I'm game for that," Joe broke in, hobbling up to where we were standing. "I still can't believe my eyes. It was beautiful." He sounded like a child who had just seen a faerie on Midsummer's Eve and I knew that he'd caught some glimpse of the wonder that the creature had shown me. The three of us stared at the ridge, pondering the secrets hidden within the depths of the world.

Murray rubbed her forehead. "I just hope the scientists and good ol' boys of the world never find it."

Bear grunted. "What are you three talking about? I didn't see nothing."

I stared at the man who had tried to shoot me. Perhaps he'd been so head-blind that he hadn't been able to sense the creature. Or maybe his fear had blinded him. Or maybe he just couldn't believe in something so incredible, even when it was standing right in front of him. Whatever the reason, it was for the best. "Nothing, Bear. Never mind."

Joe pointed to Bear. "So who the hell is he?"

Murray scratched her head. "An ex-con. Name's Ian Hannigan. Ian, we know you killed Scar—we know you and he were in on several robberies back in Michigan together. Why'd you do it? Was it because of the Tempah City Credit Union job?"

"Yeah," Bear grumbled. "He got away with the money. I got caught. He promised to put it away, to wait until I was out of jail. I agreed to take the heat and he was supposed to save me seventy percent of the cash. I figured, what did I have to lose? If I ratted him out, I'd still have to do the time. If I kept my mouth shut, I'd at least have money waiting for me when I got out."

"But it didn't work that way, did it?" Murray said.

He shook his head. "A few months later, he up and took off with everything. When I found out, I decided to keep quiet, to be a model prisoner so I could appeal for an early release. I kept in touch with our buddies, they told me whenever they saw him on the road. When I got released early for good behavior, I just had to pick up the trail."

She sighed. "Sounds like the old saying is right. There is no honor among thieves. I'll bet he was surprised when you showed up, Ian."

He almost smiled. "Damned straight he was surprised. Tried to tell me that he'd spent all the money. I figured he was lying, so I lured him out to the caves and conned him into admitting there was still about a hundred grand left."

"And that's when you killed him?"

Bear paused, he stared at the ground for a moment before speaking. "He backed out of our deal. He lied to me and left me to rot in that prison. We were supposed to stand up for each other, to hold to our code, but he . . ."

I thought I could hear a tinge of regret in his voice, but then it vanished.

After a moment, he said, "I dragged his body down to the lake so nobody would make the connection. The boys over there in the enclave had been talking about some weird shit going on in the woods. It gave me an idea. I tried to make it look like Scar might have been killed by a cougar or a bear or something like that. When people started talking about all that monster crap, it bought me a few more days to look for the rest of the money."

"What about Clyde?" Murray asked. "Save yourself a lot of trouble and cooperate."

Ian gave her a long look. "I don't know what you're talking about."

Murray cleared her throat. Her voice impassive, she said, "You know, Ian, we're going to get you one way or another. It's only a matter of time. We do have the death penalty in this state. If you cooperate, you might just be able to walk out of this mess alive. If you don't, well . . . who knows?"

She gave him a cold smile. "And you might think about this little fact: A number of the boys out there in the enclave end up in jail every so often. It's easy for us to find a reason to arrest one of the guys. And wouldn't it be a pity if that biker were to be put in your cell, knowing who you are, and what you did? The boys have their own honor code, you know."

I stared at her, glad she was on my side. Ian's eyes flickered and, for the first time, I saw fear wash across the big man's face. Murray was playing good cop–bad cop all by herself.

"However, if you cooperate, well, I can probably arrange for you to be held in a private cell, away from Clyde and Scar's friends." She let her words drift off.

He sank to the floor of the cavern and hung his head. Nobody said anything for a moment. The silence was so thick we could hear the occasional squeak from the bats, and the continual splash as the water dripped through the ceiling shaft and fell into the pool below.

Finally, he cleared his throat. "All right, just don't let those guys get me. I know all about the honor code."

"Did you kill Clyde?"

Ian huffed, but finally broke. "Yeah. Dude saw me going through Scar's trailer. He managed to find out who I was, and when I was getting ready to take off, he confronted me and demanded a share of the loot—it was hidden in that old mining shack in the meadow. I didn't have a choice. I told him sure, that I had the money in the caves. That got him down here."

I was beginning to get the picture. "And George saw what happened?"

He nodded. "It seemed perfect—an easy frame up. I found Clyde's roofies and decided to make it look like the kid OD'd. I figured I could confuse matters enough to buy myself more time. Maybe make it to Mexico. With Clyde dead, I was the only one left who knew that Scar had all that money. I caught the kid in the caves here, watching me. Didn't take much to run him down and force a handful of roofies down his throat. The pipsqueak can't fight worth a damn."

Murray was scribbling down notes as fast as she could write. "Go on."

"Once the kid was out of it, I got him started on the whiskey. He was so high that he didn't have a clue. I thought for sure he'd die, that it would look like a drug deal gone bad."

"But he didn't."

"No. And then you were all were in the meadow. When I heard you arrested him for the murder, I decided I still had a chance. Figured I'd just lie low for a couple days, then pack up and take off. I'd pick up new wheels in the city, and take off for Mexico. I was getting ready to head out this morning when *she,*" he pointed at me, "and her friend decided to nose around out here."

A thought struck me. "When Cathy and I were outside the cave, were you making noises in the bushes to scare us?"

Ian gave me a strange look. "I don't know what you're talking about. I heard somebody scream when I was in my hideout."

So it had been the monster outside the cave. Or perhaps a cougar. I doubted that we'd ever sort out some of the things that had happened.

"I guess that's it, then," Murray said. She pulled him to his feet. "Come on, time to get you up to the squad car."

"Remember your promise." His voice quivered.

Mur snorted. "Yeah, I remember. Now shut up and get a move on." She motioned to me. "Wait here, Em, and I'll be back to give you a hand with Joe."

She left us a spare flashlight. When we were alone, I walked over to where Joe was resting. "Joe, you haven't said much."

He thought for a moment, then nodded. "What can I say? My world has been turned upside down. We almost got killed, but that seems a moot point compared to everything else. The things I saw when the Klakatat Monster touched my mind—Em—they made me want to cry. I saw things no living person has seen."

Taking my face in his hands, he searched my eyes. "Honey, is this what you live with all the time? How can you handle the intensity of it? How can you face your daily routine after you've touched this kind of energy? How can anything you do measure up to what you must feel and sense? How can I matter to you when you've met a creature like that? When you've seen the wonders of this world that most of us don't even know exists?"

I bit my lip. He was struggling with what I'd had to deal with all my life. "You nit! I can't kiss the Klakatat Monster, and it can't hold me when I'm crying, or rub my back when I'm tense, or make love to me. And look at what we've shared here today—so few couples ever get to share anything like this. So don't ever dismiss what we have together. Remember babe—love is powerful magic."

He took a deep breath and let it out slowly. "I guess you're right. I just don't know how you manage to juggle both worlds all the time like you do."

I strove to explain what my Nanna had taught me. "Joe, life is a composite of the incredible and the boring, of the primal and the routine, of the ecstatic and the traumatic, and all that exists in-between. Nanna taught me to value everything that happens to me. Every experience—be it mundane or magical—has something to teach me. And if life were a constant barrage of wild roller coaster rides, I'd burn out faster than a birthday cake candle."

He gave me a thin smile that broadened out until he was laughing. "Okay, okay . . . you made your point. I'll let it go, and let it be what it was."

"And you're thankful you were a part of it?" I said, unable to stop myself.

He grimaced. "Well, I'd have been happier if that creep hadn't started taking potshots at us, but, yeah, I'm glad I was here. I think I understand your world a lot more now. And even though my ankle's banged up, we're alive, we saw something pretty darn incredible, and justice has been served. I guess it can't get much better than that." He held out his arm and I slid into the comforting warmth of his embrace. I leaned my head against his shoulder for a moment, and we sat silently, basking in the warmth that flowed between us.

When Murray returned, she had Sandy and Greg with her. The two men formed a chair with their arms and carried Joe out of the cavern.

Murray and I hung behind. I looked up at the ridge. "Mur, I want to go up there for a moment."

"I dunno, Em. This cave is really unstable."

I closed my eyes and reached out. No menace, no threat. Just that ancient and wondrous energy that lingered behind.

"It's all right. I'll be down in a moment." I carefully edged my way up the path, holding close to the cavern wall as I navigated the steep embankment. When I reached the top, I saw a tunnel leading into a dark passage. I stood at the entrance for a moment, wanting desperately to throw caution to the wind. Hesitating, I stepped forward, but a shimmer of ebony blocked my way.

"Go no farther," the Warrior said.

I pulled back. "The intruder is gone."

It nodded, slowly. "And now the lore-keeper may once again sleep and dream and remember."

As my eyes adjusted to the darkness, I saw the skull once more—the astral embodiment of the lore-keeper. It hovered just behind the Warrior, staring at me with a sagacity far beyond any mortal's grasp. Salt grazed my lips and I realized I was crying. Murray was right, if they ever caught this creature, they'd dissect him, tear him apart, shoot him down like a rabid dog and the world would lose a wealth of knowledge and compassion. We simply weren't ready to accept creatures out of legend and lore. Not while fear still ruled the world.

Taking a deep breath, I wiped my eyes and nodded. "Thank you."

And then, the shadow was gone. The cave began to shake and Murray rushed up the ledge and grabbed my wrist.

"The cave's gonna go! We have to get out of here!" She dragged me down the precarious slope at a mad dash. We hip-hopped through the bat-poop soup as the bats went winging overhead, gliding out of the ceiling shaft. Rocks and pebbles began to shower down as we reached the entrance to the main tunnel. As we exited the chamber, a loud roar filled the air and the ceiling began to crumble.

We raced down the passage, slowing only to skirt the sinkhole. By the time we reached Bear's hideout, the whole complex was rocking like a boat in a tempest. Murray pushed me up the ladder, hot on my heels, and we scrambled out of the chute and raced down the mountain to the squad cars below.

As we reached the bottom, she turned to me and said, "Em, our secret . . ." she paused. "*His* secret . . . is safe. We'll never tell anybody."

I turned for one last look. From where we stood, the quaking had stopped, but I knew that the cave was sealed. The Klakatat Monster would go back to sleep. How many eons would pass before it woke once more? I doubted that we would ever know.

Chapter 21

⁂

A MEDIC UNIT was in the meadow. Deacon was sitting on the bumper, a bandage covering his shoulder. He looked at Joe, who sat next to him, his ankle in a splint, and said, "Man, you smell like shit. What'd you go and do?"

Joe glared at him. "Slipped in a pile of guano. I heard you got tagged by mountain man over there." He pointed to the squad car next to which Sandy and Greg were standing. Murray told them to run Ian in and book him, while I put in a call to Triple-A to come tow Joe's pickup into town.

As I sat on the bumper of my Mountaineer, staring at Klickavail Mountain, Mur wandered over to join me. "You okay?" she asked.

I shrugged. "I guess. Sometimes I wonder why we bother. Why do we build cities and fence ourselves in when the world is so much more complex and wild than we are? We chase out the mysteries, we fit our lives into little boxes and ignore everything that is beautiful and primal about life." I'd managed to shore up Joe's depression, but now my own bout was settling on my shoulders. I knew Nanna was right about honoring all experiences for what they could teach us, but sometimes we had to mourn the incredible in order to let go of it.

Murray settled down next to me and shoved her hands in her pockets. "Yeah, I feel it, too. Once you've seen what exists, how can you just go about the daily grind of living?" She paused, then looked up as the medic unit pulled out, carrying both Joe and Deacon to the hospital. "I guess it's time to go." She glanced up at the mountain. "What do you think he's doing now?"

The memory of those topaz eyes, glowing with a primordial wisdom, flickered back into my mind. "Sleeping. He'll go back to sleep and dream of the world that is changing around him. He lives there, you know, the Dream-Time. Inside and yet outside of our world."

She nodded. "I think you're right. It feels weird, though, just leaving without saying goodbye." She looped her arm through mine. "You'll never forget this. Neither will I."

She was right. Somehow ghosts seemed almost mundane compared to what we'd just been through. "Maybe we should. Say goodbye, I mean. He'll hear us, you know he will."

She stood up and stretched. "Lead the way."

I made my way over to the mountain slope, where I knelt and placed my hands on the compacted dirt. Murray joined me. As the energy settled, I quietly said a prayer.

"Blessed are those who watch over the land, blessed are those who protect the secrets of the earth, blessed are those who remind of us of who we are, and those who remember us after we've gone." And then, I sat back on my heels, looking up at the meadow. The colors seemed so bright, so vivid. "From the earth you have risen . . . to the earth you return."

Evening was on its way. It was time to go home.

• • • •

WHEN WE WERE in my car, I punched in my home number. Horvald answered. "Horvald, what are you doing there? Is Harlow there?"

"No, Missy, she's not. Her water broke and the baby decided to put in a hasty appearance."

"Oh good God, Harlow's having her baby?"

He chuckled. "Having it? Not likely. She had it. Took less than fifteen minutes. Your daughter was the one who delivered it. Kip ran over to get me, and by the time I called the paramedics and hightailed it over to your house, Randa was sitting there with a squirming baby in her arms, while Harlow was cursing up a blue streak about how much she hurt."

"Holy hell! Randa delivered a baby? Is everybody okay?"

"Yep. Ida took off to the hospital to keep track of things; and she called not ten minutes ago. Both mother and baby are doing fine. I decided to wait here and keep an eye on your youngsters, along with biker-boy here." I heard the scolding in his voice, but just smiled. Horvald was still mighty ticked at Jimbo for scaring me and breaking my window.

I thanked him and told him that we'd be right there. After I hung up, I filled Murray in on everything. She stared at me, mouth agape. "Randa delivered the baby? Oh man, I would have given anything to see that."

As the ambulance pulled out, we followed in my Mountaineer. I wasn't sure if I ever wanted to see Klickavail Valley again, and yet I knew I'd be back.

WE RACED INTO the house. Jimbo was still stretched out on the sofa, with Horvald sitting next to him. Root-beer cans and chips littered the coffee table. Horvald motioned to the kitchen.

"Kids are in there, having a snack. I cleaned up the

kitchen for you. There was a bit of a mess on the floor but I made short work of it."

I thanked him and hurried into the kitchen with Murray right behind me. Randa and Kip were eating toasted cheese sandwiches and drinking big glasses of milk, their faces still registering shock. Neither one had ever even witnessed kittens being born, let alone a baby.

"Mom, Mom, I helped Harlow have her baby!" She started to hug me, but stopped cold. "Ewww! You still stink, Mom. Worse than before. So do you, Aunt Murray."

I grabbed her and gave her a hug. "Never mind that. So you played the heroine today! What a wonderful gift to give Harlow."

"Gift?" She looked at me oddly. "What do you mean?"

"Well, without you things would have been far more difficult. You helped her baby be born safely. And that, my dear, is the greatest gift you can give any new mother. Now, we'll all go to the hospital just as soon as Murray and I take quick showers. How about that?"

I took off for my shower upstairs while Murray availed herself of the downstairs bath. Nothing of mine except skirts and tank tops would fit her—she was far too tall for anything else I owned. Murray seldom ever wore dresses, seeing her in a gauzy broomstick skirt was almost more than Jimbo could bear.

Still high on painkillers, he looked at her, his eyes shining. "I love you, Anna. You know that, don't you? You know that I love you?"

"I know," she said, blushing. Then, with a cough, she gave us all a stern look. "Not a word about this to anybody, please. This is supposed to be a secret right now and you could really mess things up if you tell anybody about us."

Kip and Randa promised, *scout's honor,* and Horvald gave his word as a gentleman that he wouldn't spill the beans. As he searched through the kitchen for more root beer, Murray gave Jimbo a quick rundown on what had happened.

I led the kids outside.

"Mom, did you see it?" Kip asked.

"See what?"

"The monster!" He looked up at me, eyes shining, and I knew I was going to have to do the hardest thing I'd ever done. I was going to have to deliberately lie to my son.

I took a deep breath. "Kip, there are some strange things out there, but no, I'm afraid the only monster we found was human."

And as I said it, I knew it was the truth. The lore-keeper was far from a monstrosity. Better he live on in legend as a dangerous fiend, though, to keep people away from the mountain. With the cave sealed, it would be a long time before anybody woke him up again. And maybe, someday when I was very old and the kids were grown and able to understand the situation better, maybe I'd tell them about the day I met the Klakatat Monster.

Kip looked disappointed, but right at that moment, Murray came dashing out, sparing me from further explanation.

When we reached the hospital, Murray and I ran a quick check on Deacon and Joe, both of whom were ready to leave. Deacon's wound was, indeed, minor, and Joe was hobbling on crutches with a fractured ankle.

After Deacon's wife led him away, the rest of us headed toward Harlow's room. The nurse started to give us a hard time but finally allowed us to go in as a group, provided we were very quiet and didn't cause a ruckus. She balked about Kip's age, but after Harlow reminded the nurse just how much money she had donated to the hospital, the squabbling stopped.

Harlow was lying in bed, a tiny, perfect baby girl in her arms. Joe motioned for the kids to join him in the corner of the room where the nurse had brought in a couple of chairs, while Murray and I flanked the new mother.

"How you doing, babe?" As I stared at the baby in Harlow's arms, a lump rose in my throat. How many years had it been since I'd held someone that small? I glanced back at Kip and Miranda and smiled softly, grateful that they were healthy and growing into beautiful young adults.

Harlow's hair was slicked back, still damp from the labor. "Well, other than the fact that my daughter decided to be born on your kitchen floor, I'm fine. Doc said it was the fastest, easiest delivery any of his patients has had. Must be a touch of your magic." She grinned at me and I beamed back.

"Randa saved the day," she continued. "When my water broke and I realized the baby wasn't waiting for me to get to the hospital, I didn't know what to do, but somehow Jimbo managed to talk both Randa and me through the birth, while Kip ran across the street. By the time he came back with Horvald, the baby had already poked her head into the world. Isn't that right, baby girl?" She kissed her child on the forehead and gave us the most beatific smile I'd ever seen.

Murray's eyes were wet. "You look so happy, you and wonder-girl there. So, what's her name? Or are you waiting till James gets back?"

Harl shook her head. "No, and I think he'll agree with me that my decision is the right one. Randa, would you come here, please?"

Randa slowly approached the bed. "Yes?" she said, sounding painfully shy. I knew we were in for a long talk to help her cope with what she'd been through. Even though everything had worked out okay, helping birth a baby would have a profound impact on both of the kids.

"What's your middle name, hon?"

"Eileen. Why?"

Harlow just smiled. "And Kip—what's your middle name?"

"Eugene," Kip said from his perch next to Joe.

Harlow beamed. "That's it then. My daughter's name is Eileen Eugenia Rainmark. You two helped her make her way into this world, so I'm going to name her after the both of you."

Randa and Kip both broke into peals of laughter, obviously delighted. I leaned down and gazed at little Eileen. Her eyes were cornflower blue and it looked like her hair was going to match her mother's, too. Her nose, though, and olive skin, were straight from James. She'd inherited plenty from her Native American heritage, there was no doubt about that.

"You're such a tiny girl," I said, kissing her fingers. "Harlow . . . you're going to make a wonderful mother." And I knew she was.

ON TUESDAY EVENING, Joe and I sat on my front porch, listening to the drone of the afternoon bees. He wouldn't be going back to work for another week yet, and Jimbo was still off his feet for a few more days, so they were both camped out in my house—with Joe on the sofa and Jimbo in the guest room. The past two days had been loud and weird and a whole lot of fun, actually.

When George had been released, he called me to give what was, for him, probably the hardest apology that he'd ever made. I hoped that the time in jail had helped him rethink his attitude. Cathy had sent me a big box of candy and had ordered several hundred dollars' worth of china from my shop as a thank you. Whether we'd ever manage more than a civil "hello" remained to be seen, but at least we weren't out for blood anymore.

The phone rang and I ran inside to grab it.

Murray's voice was an odd mixture of sober and bubbly. "Em, you'll never guess what happened!"

"After the past few days, I'm not even going to hazard a guess. What?"

"First things first." Her voice softened. "You know Coughlan didn't make it?"

"Yeah." Even though he'd been a jerk, I still felt bad

when she told me that he'd died shortly after surgery. But the man had sown a life of stress and anger and it had caught up with him.

"Well, today Tad Bonner called me into his office and he promoted me. He wants me to take over Coughlan's job tomorrow."

Stunned, I stammered out, "Congrats, babe! How wonderful! Uh . . . how are the men taking it?"

She coughed. "Well, two have quit in protest, but everybody else seems to be rallying around me. I don't know though." She lowered her voice. "I haven't accepted yet. I've got Jimmy to think about. If I took this job, we might have to split up and I don't want to do that. I haven't told him yet, so please, don't say anything."

I reassured her I'd keep my mouth shut and wandered back out to the porch, wishing I had some way to make her decision easier. But there was nothing I could do.

Joe glanced up. "Party plans?"

I nodded, not wanting to break my promise to Murray. Friday was Randa's birthday party and as I planned out the last-minute details, I tried to make sure that we hadn't forgotten anything. Joe rested on the porch swing, folding his arms behind his neck. The kids were at the movies. A calm evening breeze played through the air, wafting the scent of late-summer flowers over from Horvald's yard. Joe yawned and sat up as a old beater of a Honda pulled up in front of my house.

"Is that her?" he asked.

I squinted. A very pregnant woman with long brown hair, wearing a pair of maternity jeans and a tie-dyed peasant blouse, awkwardly stepped out from behind the wheel. "I think so."

"I'll let you two talk," he said, and hobbled into the house, using his cane. Together with the walking cast, it was keeping him on his feet, albeit clumsily and slower than a snail on a cold day.

As the woman approached I sensed a flash of grief, but

also the stirrings of new life, coming from her aura. I stood up to greet her as she climbed the stairs. "You must be Traci," I said, holding out my hand.

She hesitated a moment. "And you're Emerald?"

"That I am." I escorted her to the porch swing, holding it still while she settled herself in it. "How are you doing? You don't have long to wait, do you?"

With a brief smile, she shook her head. "No, not long now. I just wish . . ." She paused, sniffing back tears. I put my hand on hers and we sat there quietly, until she was ready to continue. "I want to thank you. That's why I called and asked if I could come over. I wanted to tell you how much it means to me that you found Scar's murderer. I don't think anybody would ever have known if it hadn't been for Jimbo and you." She gave me a radiant smile, and then I could see why Scar had loved this woman. There was something inherently sweet and loving about her, without an ounce of guile in her energy.

"I'm happy we could help. So what will you be doing now?"

Traci shrugged. "I don't know. I don't want to leave the enclave, but I think my baby needs a stable home, now that he's not going to have a papa. I've been thinking of going back to school to study environmental issues and become an activist. Thanks to you guys, I can afford to do that."

There had been a reward for finding the rest of the money from the robbery. Joe, Murray, and I had been offered the cash, split three ways. After a long talk, we signed it over to Traci. Scar's baby would have a brighter future if his mother had a nest egg. I was glad to hear that Traci was planning on putting it to good use.

"I think that's a wonderful idea! Traci, if you ever need to talk, you know you can come to me," I added as she readied herself to leave.

"I can't thank you enough for all you've done. But, you know how much it means to me, don't you?" Her voice was plaintive. I held out my arms and she fell into them, crying softly on my shoulder. "I miss him, I miss him so much."

"I know you do," I said. "I know." I smoothed her hair and gave her a kiss on the forehead, thinking that Scar and Traci had been a lucky pair. And even though we'd found out that Scar was a fugitive, I couldn't help but wish that none of this had ever happened, that they had lived out their days together, raising their family, loving in the way that makes the world a better place. But life wasn't always fair. Sometimes, we just had to do the best we could with the hand we were dealt.

Traci glanced at me, almost as if she had read my mind. With a gentle good-bye, she headed back to her car, where she honked and waved before driving away. What would the future hold for Traci and her baby now? Whatever it was, the energy felt optimistic, and I whispered a prayer to the universe that the two would be protected from further mishap.

When Joe returned, I told him about our talk. He gave me a peck on the cheek. "You are one of the most amazing women I've ever known. So, Ms. O'Brien, do you want to see what I've been up to?" The look on his face told me that he'd been up to some sort of mischief.

"What did you do now?"

"Bought something. Rather expensive, too."

I squinted at him. "What? A new truck? You haven't even paid off your old one yet." Joe had been talking about buying a new pickup ever since he saw one that had bigger and better wheels than his own. My boyfriend wasn't immune to the testosterone monster, even if he was sensitive and sweet.

"Come on, I'll show you." He hobbled down the stairs. I winced as I watched, remembering how painful my own knee injury had been. The doctor said he should heal up quickly, but still, it had to hurt like hell.

We meandered down the driveway to the sidewalk, where he turned left. A few more feet and we were standing in front of the bramble-infested lot that bordered my own home. Joe stopped and waved his hand toward the towering blackberry bushes.

"There."

"There what?" I asked, still not getting it.

"That's what I'm buying. I called the realtor and she brought the paperwork over today while you were down at the shop. When my ankle's better, I'll start clearing away the blackberries, neighbor."

Neighbor! I stared at him, not sure whether he was pulling my leg. "And just why are you buying a bramble-infested lot? Do you realize how much work it will be to get it ready for a house?"

"No problem." He slid his arm around my shoulders. "I figure that when we get married, I'll just move into your house. Together with this lot, we'll have plenty of room to plant gardens and make a little pond . . . whatever else we want."

It took a moment for what he'd said to fully dawn on me. When it did, I started to cough so hard he had to give me a good thump on the back.

"*When we get married?* You want to marry me?"

Joe leaned down and brushed the top of my head with his lips. "Ms. O'Brien, I have wanted to marry you since the first day we went out for coffee. I want to be a father to Kip and Miranda—as best as I can. I'm not going to ask you right now because I know you need time to get used to the idea. But come your birthday, you better plan on the fact that I'm going to get down on one knee with a bouquet of red roses and propose, and you're going to say yes. At least," he whispered, "I hope you will."

My heart racing, I stared at the brambles, trying to make sense of all that had happened over the past couple of weeks. "I'm . . . speechless. I don't know what to say."

"Remember in the cave? You told me that we'd shared something incredible, something most couples never get to experience. Well, I thought about that and I realized that we share a lot more than that. We're good together, Em. I knew we would be from the first moment we met. So, just say you love me. For now, that's enough." He flicked my nose playfully.

I smiled up at him, melting into his embrace. "That, I can do." As I stared at the sprawling brambles that had laid claim to the lot, everything hit me at once. I'd seen the Klakatat Monster and helped solve the murders of two men that the system would have otherwise ignored. Harlow had a little girl, and Murray was in love. And best of all—Joe wanted to marry me. He loved me enough to want to spend the rest of his life with me and my children.

All my melancholy of the past few days slid away, and I threw back my head and laughed, my voice ringing out into the lazy afternoon. Autumn was on its way, my family was safe and happy and healthy, and everything felt alive again. Maybe even the most mundane of days had its miracles after all.

Mystic Moon Dreaming Pillows

❖

Sometimes, when we are in need of extra rest, or when we just want to reach a deeper sleep state, we can achieve this by the use of dreaming pillows—small sachetlike pillows that we can tuck inside of our pillow cases. Depending on the herbs, the pillows can encourage vivid dreams, astral work, or restful sleep. This recipe is designed to help promote peaceful slumber, since so many of us don't get enough time in bed in this fast-paced world.

You will need:

> 2 seven-inch squares of sturdy, purple material—linen
>   works well
> Gold thread and needle or sewing machine
> Cotton batting
> 1/2 cup each:
>   dried lavender
>   mugwort
>   rose petals
>   lemon balm
>   chamomile
>   valerian root

3 drops lavender essential oil
3 drops lemon essential oil
2 drops rosemary essential oil
Small spike of quartz crystal

Mix herbs together in a bowl, focusing on your desire to encourage deep slumber and to work with your Higher Self while asleep. Focus on the nature of dreams, how they can solve problems, and ask that this energy infuse the herbs and bring out their natural magical tendencies. Add drops of essential oil and mix again. Place quartz spike in the middle of the herbs and set aside (in a bottle with a lid if you are going to wait to finish this charm).

Place cloth pieces together, wrong sides out, and sew to form a pouch (use a 3/8" seam allowance), leaving on side open. Iron seams open, then reverse so pouch is right side out.

Fill halfway with cotton batting. Add herb mixture and crystal, then pack with rest of cotton batting. Sew the end shut.

Place this inside your pillowcase at night and, before you go to bed, focus on some thought you'd like to explore in the dream-state, then go to sleep as usual. Write down your dreams when you wake up and eventually, you should see them responding to your requests.

You can recharge this pillow by adding two drops each of lavender oil, lemon oil, and rosemary oil when the fragrance starts to fade.

Remember: It is up to us to solve our own problems, but we can call on the power of our Higher Self when we need help, or when we seek more information on a subject. Eventually, through focus and determination, we can enter the Dream-Time and learn to hear our inner guidance when we're awake, not just during our sleep.

Bright Blessings and Sweet Dreams,
the Painted Panther
Yasmine Galenorn